Hard Worked Days

Also by Lawrence Patrick O'Brien

Mischief Makers
Swallowing the Muskellunge
Clochán

Hard Worked Days

A Novel

LAWRENCE P. O'BRIEN

2026

LIBRARY AND ARCHIVES CANADA CATALOGUING IN PUBLICATION DATA

Hard Worked Days
O'Brien, Lawrence

ISBN 978-1-7778155-8-5 (hardcover)
ISBN 978-1-7778155-9-2 (paperback)
ISBN 978-1-0696817-1-3 (EPUB)
ISBN 978-1-0696817-0-6 (PDF)

I. History—Refugees—Science Fiction—United States—Fiction
I. O'Brien, Lawrence II. Title

Hard Worked Days is a work of fiction. The characters, incidents, and dialogue are drawn from the author's imagination and are not to be construed as real. Any semblance to actual events or persons, living or dead, is entirely coincidental.

Cover design by Damonza.com
Published in Canada by LoonCE

Dedicated to Devin

Once upon a time, refugee meant somebody who has a refuge, found a place, a haven where he could find refuge.

Interview with International Campaign for Tibet, Elie Wiesel (2007)

The last refuge of the insomniac is a sense of superiority to the sleeping world.

The Favourite Game: A Novel, Leonard Cohen (2003)

PART 1

Looking Up

Fares gritted his teeth and put the last nut in his pocket. He lifted the toilet and put it to one side. When he opened his eyes this morning, he knew it was going to be a black day.

"Is it done yet, Mr. Khalil?" pleaded Mrs. Juliet Fabbrini from the other side of the bathroom door.

He heard her shuffle back and forth. She dropped her cane.

"Mr. Konstas—ask him," Fares said. "He won't mind."

"I don't know him."

"He's in 312; just three doors down."

"He's got that godawful dog."

"Missus Taylor, try her. She's in 316. I'm sure you will get along. Mrs. Fabbrini, you asked me to fix the toilet, and it's in parts. You've got to go see Missus Taylor."

He heard her feet scurry out of the apartment.

A pipe burst. Caught by surprise, he bumped the disconnected porcelain toilet, and the back lid smashed the floor and broke in half.

"Ya Allah! Fuck, fuck. Fuck!" he screamed. He got up and yelled,

"What useless shit!"

"Fuck it," he moaned and patted his pockets for smokes. "Shit," he groaned. He realized that he was out, and that he wasn't going to get any more because he couldn't afford it. He peeked into Mrs. Fabbrini's living room to confirm that she had gone.

With the toilet broken, he was half expecting to find evidence of rats. *That's all I'd need. I hate rats,* he thought.

After walking into her living room, he looked towards the ceiling, waved, and muttered, "Alhamdulilah"

"Still, she's going to hate me more than Mr. Konstas, isn't she? And I don't even own a dog."

The mid-morning customer lineup stretched to the front door of ***Monica's Bakery.*** Monica Gioli was getting old. Although the shop was always busy and understaffed, she couldn't convince her employees to stay around for what she was willing to pay.

Monica looked for Ionna. "Where is she?" she muttered.

"Are the blueberry muffins ready?" Ossie yelled.

"You just asked sixty seconds ago," Ionna Sari replied.

"But—"

"The taste is worth waiting for. And there's Cherry," Ossie told a customer.

Monica left the front counter and went to the kitchen at the back. She noticed that there was a plunger in the sink. "The sink is plugged again," she groaned.

"Yeah, sure," Ionna said as she hustled a tray of muffins to the front.

"Where's my toasted tomato?" a man in a plaid shirt hollered.

"Hey. And my egg sandwich. It was two orders ahead of his."

"Egg sandwich and toasted tomato," yelled Ionna, and she dropped a tray of muffins on the counter behind the new young Black hire.

"What am I supposed to do with that?" Ossie asked.

"You could have offered cherry," she said.

"Ionna," moaned Monica.

"Got it," she replied as she rushed back to the kitchen and pushed on the plunger.

"Damn it," she yelled when she got a splinter from the decrepit handle.

She set it over the drain. Six pumps were what it took, but she managed to clear it.

"Ionna," groaned Monica.

"The cookies, I know. There's an alarm."

"They're burnt," Monica said. "You didn't set the alarm."

"Holy Mary…" muttered Ionna. "I'll be right there." And to herself, she muttered, "Lord Almighty, I really need a smoke."

Monica, out of reflex, touched a pack of smokes in her apron. She watched Ionna quickly hang up her apron on a coat hook, next to the picture of her recently departed children, as she desperately moved to make her escape.

Monica reached the back of her neck and twisted her head to get the crick out. As Ionna tried to open the front door, an old woman of substantial girth smashed the door into her.

"Sorry," the woman said, but before she pointed to the other door, a child used it to go outside.

Ionna slipped out and muttered, "Where are my smokes?"

Monica rushed to serve her client's orders, but she kept a watch on Ionna. She didn't hear what she was saying, but she knew her tone. '*Jesus, my purse,' was what she was saying.*

Again, Monica smiled as she bagged a loaf of raisin bread. *She's just realized that she forgot it at home and that her lunch is in it and rotting.*

She's not long for this place, she thought. To the irate man in a light brown suit, she said, "The taste is worth waiting for. And there's Cherry."

Fares Khalil took an apple and a sandwich from his fridge and stuffed them in his pockets. He blessed his brother's family picture and rushed down two flights before bumping into Charlie O'Keefe. The man was a big fella, and Fares spun back and hit the railing.

Charlie grabbed him.

"Fares, where's your head? I can see you are in a hurry, but flipping out is not going to help, is it?"

"Sorry, Charlie, I was just somewhere else. That's all."

"Time to get another baseball cap, don't you think? Yellow, pink, and orange. That's no hat for a Yankee fan. I know it was blue once upon a time. Maybe a Japanese team—is that it?"

Fares tried to scrape off a small bit of hardened paint from his finger on his hat. "Of course, Charlie," he replied. "Sorry. And I'll get to the drywall. I promise."

"Of course, you will."

Fares adjusted his hat. "Tomorrow, I promise," he said and kept rushing downstairs. When it came to opening the door, he noticed that a little bit of green paint had come off on his fingers.

Outside, he took a breath of the summer's hot, muggy air. It was Brooklyn's usual—thick, hazy, and smoggy. He sensed that to-day something was off.

He took another whiff. The air had a sulphurous smell to it. Looking at the street, he hesitated and decided that was not it.

Fucking *dead cat in the dumpster. That is what it is,* he thought. *Who in their right mind? It's someone else. Not someone from here. I've got a sense for it.* He put his hands on his hips and looked around.

There are four more days until garbage day. Well, damned, I'm not going in there, he thought. *Is someone trying to get me to leave? Well, fuck 'em.*

Something startled him from behind. He looked but didn't see anything. Stumbling sounds coming from the inside stairwell persuaded him to quickly move on.

Fares lived in the Windsor Terrace part of Brooklyn. The thin parcel of about a dozen blocks was squeezed between a cemetery and a park. After getting a coffee from Monica's Bakery, he came to an intersection. He looked left, which would have taken him to the cemetery. A large crowd of people approached from that direction.

Nope, he thought and raised his cup of coffee. He was going right. *Prospect Park, it is.* He quickly stepped out of the way of a falling bit of bird shit. He watched the avian bomber make its escape.

Maybe it's not such a black day after all, Fares thought. He raised his coffee cup again.

To-day's petty delays weren't giving him much time to get to the park. He had a long list of repairs and not much time for a break. Eating something while watching squirrels, birds, and trees was the only thing in his day that offered a sense of freedom. Wildlife—as in the living kind—distracted him from a dismal, ever-repeating existence that felt like a broken toilet.

Javex, he thought as he tromped into a new day. *I'll bury it in Javex and cardboard.*

An old woman, who was wearing shoddy, patched clothing and pulling a two-wheeled shopping cart behind, smashed into Ionna. "Aren't you going the wrong way?" she asked.

Stunned, Ionna spun and stared at the women. Since she considered that she might be homeless, she replied, "Aren't we all?"

They both looked up at a fireball that moved across the sky. The white smoke trail was shadowed in grey. The fireball was bright white and was lined with yellow.

"You'll not see many of those. You should make a wish."

"It's a big one," Ionna said. "Yeah, I'd like to get out of here."

"You're not supposed to tell," the lady said.

"Doesn't matter. It won't happen. Have a nice rest of your day, ma'am."

The old lady didn't say anything and just kept on going.

"That someday, I can escape what I did to Thea and Nikos was my real wish," Ionna said.

She could see the park's stand of trees that was just a few blocks away. As she began to walk across the street, a chill came on. The hairs on her neck and arms felt like they were standing up.

If you asked anyone who worked in Manhattan, pretty much on any day, they'd tell you that they were busy. They worked hard and always had too much to do.

Fares and Ionna lived and worked about seven miles from Manhattan, which was on the other side of the East River. Fares and Ionna were among the many who intended to head to the green spaces to escape city life.

Unfortunately, just before the lunchtime rush, on the first Thursday in March, the disaster hit. It was in Midtown Manhattan, about a dozen blocks south of Central Park, where it happened. It was the day when something like Hell came to town.

A flaming fireball crossed the sky, crashed, and erupted in an explosion of light. As the shock waves rippled away from the blast point, everything in Manhattan was vaporized.

A nuclear-like explosion in seconds carved out a crater over a kilometre wide. Debris and dust were thrown into the stratosphere and covered the city in darkness. The city was set ablaze.

Most of the buildings in Windsor Terrace were less than three stories and tightly squeezed together. The streets were narrow and aligned in a northeast direction. The buildings protected pedestrians and drivers from the worst parts of the initial shock wave. The tops of trees and vulnerable roofing got ripped out. More than a few windshields were destroyed. Debris and cars from parking lots sailed through the air like flocks of ravens.

Ground tremors shook Fares and everyone around him off their feet. He lost his coffee and almost lost his lunch. A garbage can prevented the wind from taking it away.

Ionna was in the southern part of the neighbourhood, where the streets were more aligned towards the crater. Despite the foul, dirty air and lancing debris, she managed to drag herself behind a short brick side wall to a tight huddle embrace with three terrified strangers.

When the worst of the dust storm passed, the people of Brooklyn were confronted with a bright, mushroom-like dirt cloud that towered into the heavens. It fed a darkness that spread across the sky.

If folks in Brooklyn were asked within the next couple of days if they considered themselves busy with work, any of them would have replied with a "go fuck yourself."

Ionna, during the storm, witnessed a body being whisked away. Afterwards, she saw a corpse impaled between two cars. The street was lined with construction materials and broken branches, mostly. She saw a motorcycle in an apartment window. She followed a line of people, shocked like her, marching to the open space of an intersection. After the deafening sound and forceful pressure from the wind, she felt very out of place. Any sound was too loud. The fear that something would take her was too real and too near.

When Fares got up, he noticed that the two young girls near him were nowhere to be seen.

"Alhamdulilah," he moaned.

He also saw a car in the middle of the street that was turned on its side. People from side streets were moving to open spaces. To get away from the crowds, he rushed to get to the park.

After the initial shock waves, many, like Ionna and Fares, sought the security of the wilderness. The tree cover in Prospect Park was extensive, and most of it still stood strong.

Fares and Ionna joined a small, traumatized group that faced a long, shallow reservoir. Ducks that were on the grass made their way back to the water. They were in the park's central open space, and the trees stood tall behind them.

What had caused the explosion was not a meteorite. It was an alien object. Unknown to anyone, there was some barely noticeable activity occurring deep within the crater.

A hole appeared, and an egg soared out of it. The tossed object travelled for miles. At the height of its trajectory, a set of wings extended. It enabled a glide towards Prospect Park. The object flew under the tree cover and landed within the park's open space, near where Fares and the others had gathered. When the white egg stopped, it gave a gurgling sound. The egg was about a meter across.

"My God, what is that?" shouted Shirley.

"Do you think it has something to do with that explosion?" asked the woman beside her.

"No, Zhao, I don't see how."

"Are we being invaded?" asked a man with a cap that had an MGM decal.

"Eggs don't fly," said the young girl, who wore a bright orange spotted summer sundress.

The crowd stepped back a couple of paces. Everyone except Fares and Ionna.

The egg's wings disintegrated.

"Maybe it's NASA doing experiments? You know those private contractors," said a man wearing shorts and sandals.

"Don't be silly. They're not going to put any eggs in space," Shirley said.

The egg rolled towards them, then turned towards the water.

"Maybe it's a giant duck," said the young girl. Maybe it needs water."

"They usually have a nest," said the Jamaican.

"That thing is huge. That would be a hell of a big duck," said the man with the MGM cap.

"Watch your mouth, mister," Shirley said.

The egg spun around and again rolled in their direction.

"That's no duck," the Jamaican boy said.

The egg cracked. Something that looked like a large armoured crustacean emerged. It looked like a cross between a crab and an ancient trilobite.

"What in the name of God is that?" Shirley said as she held her purse close to her with both hands.

"It's not natural," said the Jamaican teenager. He took another three steps back.

The crab-like thing moved slowly towards the crowd. It moved with legs that were similar to a millipede's. Two thin, crustacean-like arms grew out. It had pincers instead of claws, which kept opening and closing. Its thousands of feet kept moving it forward and back.

"Keep away from it," the man with the MGM cap said. "It's not American."

Everyone in the crowd stepped back again, except Ionna and Fares. The pair was now in the front row of the crowd.

The extraterrestrial visitor stopped.

"Maybe we should notify the zoo," said the little girl.

"The police," said the guy with the MGM cap.

"The army, you fool," Shirley said.

Fares crouched to see it better.

From the front of the trilobite-like thing, stalks emerged. Eyeball buds formed.

"Mister, you shouldn't stare at it," Ionna said. She preened her hair when Fares looked at her.

Ionna got closer and whispered, "It might feel threatened."

Both eyeballs on the stalks rotated to stare at the crowd. The thousands of feet rotated the creature to face them.

"I wouldn't stand so close, if I were you," Shirley yelled.

"I think it's cute," Zhao said.

A hose-like appendage grew out of the crab-like creature's back. It spewed far into the air.

"Pee-yew. It's taking a leak," said the man with the MGM cap.

"Or maybe something like a skunk," the young Jamaican teenager said.

"What the fuck?" yelled Fares when the foam-like substance landed on him. As he stepped away, the creature's spray kept landing on its target.

"Ooh gross," said the Jamaican when it stopped.

"Fuck off," Fares said.

The crab-like creature moved forward, and everyone took steps back, except Ionna.

"Somebody, phone someone," Shirley said. She ran back into the trees.

The crab-like creature spewed again.

"Hell no," screamed Ionna when it got her. She tried to dodge it by moving left, then right, and then back, but it kept landing on her. "Stop it. And damn it, does it ever stink? It's worse than a skunk."

"Everyone into the forest," ordered the man in the MGM cap as he turned to run away. Everyone but Fares and Ionna followed him. From behind a tree, Shirley yelled, "Well, don't just stand there; get away from it."

The creature stopped spraying and moved a dozen feet back. It gave a gurgling sound and then disintegrated.

"Did you see that?" said the man with an MGM cap. It just turned to dust. I didn't see no flames or anything."

"You there. Both of you, go get washed up. Hurry, before you get sick," Zhao said.

"Yes, the small waterfall, and it's got a small pond," Shirley said. "Hurry up. Don't think about it."

"Yeah, it's behind those trees," said the little girl as she pointed.

"Don't just stand there; you have to wash it off," said the man with the MGM cap. "It might have asbestos."

"Might get herpes," said someone.

"Rabies," says another.

"Or bird flu," says another.

The man with the MGM cap called the police.

Fares, believing his life depended on it, rushed into the stand of trees to find some way of washing the stuff off. Fares had a good start, but Ionna reached the waterfall at the same time. He stepped directly into the pond and bent down to wash his hair. When she stepped in, she elbowed him and ordered him to move over.

Fares sat down in the pond and made sure he was good and wet. He tried to rub off every bit of goo.

"You're shaking," she said.

"You think?" he replied. "This is something that might kill us." He dunked himself underwater.

"One minute, it looks like the world is coming to an end, and then this. I don't know what to think."

"I saw a dead person," she said as she scrubbed her hair.

"You're green," he said.

"Fuck off," she said. "This is a fucking nightmare."

"I mean, really," he said.

She stared at him and then at her hands. "Christ Almighty. By the way, so are you."

"Quick, rub it all off," he yelled. He looked at his own hands and then tried to wipe the colour away with leaves.

She dunked herself in the water like Fares had done.

"What the fuck?" he groaned. "What are we going to do?"

"Does your health care include bug infestations?"

"Ha," he said. "As if."

"Did you see the movie Alien?" she asked.

"Eggs in the skin, and things moving around, you mean."

"Stop it," she said.

"You brought it up. Or maybe something like a tapeworm," he said.

"What?"

"It starts as a bug and feeds on what you eat."

"Or we got sprayed with something that's just poisonous," Ionna said.

He dunked himself again and tried washing the colour off with mud. He applied slime and roots, but nothing seemed to help.

"Looking on the bright side, are you? Fares said. "More to the point—if we go to the hospital, and we don't go bankrupt, who do you think will take responsibility for us?"

"I give up. Who?"

"The Army." Fares kept rubbing himself with mud. He got up and climbed out of the pond. "How do you think this country will deal with infected immigrants? Ma'am, I am sure you're a nice person, but really, I hope we never see one another again. That twit back there called the police, and I have no interest in being locked up in someone's medical prison for the rest of my life. Things are rough enough as they are."

"Me too. I can live with that," she said as she got up. "Fucking green. Lord love us. My skin is fucking green. Not French, nor fucking Irish. Greek, and I'm fucking green."

After she finished complaining, she noticed that she was alone. It wasn't just him who moved away. It was everyone from their small group. "Nothing here but bad news," she mumbled.

"So, how the fuck am I going to burn these fucking clothes?" she muttered as she hurried home. "Hmm, who do I know that has a barbecue?"

As Fares entered his apartment building, he noticed that two windows were broken and a tree was split in half. "That's all I need," he muttered as he opened the door and headed for the stairs. "I don't even want to think about the roof."

On the stairwell, he looked back at the darkness that he saw through a pane. "Or the fucking sky or damn fucking life on earth as we know it," he added. After taking another couple of steps, he said, "That green lady was cute, though."

Once inside his apartment, he tossed his wet clothes into a garbage bag. He grabbed some dish soap and took a shower. Due to exhaustion, he tripped on a rug. A vision of eggs moving under his skin stayed with him until he reached his bed, where he blacked out.

Ionna returned home and tried to scrape away the strange tinge from her skin. Exhausted, she intended to get something to eat and go to bed, but she dizzily meandered towards her sofa. She fell into it. The last thing that came to mind was the word 'tribute.'

Disassociated Retreats

A loud smashing on Fares's apartment door woke him up. He slung on a blanket and groggily trudged towards the door.

"Hold on to your horses," he yelled. "I am coming, I am coming." He lmost tripped and hit the door frame as he attempted to put on some slippers.

The senior looked perturbed. There were a couple of missing buttons, which evealed that he had a modest potbelly.

"Mr. Moretti, what's up this time?"

"Anthony, please."

"Yes, sir."

"Fares, you promised to fix the hole in the wall in my apartment on Friday."

"Yes, I did. I will get to it."

"Today is Sunday."

"It's been three days?"

"Are you alright, Mr. Khalil? You don't look well."

Fares looked at his arms and laughed, "They're not green."

"Really, you aren't yourself to-day."

"It's a holiday. And I've come down with something. Tomorrow. We'll talk tomorrow." He slammed the door. He swiped a hand over his head and glared at the ceiling. "It's a holiday. Thank God," he said as he dragged himself towards his living room. He flaked out on his couch.

The word **tribute,** like a musical ringworm, kept coming to mind. After a short nap, Fares rolled naked off the couch and tried to wipe the sleep out of his eyes. There wasn't much that was appetizing in the fridge. That was because inside, there wasn't much of anything.

Friday was payday, wasn't it? he thought. "I need a coffee."

After he had his jeans on, he grabbed a T-shirt from a drawer. He looked at himself in the mirror. Fuck, that doesn't say Bristles. It's not even a rock group. It's a commercial for Bristol. He swapped the black T-shirt for another.

While pulling on socks and shoes, he remembered *those windows, the ones in front—they're broken. The storm got them. Must be a hot house now."*

Standing up, he stretched towards the ceiling. "I really need some caffeine." He swept his curls to one side and put on his baseball cap. After locking up, he gave a sign of relief after confirming that his wallet was in his back pocket.

Once outside, he noticed that the tenants had covered the windows of their apartments with cardboard.

Both are going to be furious, he thought. *I could say I was out of town. But obviously, they would have called the owner. And Mrs. Fabbrini and Mr. O'Keefe would have said something about that, wouldn't they?"*

"I need something to eat," he muttered. Fares headed to a bakery that he knew was only a couple of blocks away.

The line inside was long. A teenage girl who was eating at a table near him asked, "I didn't know there were mountains in Colorado."

Looking at it, Fares understood that she was right. "Goats and sheep," he replied. "They also have goats and sheep." He scanned the counter searching for the coffee machine. He really needed a jolt.

When his place in line got close to the cash, he saw Ionna walk out from the kitchen.

That's the woman from the park. He removed his cap.

"Are you going to get something or not?" said the man behind him.

To Ossie, who was at the cash, Fares ordered a couple of spinach croissants, a pita sandwich, and coffee. After paying, Ossie told him that he was going to have to wait for the croissants. "Those are only for show."

Fares saw Ionna look at him.

"What are you doing here?" she asked. "I don't want you here."

"Ionna, don't be like that. Why has he been bothering you? Do you know him?" Monica asked.

"No, we don't," protested Fares. "She must be mistaken."

Ionna stepped back, glared at him, and shooed him away.

"Well, the green has come out," he added.

"Two spinach croissants," Ossie yelled.

"I know. I know," she yelled.

Fares noticed that Monica, the manager, had a quizzical look on her face.

Ionna came back and put the croissants in a bag and left it on the counter.

Fares moved his hand towards the counter, and the bag of croissants moved towards him.

"Wha?" Fares mumbled. He quickly picked it up, along with his coffee. He tried to quickly leave, but he heard Monica yell, "Hey, sir."

From the door, Fares turned around. He saw her wave a sandwich. "You forgot this."

"Of course I did," he muttered.

He returned to grab it and quickly left.

In the afternoon, Fares headed to the basement to look for some building supplies. After a blink, he stumbled. He felt unusually groggy. Fares found himself standing outside on the sidewalk. The apartment building was behind him. He couldn't remember how he got there.

"What?" he muttered. He didn't see any tenants around.

If I black out when I'm on a ladder, I'm finished, he thought.

"Fuck," he moaned.

He looked at his hand. *It's not green,* he thought. *And it doesn't look radioactive.*

"Nonsense," he said. "Stress. Yeah, it's just nerves."

On the opposite side of the street, he saw Ionna appear, and she was heading in his direction.

"Not again," he muttered.

Fares quickly returned to the apartment building. From inside, he watched her walk by, through a glass pane in the door.

"What's going on?" he muttered. "Was she following me?"

He headed downstairs to get a jug of Javex for the dead cat.

In the middle of the night, he found himself walking outside. He was wearing pyjamas and slippers. And again, he recognized Ionna. She was also walking at night in Brooklyn, wearing a bathrobe and slippers.

"Ya Allah! This can't be real."

He turned and rushed back to his apartment, thinking, *What is happening to us?*

"I am never going to see that woman again," he promised. "This has got to stop."

When he got back, his clock confirmed that it was 2:30 in the morning.

A blackout and a chance meeting happened again on the next afternoon and during the next night. In both instances, he hurried away, hoping that he wasn't recognized.

When Fares got up the next morning, he felt miserable. He went to his mirror and checked to see if there was anything crawling under his skin.

How am I going to avoid that woman? he thought. *Maybe I need to get out of here?* Without making himself something to eat as he usually did, he grabbed his wallet and left.

Without remembering how he got there, he found himself staring at the entrance door of Monica's Bakery.

"Ya Allah," he cried. After looking at the sky's thick rolling darkness, he decided to go in.

Once he reached the counter, he ordered a coffee and some croissants. He waved at her, but she was trying to ignore him. "Ionna, we have to talk," he yelled.

"Why do you keep bothering me?" she asked.

"This is serious. We have to talk about it. It's something that won't just go away. We need to talk out there," he said as he pointed outside.

"You're trouble, and I've got enough problems. Did the bugs come out?"

Fares raised his arms wide and twirled around.

"I take that as a no," and she laughed.

Ossie and Monica looked at each other. She rolled her eyes. "Do it at 11:00," she said.

"Sure," said Fares and left with his coffee. As he exited through the door, Ossie waved his croissants. Monica brushed her nose and pointed to the shelf behind the glass.

"And make it short," yelled Ionna.

Ossie chuckled at her when she returned to the kitchen. Monica admonished him for keeping the cash register open.

When Fares returned to Monica's Bakery, he removed his hat and cajoled Ionna into joining him outside.

"You're late," Ionna said.

"I know, but it's been busy."

"I'm busy," she said as she wiped her hands on her apron.

On the sidewalk, she asked, "So, what's so urgent?" She lit up a smoke. She didn't offer him one.

Fares paced about on the sidewalk and looked back at her.

"Don't you find that it's strange that we keep bumping into each other?" he asked.

"You keep bumping into me." She blew a smoke ring at him.

"No, that's not true. And I don't mean here. I saw you four times after work."

"Are you stalking me?"

"No, you don't understand. OK, you explain to me why you were walking on the sidewalk last night, in the middle of the night. You were wearing bathrobes and slippers? I was there, and I have no idea how. Do you?"

"You were wearing a bathrobe?"

"Well, no. Pyjamas."

"You wear pyjamas? With little shorts?" She blew another smoke ring.

"No, that's beside the point."

"I suppose it is. It sounds a bit off."

"But we are."

"How do you know what I sleep in?"

"You wore a bathrobe."

"Oh. Well, I didn't see you."

"Ionna, do you remember walking there? I guess not. Well, after getting sprayed, I crashed and didn't get up for three days. What about you?"

"You've been forgetful," she said.

"Maybe, but what about after the Park thingy?"

"Yes, I slept in until Sunday."

"Since that day, I've had a word keep coming up," Fares said. It's like an earworm jingle."

"Tribute?" asked Ionna.

"Yeah, that's it. I am finding this to be hauntingly strange."

Ionna offered him a cigarette. "How are you feeling?"

He waved it away. "Nothing moving around inside, if that's what you mean. At least not yet. When I lived in Lebanon, I took a couple of years of medical school. I had to leave, and once I got here, it was too expensive to start again. So in case you were wondering, I do have an idea how things work."

"Me too," she said and blew another smoke ring.

"I lived in Greece; I ran my husband's restaurant."

"What does he think about all of this?"

"He drowned." Ionna was hesitant, but then she dropped her cigarette into a garbage can.

"I lost everything and came here to start over."

"The park and cemetery are nice," Fares said. It made her smile.

She looked at the dark sky. "It's amazing how bad it still is north of here. We got off relatively lightly."

"I heard that more than a million people died in the explosion, but I know what you mean. The dense, low-rise buildings and the downtown towers protected us from the worst of the blast. That was a good thing for us. That Manhattan is now just a hole in the ground—not so much for them."

"The air here has never been great. Should we worry?"

"It's not radioactive. It's just dirty. Wouldn't hurt to wear a hospital mask. I have one, but I keep forgetting it on the counter."

"Do you think there are any more of those bugs?"

"I hope not, and I am damn sure I don't want to see any more of them."

She threw the pack in the garbage can. "I have to go back," she said. "It looks like we're destined to talk again." She waved as she went back to work.

"Tribute," Fares repeated.

Ionna, on her walk home, saw Fares watching her. "How did you know when I got off work?" she asked.

"I didn't. Why did you come here?"

"What do you mean?"

"You are standing in front of where I live. I just happen to be here because this tree is going to fall and destroy my building. I can't get anyone to safely take it down. Did you bring a chainsaw?"

Ionna showed empty hands by her hips to imply empty pockets.

"I am also the custodian and superintendent of this apartment building. Anyway, what is happening here isn't a coincidence. Something is messing with us. How about grabbing a sandwich? I'm hungry. Chinese?"

"Strange is right. This isn't on my way home. OK. How about Andy Li's?"

"Sure."

After they ordered at the restaurant, Ionna asked why he thought this might be the start of something. Her long, wavy, light brown hair draped over her shoulders, and she nervously curled the ends with her fingers.

"After an alien bug marked us, strange things happened."

"Do you really believe that thing was extraterrestrial?" she asked.

"It turned to dust in front of our eyes—twice, and do you remember the kid who yelled, 'Eggs don't fly.' I mean, that's a pretty good point."

"I suppose."

"And then there's the word—tribute."

"So you believe that the bug gave us something?" Ionna asked.

"I think that it wants us to know that we are being given to something as a gift."

"That's being paranoid. It could be like raising a glass or tipping the hat."

"Maybe, but a tribute is normally given to a conqueror."

"Let's just stick with what we know, which is plenty scary enough."

He watched her scratch her arm.

"If you're quitting, why don't you try a patch?"

"It takes my mind off other things," she said and laughed. "You look puzzled," she added.

Fares just put his hands in the air and shrugged.

"So what are you suggesting we do?" she asked.

"I think we should get as far away from here as possible. When we get to a safe place, we could notify the authorities on the internet."

"It's just one word. It could be a misunderstanding."

"Probably, but I don't like being pissed on," Fares said.

"Kind of crude, but I see your point."

The food came, and they remained quiet while eating.

"And they sent one of their own, and what did they do? They killed it. I don't think we are dealing with nice folks."

"There is another way of looking at it. If the bug laid its eggs in us, we'd be tribute to its offspring, wouldn't we?" Ionna said.

"Ugh, enough with the crawlies, please," he said as he chewed on a chicken ball. "If that were the case, there would have been a lot of eggs released, and someone would have reported something on the internet or the news. So far, I haven't seen anything. Everyone is still convinced that it was an asteroid that created the crater."

"Leaving is not something I can afford to do right now," Ionna said.

"Me neither, but we might not have an alternative," Fares said.

They both sulked quietly while spooning their ice cream.

After they paid, Fares noticed that the cook returned Ionna's wave.

Both of them left the restaurant quietly and in different directions. Fares's shoulders were slumped, and his hands were in his pockets. It wasn't cold, but Ionna's arms were tightly wrapped as she walked slowly and occasionally took a bite of another egg roll.

The next morning at the bakery, Monica said, "That Lebanese fellow looks nice; I mean, you could do worse."

"He wants to leave," Ionna said.

"Are you going with him?"

"He didn't ask. No, I don't think so."

"He doesn't like it here?"

"No, it's not like that. The meteor has something to do with it."

"Nervous people appreciate coffee and fresh-baked goodies, so I'm good with it."

"Do you believe in aliens?" Ionna asked.

"You mean like us?"

"Yeah, sure," Ionna said, and she brought the tray back to the kitchen to get another batch from the oven.

Fares grabbed his knapsack with the intention of never returning to his apartment. He reasoned that once he got a place on the mainland, he could call her and persuade her to follow him.

On his walk south, there was a lot of debris set out for garbage pickup. He kept an eye out for a bike. It was going to be a long walk to the other side.

He looked up and wondered if something was looking for him. He shivered at the thought.

Fares meant to leave the island by crossing the Verrazano-Narrows Bridge. After walking less than a kilometre and a half, he got disoriented. Although Fares had never turned around, the street signs confirmed that he was walking north, not south. He turned and went south again, but almost immediately, the signs again confirmed the same turnaround.

"Ya Allah! No fucking way," groaned Fares. "The fucking bug is trying to lock me in." He paced around. There wasn't any sign of a fence or a marker. "Not very helpful, is it?" Fares said.

While looking at his map, a cyclist went past. Fares persuaded him to stop. "How long do you think it would take you to ride to the end of the block and back?"

"Five minutes," the boy replied.

"If you do it in four and a half, I'll give you a buck."

Fares walked with him, and the switch happened again. The boy was slow in getting back, but he got his reward.

The boy proves to me that I am not going insane. The reality is unfortunately probably worse. Anyway, back to work, I guess, thought Fares. *Mr.*

Moretti might be pleased.

Fares got Anthony Moretti's wall repaired. During the touch up, paint spilled on his recently bought secondhand runners. *So much for street shoes*, he lamented.

He found from the tree services company that it would take another week and a half before they were able to cut the damaged tree in front. *And in the meantime, it's going to fall over and smash the building,* he thought. *Then what are we going to do? Kick the tenants onto the street because a tree on city property destroyed our building. The city will say it's an act of God, but if they got someone here and did the work like they are supposed to, the fucking tree wouldn't have had time to fucking fall over, would it?*

Fares relocated tenants that had broken windows. He arranged for a window repair company to replace the broken thermopane windows. In the meantime he avoided answering his phone and planned to spend the rest of the day painting the units.

In the late afternoon, it didn't take much for him not to fight the compulsion to return to the bakery. Once again, he met Ionna on the street.

"How do you know I was leaving?"

He shrugged.

"You told me that you were leaving."

"I did."

"And? Oh, I know why. It is because you didn't know that you can't walk across the Verazano-Narrows Bridge," she said. "You have to go across it by bus."

"I need to show you something."

"It doesn't involve you wearing shorts?"

"Do you have a thing about my pyjamas?"

"I told you I never saw them."

"Let us get on with it. I need to show you something."

"Which is?"

"Trust me. You wouldn't believe me if I told you. You go south, and I'm going to go east towards the Bay."

"But that's kilometres away. Is it like turning green?"

"Well, no, not quite," Fares said. "And when you're done, I'll be waiting for you at Andy Li's."

"What? 'Not quite'—what's that supposed to mean? There and back is more than a few miles. You're delusional," she said.

Fares walked off without answering her.

Ionna returned to the restaurant before Fares. She stopped sipping her soup when he came in.

His jean jacket and pants, like his sneakers, had paint stains. The dried smudge on his hand must have come from wiping the side of his head. He was clean-shaven, and his wavy dark hair swept across his ears and over the collar at the back. He stood with his cap in his hand.

Fares took a breath and then sat down.

"Now what the fuck was that?" she asked. She firmly grabbed his arm. "What the goddamn hell is going on?"

He put a hand on hers and replied, "I have been thinking about that all the way here. I have more questions than answers, and frankly, this is scaring the shit out of me."

"Yeah, I walked about a mile, and then I got turned around. I repeated the walk four times, and it kept happening," she said. "Was it a mind trick, or was it real?"

"I don't know," he said. "But something is fencing us in. Going east, I got almost two miles."

She wrapped her arms tightly.

A server brought over Ionna's order.

"I'll have what she's having," Fares said.

"Thanks, Andy," she said.

"I thought that it was self-serve?"

"He knows me. You should be nice."

Fares noticed that the man, who looked like a beefy wrestler, kept looking back.

"So what are we going to do?" she asked as she ate a forkful of noodles.

The server sat down and looked back at her.

"Actually, I'd like to get something to eat, pretend this isn't happening, shoot the breeze, and be a million miles away, and you?"

She smiled and replied, "You have a point." She raised a fork and kept eating.

After leaving Andy Li's, they agreed to do another walk south and see what would happen when they walked south together. They only got about another kilometre further. After that, Fares started stepping backward, and Ionna followed in kind. They did this for about sixty meters.

"Ionna, what do you see?" he asked.

"Not much, but it's kind of quiet. Actually, it's spooky quiet."

He pointed to the sky and said, "Look at that." It was a crow, but it was frozen in the air.

"Oh my god," she said.

"I see someone in the window of that apartment, but they're not moving."

"Same with that car that's coming towards us, but it's not moving."

"Are we fucking dead?"

"No—at least, I hope not. If we turn around and walk the way we came, they should all start moving again," he said. "Ready, one, two, three, go."

And just like he said, the car passed, the head in the window moved, and the bird flew on.

"Looks like we're not leaving the island," she said.

"Personally, I found that last trick a little excessive," Fares said. "It was like the aliens were showing off and letting us lesser folk know what we're up against."

"Well, it scared the bejesus out of me, so it worked."

"Tomorrow, why don't you do another walk with someone else?"

"And what do you think will happen?"

"They probably will keep moving on, and you will have seemed to disappear. When you turn around, though, you should be able to see them."

"If something else happens?"

"It would mean that bug has given us something that affects other things, and that would probably not be a good thing."

Eggs Don't Fly

Ionna and Fares decided to let others know about their secret. A walk was arranged after the bakery's closing. By the time everyone arrived, it was late, and night was setting in. Ionna invited Monica and Ossie. Fares introduced them o Charlie O'Keefe. Charlie was tall, beefy, and in his late twenties.

Ionna had just told the group that they were going to see something truly mazing. When Ossie asked if it was magic, she just said, "Sure."

Fares and Charlie watched from across the street. Ionna started in a rushed valk. Ossie and Monica trudged behind.

"Have you ever seen her this wound up?" Ossie asked.

"Bitchy all the time," Monica whispered. "She's got to get out more. This Mr. Khalil has really gotten her revved. It's like she's drinking too much coffee. How long has she been doing magic tricks? Personally, I think this is her first ttempt. Best we support her, no matter how it turns out."

"Monica, are you sure you don't know what she's going to do?"

"Don't have a clue."

"Houdini wrapped himself in chains and jumped off a bridge; you don't hink?—" Ossie asked.

"Don't be so melodramatic. Besides, we're going in the wrong way."

They watched her move faster, and then she vanished.

"Well, holy smokes," Ossie said.

"Well, I'll be damned. Look, she's appeared way back there," Monica said.

"She couldn't have run back there in that kind of time, no matter how fast she ran. There must be two people doing that," Ossie said. "I wonder if she can do it in the daytime."

When Ionna got close, Monica asked, "That was impressive. So how were you able to do that?"

"I got sprayed by a bug," she replied.

"Whoa," Ossie said. "That's a joke, right?"

They followed Ionna to where Fares and Charlie were waiting.

"That was not a trick," said Fares." He told them what happened.

"But that's not possible," Monica said.

"Charlie, you and Ossie stay here to watch what happens. Monica, please walk with us."

"Am I part of the trick?" Monica asked.

"No. Unfortunately, it's real, and it has got me worried," Ionna said. "Well, terrified, actually."

Monica walked in line with the others, keeping out of reach of Ionna. She stopped when she heard Ossie yell, "Whoa!"

"Oh, my god, I can't believe it," said Charlie. "You were with Monica, and then you showed up here. That's one hell of a messed-up thing."

"It won't let us out," said Fares.

"You mean that you can't go that way?" Monica said.

"Or that way," Fares said as he pointed east. "It wants us to go to the crater."

"Holy shit," said Ossie.

"Dear Lord," Monica said as she blessed herself. "Maybe we should get a priest," she said.

"It's an alien thing," said Fares.

"A physicist is what you need," said Charlie.

"The Jesuits might have some," said Monica.

“We definitely need something, and fast,” said Ionna.

“That calls for drinks,” Monica said as she stared at Ionna, who had her arms crossed.

“Hot chocolate for me and this lad,” said Fares. “Why don’t you all come to my place? It’s not special. It is what it is. We’ll pick up snacks and whatever at a convenience store along the way.

Fares’s apartment was a small one-bedroom. The living room had a couch and a chair. Fares brought out a fold-out chair from the closet. A kitchenette was part of the same space. A single framed icon was hung on the wall.

“Greek Orthodox,” Monica said as she looked at Ionna.

“No. St. Maron,” he said.

While he passed out mugs, Charlie brought in an extra chair and some sherry.

Fares put on the kettle while everyone else dealt with soda drinks and snacks. Ossie cracked open a bag of barbecue chips for himself and asked, “Now what is it that you needed to figure out?”

“We’re trapped here, and Fares is convinced that we have got to get off the island. Something is drawing us toward the crater. Fares believes that once that happens, aliens might invade.”

“What’s that got to do with you disappearing?” Ossie asked as he crunched more chips.

“If we try to walk away from here, we’re forced to return,” Fares said. “You saw us disappear, but what we saw was the road we had already travelled. Something turns us around, and it does it in a really creepy way.”

“Charlie and Ossie saw you disappear, and then in another minute you appeared behind me,” Monica said.

“And about time stopping—” Ionna said.

“They’re not going to believe that,” Fares said. There’s no way of showing them.”

"So what happens?" Ossie asked.

"Please do," Charlie said.

"When we stepped back, everything had frozen in time. We could move, but nothing else did."

"What would happen if you kept walking backwards?"

"Don't know. We'd probably be thrown out of the loop, I guess. I don't know at what stage this can affect our well-being."

"You think you might get snuffed?"

Fares just shrugged his shoulders.

"Maybe you could get a video of it on your phone," Charlie said.

"It might just be unique to us and not devices. It's something we could try, I suppose."

"How about we try this in the morning?" Ossie asked.

"Are you quitting?" Monica asked.

"You could close up just for a bit. Do you really want to miss out on this?" Ossie asked.

"10:30," she replied.

"If it wasn't for the fact that Manhattan was destroyed last week, I would say that all of this sounds pretty whacked out," Charlie said. "Fares, what's the point of all this?"

"Ionna and I believe that they're going to collect us."

"Alien abduction? Not like it hasn't happened before, but why you?" Charlie asked.

"We were in a crowd, and everyone else moved but us, is my guess, but honestly, I don't know. We weren't even next to one another."

"So what's picking you up?" Charlie asked.

"No idea."

"From what I've read, it would be something from the crater," Charlie said.

"How's that?"

"If someone wanted to send people long distances, they would need a receiving device. It might take a long time for the original object to be sent somewhere, but once it lands, living things could be transported to the original location at speeds near the speed of light. Once they have proof of delivery, they could send explorers."

"Or soldiers," said Ossie.

"Or soldiers," repeated Charles.

"What's proof of delivery?"

"You. If the two of you return to them unharmed, that proves that the doors are open. Your ability to survive in slowed time might suggest how they have prepared you for surviving the trip.

"Sounds like we should all get out of here while we have time," said Ossie.

"You have to give me notice," Monica said.

"It's hard to believe any of this, but I'm looking forward to going with you guys tomorrow," Charles said.

"Personally, I'd like not to think about any of this," Fares said.

"Charlie, where do your ideas come from?" asked Fares.

" *War of the Worlds* and *It Came from Outer Space*, I guess."

"Charlie, really? And what about the receiving device?"

"Comics mostly."

Before Fares could swear, Ossie passed him his almost empty bag of chips.

"Charlie, you were going to tell me what you do," Monica said.

"I am a student. I major in Geology. I read a lot of Science Fiction."

"I like murder mysteries," Monica said. "Especially on the seedy side."

Charlie gulped what was left in his glass. "I don't think any of you are taking this seriously enough. Aliens destroyed America's largest city, and they are preparing to launch an attack. This is like the beginning of World War III. Life isn't going back to normal. Monica, it is going to be the end of your business as you know it."

"Maybe, they just want to talk," Ionna said. "They told us this is a tribute. Maybe that just means they want to be sociable."

"You don't really believe that, Ionna, do you?" asked Monica.

"No, but it was worth a shot. Charlie, great sherry, by the way," Ionna said. She stroked her hair. "Fares, how's your hot chocolate?"

He smiled and answered with, "Absolutely marvellous."

Ionna and Fares made another public attempt to walk past the boundary in a different direction in the morning. The attempt failed again. The group returned to Monica's Bakery. Fares and Charlie ate and talked at a small table while the other three went behind the counter and got back to work.

"That was awesome," Ossie said as he loaded a small box with muffins. "You weren't there, and poof, you appeared."

"Too bad about your phone," Charlie said. "Poof, just like that, it disappeared."

"Yeah, I should have brought yours.

"Good that neither of you had a pacemaker," Monica said. She handed a little girl a bag of cookies.

"I don't know if any of you were paying attention, but this time it happened two city blocks sooner," Ionna said. "Soon, Fares will not be able to return home." After putting another couple of trays in the oven, she came to the counter and said, "OK. Scooting us along—Do any of you have any useful ideas?"

"Me? No, not really," Fares said.

"I know you have a good reason not to trust the government, but I think you should still consider going public," Charlie said. "There is a good case for bringing a lot of good, smart people into your circle. If you're forced to go to the crater, maybe someone can figure out how to break the control it has over you."

"I know someone who would love to interview you guys," Ossie said.

"I was thinking more like CNN or CBS."

"Charlie, you've got to start somewhere," Ossie said.

Fares quietly finished his coffee.

After work, Ionna and Fares shared pita sandwiches during a walk through the park. The others were making them feel claustrophobic. They had a shared need to get away.

"I know they think they're helping," Fares said. Ossie has us booked to speak to Woody Diggs tomorrow night. There are so many ways that this could go wrong."

Ionna tossed pieces of bread to the ducks. Fares was sketching.

"Not bad," she said.

"Better if the duck didn't keep moving," he said.

"When I saw the crow, it reminded me of how poor an artist I am at capturing life drawings," Fares said. "In medicine, it helps to be able to draw. It was like the bird stopped like that, so I could take my time to capture its flight on paper. It was really strange."

"So, what did you leave when you came here?" she asked.

"I lost everything. My parents and my sister were in our house when we lost it. There was nothing left. My brother arranged for me to get here. I left school and everything I had except a pack on my back. He joined my sister in Gaza. You know how bad things are there now. I've been sending them everything I can, but I've never been able to verify if they've received any of it. You didn't tell me what happened to your family."

"We were on a boat cruise with friends of my husband. It was the worst time in my life. I got badly wasted and fell asleep. When I woke up, I was in the water. Someone put a life jacket on me. I was there alone. Everyone else disappeared with the boat. My Thea was three years old. And my precious Nikos was five. I completely fell apart. I never could forgive myself. The business went bankrupt, and I didn't sober up until I came here."

For the first time, Fares held her hand.

"When time stopped and I saw that crow, it reminded me of when I awoke on the water. Both things were unreal," she said.

"How did you end up working with Monica?"

"I needed to find work. Any work. I came in to get a coffee. She swore in Greek, and then I asked her for a job. I just needed a place to hang my hat."

"She's Italian. How did she come to know Greek?"

"This is Brooklyn. You meet people. You pick things up. Lots of people come to America. Look at us."

"We'd better go," he said.

She took another drink of her coffee and looked at him. "Let's do that again. Bring your drawing pad," she said.

"Maybe charcoal," he said and laughed.

The sky was still dark and menacing, but for them, it felt like it had gotten brighter than it was.

Ossie brought the group to Woody's apartment in the evening. The broadcast was set up in a small spare room in Woody's apartment. The five of them sat on simple fold-out chairs and were tightly squeezed together.

"Welcome to *Woody's Net Raves* and your man, Woody Diggs. To-night we have special guests with us. Everyone out there is familiar with the biggest story of our time—the destruction of Manhattan. Well, our guests are here to tell you that it wasn't a stone that made that big hole; it was an alien object.

"Fares Khalil and Ionna Sari are here to explain tonight why everyone else has the story wrong."

"My name is Fares. After the initial shockwave, I headed to Prospect Park. It looked like a better place to be than near the buildings. A crowd collected in an open area. Something came in from the trees. To me, it looked like an egg. When it hatched, a plated bug emerged. It sprayed Ionna and me and then disintegrated. The remaining material looked like very fine dust. It stained our skin. After that, each of us went home and slept for days."

"So what makes you think that the thing was related to the crater?"

"Eggs don't fly," Ionna said. "And how many bugs with armour do you know that are a meter long? And that thing sprayed foam twice from at least six meters away. And how many animals of any kind just disintegrate? That clearly wasn't from New York."

"When Ionna and I tried to leave, something stopped us," Fares said.

"What do you mean?" Woody asked.

"It's better that someone else who has seen it explain," Fares said.

"My name is Charlie O'Keefe. I know their story sounds hard to believe, but there are three of us who can confirm that something very strange is going on. We watched these folks go a few blocks, and they just disappeared. A minute later, we would see them appear behind us but walking in the opposite direction."

"They told me that they believe that aliens have selected them to test their transportation device that's buried underground," Charles said. "If the machine works, we expect that those returning will come back armed. We don't believe they're friendly or especially good people."

"What happened last Thursday was bad, but to hear that things could go unimaginatively worse does not sound good," Woody said.

"You people shouldn't be putting words in my mouth," Fares said. "There's a lot that we don't know, and we don't want people out there acting crazy. People could get hurt.

The broadcast went on for another fifteen minutes. Much of the subject matter involved Woody quoting social media stories from New Yorkers who shared how they were affected by the crash and how afraid they were of the future. Fares closed by saying that the main thing he wanted from the authorities was for them to at least dig the alien artifact up.

Woody closed with, "I am glad you are all listening to my channel. Please remember to tag a like if you found this useful. Thanks again for listening. This is Woody Diggs for *Woody's Net Raves.*"

Fares and Ionna, along with the other three, walked back to the bakery. The recording studio was only a couple of blocks away.

"I think that went well, considering," Charlie said.

"I don't expect that government officials will be coming for you, Charlie," said Fares. "Bringing up the story about alien invaders was a mistake."

"Yeah, well, it's true, isn't it?"

"It's an opinion, but it's not a fact."

"Why are you both wearing backpacks?" Charlie asked.

"I can't go home. The barrier by tonight will stop me from returning to my apartment."

"He's staying with me tonight," said Ossie.

"Ionna might have another day or so, but she packed just in case."

"So I'm supposed to hire someone else?" Monica asked.

"They need our help. I mean, they're Americans," Ossie said. "They're one of us."

"Yes, of course, dear. Shock makes people say foolish things, doesn't it?" she replied.

"I'm not an expert, but I believe these things just send bodies, not things," Charlie said.

"If they return, wouldn't they bring weapons?" Fares asked.

"Maybe you're right. What I do know is that when I fly, I only bring carry-on luggage," said Charlie. "Anything else, you get charged, and it just disappears."

"Just disappears," repeated Fares, with a grin.

At the bakery, Monica unlocked the doors. She served up coffee and sandwiches. The five of them sat around the same table. The talk changed to idle chit-chat. For a brief interval, anything related to the crater was left outside. They shared a last meal before having to say their goodbyes.

Leaving Brooklyn

The Diggs interview was initially picked up on conspiracy channels. The flying egg comment was widely replicated in comedic Mojo vids. When heavy machinery moved onto the site, the media frenzy began. A week after the Diggs broadcast, the invisible wall had forced Fares and Ionna through Boerum Hill and into Brooklyn's downtown.

When the couple reached lines of cameras and media trucks, a large crowd of followers had collected around them. In spite of complaints and swears from Monica, she was joined by Ossie, Charlie, and a half-dozen people from Fares's apartment. Fares thought that they couldn't stand him, but he was mistaken. Even Mrs. Juliet Fabbrini was there. She caught a ride with Mr. Konstas. Charlie and Andy sat in the back with his dog.

The line of media blocked an intersection. Behind them, the downtown lay in ruins. Anyone in a vehicle got out and joined the onlookers.

Mrs. Fabbrini joined Monica and told her, "That Ionna Sari will set him right. I'm sure of it."

Monica kept close to Charlie, and Ossie, not wanting to lose his job, followed her lead.

To legitimize their time, the media demanded to witness their disappearing act. They asked to see it again so they could get footage of it from a chopper. The story quickly became front-page news.

"Do you believe they are friendly?" a woman from CNN asked.

"They're taking us against our will. What do you think?" Fares replied.

'*Two Recent Immigrants, an Arab and a Greek, Are Being Taken Away by Aliens*,' was the story line that appeared in right-wing media. '*Aliens Taken by Aliens*' was one headline. '*Who Really Was Behind 9/11?*' was another.

After the media were given what they asked for, they moved out of the way. The couple with their entourage kept strolling towards the East River.

"Do you believe that the Statue of Liberty survived?" Ionna asked.

"I don't know. If it was damaged, it will need to get fixed. In these times, will anyone want to bother?"

"Not everyone is like that?"

"Are you sure?" he asked.

Ahead of them, entire office towers had fallen. Breaks in the ruins still provided a view of the remains of bridges. Fares tightened his hand on Ionna's and pointed to the Manhattan Bridge and then to the Brooklyn Bridge.

"They're in bad shape. I wasn't expecting this. We might be able to get across, but it looks pretty scary."

A convoy of black cars and vans meandered around the ruins. It stopped a city block from the pedestrians. A group of men in black suits marched towards them. When the first two got within six meters of them, they stopped and waited.

A man with sunglasses and a black suit, who looked like a beefy bouncer at an expensive club, had a microphone clipped to his lapel. He asked, "Will you come with us?" He pointed to an open car door. Black glass did not reveal who was driving.

"No," Fares said. "But you can come with us and our friends."

"That's not how this is going to work," he said. The man waved for the two bulky men behind him to take them.

"Stay back. You don't have the authority."

Ionna moved behind him.

When one of them tried to grab him, he stepped back and waved for the media to move in.

"Don't make this more difficult than it has to be," the man in black said.

"Louder, for the cameras, please," Fares said.

The media, who followed behind, slipped around them and moved ahead. The crowd opened like the parting of the Red Sea to let Miley Springfield from CNN come into the scene.

"Who are you, and by what authority are you attempting to grab people off of our streets?"

"That's not your concern."

"Are you with military intelligence? Why isn't our government addressing our concerns?"

While the men were distracted, Fares and Ionna and their procession quickly moved on.

When they got to the other side of a fallen building, everyone could see that there was a blockade waiting for them. Heavily armed soldiers stopped them and told them that they weren't allowed to go any further. From beyond the line, a soldier came up to meet them.

When the man got close, Fares said, "Hello, officer."

"That's Major," and he pointed to his name tag. "Major Branagh.

"Major, if you watched the news, you'd know that there's nothing that you can do to prevent us from getting there," Fares said.

"We could shoot you," he said.

"And then maybe, it would take you," Fares replied. He was distracted when he overheard Monica whisper to Ossie, "No talking to him. He's clueless and has fungus for brains."

The soldier apparently wasn't paying attention. Something from his earpiece caught his attention. He quietly returned to somewhere beyond the roadblock.

Fares sat down on a block of concrete, where he pulled out a book and a couple of sandwiches from his pack. He gave the latter to Ionna.

"What are you reading?" Ionna asked him.

"Charlie gave it to me. It's called *The Grapes of Wrath.* I believe that we are waiting for someone in charge. This might take a while."

Ionna watched a growing media circus in front of her. None of the interviewers seemed to get much. Onlookers just ranted about their government and their lot in life while the soldiers said nothing and tried to look unwieldy and manly.

"What is happening isn't normal," Fares said. "The military should have shown up long before now. Someone political has put a thumb on how they want things done."

"What if the barrier comes this far?" asked Ionna.

"Then time will stop, and we can do what the fuck we want, and maybe for as long as we want, assuming how and if we could survive in it. And then, of course, when we left, we would probably come out beyond the blockade. But honestly, who knows? If there were a lot of people back there, maybe we would land inside somebody."

"Good God, why would you bring that up? That is so gross," she replied. After folding her arms and pacing around, she waved for the media to come over.

To the reporters she said, "These walnuts are preventing us from approaching the crater. Why don't you uno-to-uno get this on tape? Or better still, why don't all of you get in on this? Isn't this supposed to be a free country?"

Fares watched another soldier come out to talk to Miley Springfield. The soldier provided a mangled and incoherent reply.

Fares looked to Ionna for an interpretation.

"He's just waiting for someone in charge to come and deal with this," she said.

Fares read, others sat eating, and a few tried to sneak beyond the blockade to investigate the city ruins. Fifty minutes later, a tall, greenish, amphibious combat vehicle drove up from behind the blockade. Lines of soldiers opened up to fully reveal the vehicle.

The soldier managing the defensive line saluted and yelled, "General George Edwards, sir."

An Amphibious Combat Vehicle drove through the swarm of civilians. The onlookers were sent running and screaming out of fear of being run over. The vehicle stopped beyond the blockade and the media swarm. The vehicle circled to point back towards the water. Lines of soldiers came running to encircle the vehicle, as the general didn't climbed out from a turret on top.

Fares watched the general march towards Fares and Ionna as six soldiers ran to catch up. The general seemed to recognize them.

"So you are the couple that's causing all this ruckus," he said.

"The alien object is responsible. You're reacting to it," Fares said.

"A smartass, too," said a man in a grey suit who came from behind Fares.

"Where the fuck did that guy come from?" muttered Fares. He looked back at him and watched him pass.

"Well, well," said the man in the grey suit when he greeted the general.

"Hello, Phil."

"We don't have a choice in this. Doesn't look like neither of you are doing much," Fares said.

"You think it's going to open up for you and give you an expense-free trip to somewhere else?" the general asked.

"If you can get someone else to go, please do. It's really something I'd rather have nothing to do with," Fares said.

"So, why don't you go back to where you came from?" asked the man in the grey suit.

"Since you don't watch the news, why don't you ask the folks back there?"

"OK, I'll humour you. Men move the barricades. We'll walk with you," the general said. "I don't need to see your disappearing trick. I've followed it up close."

"Not too close, I hope," Ionna said, as they all hurried to get beyond where the amphibious personnel carrier was parked.

"So you don't believe they are folks that we can get along with?" the general asked.

"I haven't met them, but so far I have my doubts."

"What's changed?"

"What do you mean?" asked Fares. "You're not boxing us in with sycophants, and I'm talking with you?"

"You don't have to tell him anything, general," the man in the grey suit said.

"They'll see it all when we get there anyway. Events have advanced very quickly. We don't have to do anything to verify your story because we've seen the craft. It dug itself out of the dirt on its own. It built a spiderweb-type lattice structure around it. The higher-ups got antsy and decided to blow it up. Every time something was shot, the projectile was returned to the source with a hundred percent termination rate."

"Time freeze barrier protection," Fares said.

"What?" asked the man in the grey suit.

"Well—" the general said.

"The barrier that limits our access uses the same technology," Fares said. "If we walk backward, we will be able to experience it."

"And you're the only ones," the general muttered. "Which is why you're the only ones that can go in there."

"So if you throw somebody else in there, they'll probably bounce back or disintegrate. I mean, a person is not a thing like an inanimate missile, so who knows what rules apply?"

"We have a good idea," General Edwards said.

"I don't hear any bright ideas about how to prevent us from going," Fares said.

"We don't want to stop you. We want you to bring a beacon," said the man in the grey suit.

"Phil, it's not the time," the general said.

"In case you were wondering, general, you work for us," said the man in the grey suit.

"Might as well not delay this," said the general as he gave a wave to someone behind. The amphibious combat vehicle pulled up behind.

When the general stared at him, Fares froze.

"Are you going to get a lift with us, or are you going to swim across?"

"We'd like our friends and respected members of the press to see us off. If you can agree with that, we'll go with you," Fares said.

Ionna nodded in agreement.

The general had soldiers wave them inside. Phil attempted to board, but the general told him that since he came with all the big bucks, he could get his own. He waved for some of his soldiers to board.

As they boarded, Ionna and Fares watched their friends wave them goodbye. When the back door closed, they were boxed in. There were no windows that enabled them to see outside.

Once the vehicle drove out, Fares asked, "Who was he?"

"He's a nobody who thinks he's a politician," the general said.

On the drive across the river, they could hear the splash of water, but they couldn't see out. There were no windows.

In the middle of crossing, a woman soldier reached for Ionna's backpack. Ionna was wearing it. The soldier told her that scientists had asked her to document what was being brought from Earth.

"Bullshit, you fool. You are not customs. The flight crew on the vessel will decide, so go fuck yourself."

"Asshole, that is none of your business. Leave her alone. What trinkets we bring are meaningless to you. You were trying to plant something," Fares said. Both glared at the general.

"Private Jennifer Banks, I am sure you meant well. I am sure that the research team had their reasons, but these folks have made some good points. This is an incredibly stressful situation for everyone. Honestly, if I were taking this trip, I would have no idea what I would take. What about you, Private Banks?"

"No, sir. I would have no idea."

Fares felt like he was moving within a metal coffin. The space was almost full. There were nine of them, not including the two on top.

After the vehicle let them off near the crater, Fares saw that the island had become a wasteland. It was covered with the ruins of broken towers. The crater was encircled on one side by an unruly, ranting mob.

Fares saw signs with their faces on them, which had writing similar to '***Aliens go home.***' A large ship and a flotilla of pleasure boats on the Hudson River had similar '***Go Home***' signs and banners.

"You allowed this shit, but you stopped the crowd behind us? And are the others coming?"

"This wasn't my doing," the general said.

"Getting us here in this truck sure was. General, I don't believe a word you're saying."

"We don't have a way of stopping you from boarding, but if you carry this beacon, I will be able to send soldiers after you. With their help, you can come back," he said. The general pointed to the object in the crater. "There was an opening, but my men weren't able to get in."

Fares saw soldiers being carried on stretchers to ambulances, which were on the other side of the crater.

"When you're ready, this tracker beacon will let my men locate you."

"Ionna, are you ready?" Fares asked.

She leaned back and folded her arms. Next, she bent forward and aimed her right hand fingers towards his chin and said, "This is just royally fucked up nonsense—What do you think?" She spun her hand around in the air and waved it away.

He shrugged and told her that he couldn't have described it any better. "It stinks," he said.

The army forced the crowd back, but the ugly, hate-infested rants continued. They were confronted with signs like '***Go where you belong, Take it with you,***' and '***Egg us alone.***'

The beacon was on wheels. It was strapped to a handle. When walking along the ground, Fares pulled it as if it were a heavy suitcase with seven-centimetre wheels. It was awkward to manoeuvre when he had to slide down the steep dirt wall of the crater.

When Fares got down to the bottom of the crater, he waited for Ionna to join him. Once she reached him, he pointed to an entrance. The site was enclosed by a black, sparkling, spider-like canopy. Thick beam-like ends punctured into the ground. Underneath the covering was a thick mesh.

Fares didn't see any snipers above, but he could sense them. They moved towards the entrance to keep out of sight.

"It's not a beacon. It's a bomb," he told Ionna. I can tell the difference between a transmitter and a weapon. This is why the soldiers didn't escort us down. They had no intention of bringing the media or our friends because they didn't want any witnesses to see what was going to happen."

"What do you mean?"

They aren't going to send someone after us because they don't know how to prevent their soldiers from getting killed."

"So nothing could have been done for us?" Ionna asked.

"No, I didn't say that. They didn't even try. Monica and Mrs. Fabbrini are good people. But so many others have lost their way. Why it's like that is something that I don't have an answer for.

"If they had bothered to earn our trust, they might have found out why we're special, and once inside, we might have found a way of sharing what we've seen. Once we're in there, we might be able to walk out again. If they bothered to make us a real tracker, it might have enabled the Americans to clone the technology and travel to the stars.

"Ionna, I have had it with the unwelcoming and self-obsessed bullshit. Looks like new folks are going to move in and really stir things up. From what I've seen, it might even be an improvement. You never know," Fares said.

"We are free at last. I'm not sure I'm ready for this, but I am glad I am with you," Ionna said.

Staring into her eyes, he asked, "May I?" She blinked, and he kissed her. They hugged each other tightly for minutes, with the consolation that each could still feel the other breathing. He caressed her hair and asked her what she was thinking.

"It's going to be a long trip. I think we should take a pee before we go."

That got him howling with laughter. After pissing on the bomb, he zipped up.

Fares heard a lot of noise at the crater's edge. "Ionna, go ahead," he said. "I will be right behind."

When Ionna stepped through the entrance, she had to bend over. The top of the door was at the level of her shoulders. Fares threw his pack behind her. He rolled the bomb out from under the canopy. A barrage of sniper fire hit near the bomb and the canopy above him. His arm was grazed. He dove into the entrance. He grabbed his pack and ran after Ionna into the darkness. He almost bowled her over. Beyond the entrance, they were able to stand up. After a couple of minutes of walking, the tunnel ended.

Ionna lit a match, which revealed a bare rock wall. "What in blazes?" she asked. "All this way for this?"

A breeze blew the light out. Something formed around them. As it grew, a very dim light was emitted. Fares put his arm around her to keep her close. A soap bubble-like thing surrounded them, and they felt it rise upward. They were forced to kneel down due to a lack of space. Both screamed as the bubble lunged forward and picked up speed fast. The dim light was turned off.

"Holy mother…" Ionna moaned.

Less than a minute after it picked them up, the force from an explosion forced them to fall. The noise was deafening. The acceleration increased. It got very hot. Both couldn't move and were having difficulty breathing. The ball didn't slow down until about twenty minutes later.

"Where's it taking us?" she whimpered.

"Not sure, but I'd guess that the launch site must be set up away from the impact crater. That would explain why they gave us a couple of weeks to get here. Earthlings wouldn't be able to mess with it if they didn't know where it was. Let's just hope it doesn't let us out at the bottom of the ocean."

"General Edwards?"

"The crowd is definitely gone. But him? I'm not sure. His chopper would have had to have been in the air, but I don't know if he would have been able to get away from the blast that fast. Maybe someone wanted to get rid of him. If I were to put money on it, I'd say that it was his old buddy Phil. I am glad the others stayed behind."

"The general was still near the crater's edge when I went in," Ionna said. "Phil was creepy. If he could get to a chopper, yes, definitely him. But why kill everyone?"

"Because they were fools. Before they really know anything, they try to blow up the artifact. With it gone, no-one comes back. They want to just forget about it."

After the ball stopped, it disappeared. They were left in an open area that was again lit with indirect lighting. Unlike the cramped space of the entrance doorway and the ball, the open space allowed them to stand. The ceiling was a meter higher than Fares was. The air was cool and musty, like you would experience in a cave.

"Where do you think we are?" she asked.

"We could be anywhere. Maybe even under the ocean."

With tightly folded arms, she paced nervously around the small, dark room. "You know, I'll never get to see the Statue of Liberty," Ionna said. "I'll never get to see Venice, nor Hawaii, nor New Zealand, even. Have you ever skied in the Alps? Swam in a salt sea? Been on a dog sled?

"And I'll never see them again. And no more cooking in that godforsaken bakery. Not just this place but anywhere."

"I have never skied," he replied. "But I have been to the Statue of Liberty. I can tell you about it. You will see it through my eyes.

"I would have liked to know if my brother is alive. Now they are going to be on their own."

"Just like us."

"Yes, just like us." Fares put up his arm and kept repeating, "Sari-Khalil, Sari-Khalil."

Ionna joined in. She grabbed, forced him to the wall, and patiently kissed him.

They were interrupted by a gurgling sound.

"Fuck," they both groaned.

A big bug similar to the one that they had seen at the park was near their feet. Holographic light shone above its back. The creature led them to adjoining seats that were against another wall. The hologram emitted from its back gave instructions. It showed them that they had to put all of their belongings, luggage, packs, and coats on the floor.

Like at an airport, it showed an X-ray of his pack. It highlighted some things. From Fares's pack, the bug highlighted a clay bust, chips, and an egg sandwich. Fares removed them and put them in a pile in front of it. Ionna, after prompting, did the same.

The objects disappeared into the floor. It was unclear if they were being collected or disintegrated. Ionna lost a phone, cosmetics, sandwiches, and a couple of juice boxes.

They were shown a place under their seats for their packs. The creature tried to explain what was going to happen during flight preparations, but Fares couldn't make sense of any of it.

"Ionna, besides being terrified, how are you?"

"Terrified."

"We'll find our way, somehow," Fares said.

"What are you thinking?" she asked.

"Tribute," he said. He removed his cap. "I thank God."

"For this?" she asked as she crawled onto a seat.

"Yes. For all this."

"Why?"

"Because, if it wasn't for this, we never would have met, would we?"

He bowed and then put his cap back on.

"If this flight served alcohol, I'd raise a toast too. You had better put your cap with your pack. You're hesitating. You might still need it. Maybe it's tropical."

After ditching it, he climbed onto his seat and said, "Well, we did have some spicy Doritos."

"Maybe, if we ask the flight attendant nicely, what do you think?"

The engines started. Fares reached for her hand, but the seats forced them apart. The seats reformed into two separate isolation pods. Their bodies sank deeply into the seat fabric. Straps wound around them so they couldn't move.

The lighting dimmed to a dull gloom.

"Stop it," yelled Ionna.

Fares, once again, felt like he was trapped in the damaged apartment building that had crushed his family. The material wouldn't budge.

Ionna struggled aggressively.

"You're not drowning," Fares said. "I am here with you."

The big bug scurried across the floor. It rocked back and forth as its many feet danced about. The couple stopped moving and didn't say a word.

From out of its head grew stalks. Big eyeballs grew out of the ends. Pincers grew out from the front.

Next, it somehow got upright. It leaned on its backside and showed all its thousands of little feet scurrying. The behaviour was not very bug-like. Next, it crawled up onto Fares's seat. It moved over him but didn't crush his chest.

Fares banged his arm against his bindings. Ionna did the same. The bug turned and faced him for a few seconds. Its antennas wiggled around. Next, it backed off and climbed off the seat.

"Looks like you had a moment there," she said.

"No idea."

The fabric retreated from their arms, and on the armrest, a pile of chips remained.

"Well, isn't that something? They have in-flight service," Fares said.

"Bug poop? You first," Ionna taunted.

PART 2

In Irons

A year after General George Edwards was killed in an explosion in New York, his daughter docked his father's boat in a remote inlet in the Caribbean. The events of that day were not heavy on her mind, nor was her father's passing. She was not particular about formalities or things that didn't concern her.

Olivia took a slow drag of air. It was fresh, briny, bracing, and vast. Not marshy like Florida. And the air was quiet; the birds weren't calling.

But this pounding , she thought.

Sunshine beamed in from the cabin portal. She tried to suppress a hangover by compressing her grip on the pillow against her cheek. The squeeze blocked her eye.

She rolled onto her back with the pillow over her face. The rocking waves caressed. So gentle, so eternal, she thought. *Am I going to survive it?*

She pushed the pillow aside and spun around to sit up, but stubbed her toes on a bottle of Jack Daniels. The bottle sloshed across the cabin sole to a corner.

"Fuck," she groaned.

She was still wearing jeans and a T-shirt.

Olivia grabbed a pair of her socks from the bed and smelled them. They got thrown at the bottle. A trudge into the head led to a throw-up. A bottle of aspirin was added to her pocket before washing her face. After glancing at her lipstick, she stared into the mirror and puckered.

"It's all about presentation, isn't it?" Olivia mocked.

A pair of socks from her dresser was slipped into her back pocket. After scooping her deck shoes from the carpet. She flung out a hand in the air as if she had just sung something and then turned the door knob. It opened the door to leftovers—to yesterday's business.

A body lay across cushions by the galley table. Blood dripped across the tabletop where he must have hit his head. There was a hole in the window glass above.

At least it didn't go through the hull, she thought.

She crouched and opened the small fridge door. She meant to reach for a bottle of water, but she was shaking. She stood up and put two hands on the counter to steady herself and took a steeped breath. "Fucked up or what?" she said.

She grabbed a bottle of water and took a swig. Olivia popped a couple of aspirin and took another drink. The coffee maker was started up. From the fridge, she dropped some strawberries into the cup and took a banana. From the sink, she grabbed her fleece jacket.

Looking at the electronics board above the radio, she noticed that the outside lights were off. *A baddy; Could have gotten a ticket,* she thought and grinned.

She stepped over the body that was reaching for the companionway. As she stepped up, she said, "At least the doors were open."

From the cockpit, she noticed that a couple of holes had pierced the bulkhead. "Cosmetic," she said. "At least the hull is untouched."

She sat on a cushion across from the helm, eating her strawberries. A man's body had washed up on shore. There were blood stains on his back.

Why would somebody want to end the world? she pondered and gave a spit.

She left the peels from her banana in her empty cup and headed to the anchor.

No-one else anchored here. Expected; considering, she thought. *This inlet was not popular even in normal times.*

After pulling anchor, she saw a body floating towards shore. It should have sunk, she thought. “Persistence,” she said. “And impassioned evil.”

She motored out until she was ready to take the wind. Her grandfather’s sailboat had two masts. She pulled the sheet ropes until the jib in front was rolled out in full. The mainmast was reefed at half. She steered away from the wind in a run and then secured the wheel to keep her course. She hurried down to the galley to get a coffee and yesterday’s half-eaten sandwiches. She returned with a map and a notebook from the shelf under the radio.

Sitting in the cockpit, she pulled the table up and laid out a course according to the coordinates she was given yesterday. The boat was rocking, which implied that the wind direction was changing. She took over the wheel and manoeuvred lines to enable a port tack. Olivia sailed the boat around to head into what was coming. She was hoping to raise the main while she could, but it was too late.

She wheeled the boat to turn to a starboard tack and quickly realigned her sheeting lines. Olivia configured a course on the chart plotter, which was above the compass. She set the boat angled slightly away from the direct wind on a port close haul. She set the autopilot to maintain her course.

Olivia got a spare line out of a locker and attached an end around a corpse in the galley. At the cockpit end, she locked the live line with a clutch and replaced its end with the the rope that was tied to the body. She wound the winch handle, and pulled the corpse up to the cockpit. She managed to shove it onto the swim shelf for a final push off.

She cleared the pockets of each corpse before introducing them to the creatures of the underworld.

“Good riddance, motherfuckers,” Olivia said. She was never one to reflect much on the afterlife. Her mother died early, and her father, the general, was never around much. And neither of them got much from her except curses.

Robert was a more considerate sort, she thought. *The oldest became a marine like General George Edwards. Six years in, and he died in a fucking helicopter crash near Philadelphia. A plane hit. Wasn’t even supposed to be there.*

Typical. Too many fuckers not knowing their ass from their face.

The other went on to study bird catching or something. Paleontology, I think. What the hell? I haven't heard from him in nine fucking years. Oh, and poor, poor Robbie. He's lost somewhere. What's new?

The General was never as much a dad as Grandpa was. "Go into the navy," he told him. And look at what it got, old George. Boom. Enjoy your retirement.

I loved hearing the sounds of Grandpa's cuts, slices, and swishes. It meant it was his turn with the best of his spices and secrets. Oh, and what my grandpa could do with our fresh catch, kelp, peppers, and who knows what. Yum, it was so good. Maybe I remember it that way because it was his turn. Our ocean gave us these things. The ocean has been the way it is since before any of us. It is what holds us up.

As long as there were fair skies, there would be no-one to hold us back. We always had a direction, but that never prevented us from changing it or what we were going to do. We would prepare for any journey to fly within the still, navigate beyond building swells, crashing breakers, and the worst of storms, and even survive the long, tedious boredom of sailing without sleep.

I remember the long hauls—the sweat, tears, and a full bilge from an ocean ready to weigh us down to Davy Jones. I remember putting this boat back together piece by piece. And I remember taking it out for the first time without my grandpa, when there was just me.

"Since the end of the world is coming, I don't expect that we're going to have time to go fishing anymore," Olivia said. "Good to have a final thought, I guess. This, I suppose, would be a good time to make an exception.

"Dear Lord, may this fish food that we offer make the sea creatures bountiful that eat them. Lord, please hear my prayer. Amen."

She noticed that there was still a pair of shoes left in the cockpit. She quickly threw them overboard and repeated an "Amen."

She stepped down the companionway, and the sight of blood spatter, scattered bottles, and garbage in her galley made her want to retch. After wiping the blood off the floor and table, she noticed the stains on the cushion.

"Damn, I'll never get that out. Damn you, fucking Marty Flowers." Olivia wished she could get that ugly face out of her head.

Olivia set sail with her four passengers from near Palm City, Florida, and headed to the Caribbean. It wasn't until three days in, that she had a chance to sit and assess her concerns. Olivia returned to the cockpit with a coffee and put her feet up.

Damn, and it was all because of that stupid chicken, she thought. *Lots to remember and wish I could forget. My husband talked about developing investment options outside his chain of car dealerships. And then I had to push dear David to actually do it.*

"Why should I do something different?" David Butler asked her. "I know what I'm doing."

"It has been eight years since you brought your ideas to Marvin and Gurney. You go on and on about what you are going to do, but it is all nothing but talk." That is when she threw the chicken at him.

"What the fuck, Olivia? I'm trying to read here, and you threw this stupid plastic flamingo at me."

"It's a chicken, stupid. Go get some air. Will do you right. Might clear that head of yours."

Unfortunately, he did exactly what was asked. He got involved in politics, and then it came back on her.

"I got something urgent," David said. "These guys need a boat, and they are willing to pay."

"When?"

"In a week."

"But I'm committed."

"Is it worth $25,000?"

"Are they crazy?" Olivia blurted. "Better not be drugs. Maybe a hundred thousand for that."

"No, apparently it's legit. Four guys want to go somewhere near the islands."

"Is this a kinky thing?"

"No, it's scientific. Real important, they say. It's urgent."

"Fifteen thousand, and those repairs you owe will all be paid for. I mean, you couldn't ask for more, could you?"

"OK, fine. They've got my interest. Ask them when I can meet up."

"I told him at one at Jimmy's."

"Fuck off. Why did you do that without asking?"

"Twenty-five G's is why. The deal is not going to wait for you. You know me. One thing I'm good at is smelling them out."

Yeah, sure, David, she thought. *You can really smell them out.*

Olivia, who was now en route, sat up and took a sip from her cup. There was a bad taste, and it wasn't the coffee.

Olivia remembered meeting Marty Flowers for the first time at the restaurant. The man didn't go into details about his project or specifically who he was. He just said that he was with the government. 'Involved scientific research,' he said. His ID said DIF. I didn't have a clue what that was and still don't.

The contract was for a two-week trip for four passengers and some scientific equipment. The men were responsible for their own cooking and cleanup. They paid five grand up front into my account and would pay for food once they got the receipt.

At this point in the trip, they had travelled for three days away from the mainland. When David confirmed that Flowers still hadn't paid for the food, Olivia started to have serious doubts about who and what she was dealing with.

Olivia confronted Marty Flowers the next day.

"Mr. Flowers, you told me that you were on a scientific mission. But why did Mr. Lewis bring along a portable television camera?"

"We're documenting our work. Nothing to be concerned with."

"The coordinates are in the ocean. Did you make a mistake?"

"No, that's right. If we need to change it, I'll tell you."

"But you didn't bring diving gear."

"No, that is OK. We'll be just fine. We have what we need for now."

When she got in range of a cell tower, she texted her husband to check her account again. She told him that she didn't trust Marty Flowers. She asked him to take a closer look at the man's background.

"That's all I need," he replied. "It's so busy right now."

"It's important, David. Please do it for me," she asked.

"I'll do what I can," he said.

Something is up, she thought. *And it's not me.*

Olivia confronted Mr. Flowers about why the bill hadn't been paid.

"Just a misunderstanding," Marty said when confronted.

"Just a misunderstanding—your ass," said Olivia. "Fix it, or I am dropping you off at the next port."

When Marty hauled out his sat radio from his cabin, he had to bend over for it. His sweater pulled up and revealed a gun holster on his back. She watched as Hugh picked at some French fries. She noticed that he had a noticeable bulge under his arm.

Why would analysts need guns, she wondered. *We are supposed to be sailing towards the people they work with.*

"Give it an hour," Marty told her after hanging up. "Why are you acting like this, Mrs. Butler? You know that your husband has vouched for us."

"No, somebody else did. That's not the same. Trust is something earned. What I have seen so far is a bit flaky. All I expect is what was promised."

Late at night, her husband confirmed that the money had finally shown up in her account.

Marty Flowers and his men kept to themselves in the galley, which made matters worse. She was wary because all of her other clients tended to huddle around a table near her in the cockpit above. Being able to hear everything allowed her to fix things before problems lit up. People who stayed above deck and kept an eye on the horizon were less likely to get seasick. She hated cleaning up barf from drunks who were too lazy to take care of themselves. Since she couldn't overhear what Marty Flowers was telling his men, she placed a small recording device under the galley table.

After mooring for the night and securing the boat, Olivia snuck a whisky bottle from a box the men left on the counter. She removed the listening device from its Velcro pocket under the table. She closed the door of her quarters and sprawled across her mattress.

Buggers, all of them, she thought.

Her passengers cooked for themselves, but they lived like pigs. Never cleaned anything. Papers and scraps were left on the table, floor, and sink countertops. Clothes were left scattered around the galley amongst the many cans and empty bottles. All but Marty tramped around in bare feet.

They had money. Why not bring your fucking deck shoes?

She poured herself a cup, popped in the earbuds, and zipped through the recording. The clip that she spent the most attention on included the men's plan to fix an unnatural disaster.

"So we have developed a black hole? LSI, I mean."

"Get your head in the game, Brad. If anyone hears about this, we work for LSI," said Marty Flowers.

"Yeah, sure, boss."

"A small black hole?" asked Earnie Saunders after pouring himself another drink.

"Big, small, they all do the same thing," said Hugh Clarke.

"Fixing climate change is all about taking carbon dioxide out of the air," said Earnie.

"How does a black hole get carbon dioxide out of the atmosphere?" asked Brad.

"Carbon dioxide gets fed into it and never comes out," said Earnie.

"What if the black hole gets loose?" asked Brad.

"It spills into the ocean and sucks up all the water until it is gone," said Earnie.

"That sounds real bad. That could create a media shit storm."

"Yes, Brad, work it from the ocean angle. What do you think, Hugh?" asked

Marty.

"The poor whales, the octopus, baby seals, and the loss of tuna. Everyone likes tuna, right? And they will all be gone. So sad."

"Has a bit of flair. Push it to TikTok, YouTube, and Facebook. Get the links to the right groups," said Marty.

"How do they stop it?" asked Brad.

"We get the military to blow the hell out of everything before it is too late," said Marty.

"But it's a black hole."

"Brad, it is a small black hole. Don't overthink it," said Earnie. "What if they don't nuke it?" asked Brad.

"When in a pinch and for the right cause, there are a lot of countries with nukes," said Marty.

"On the positive side, without water, ecofreaks will be able to walk to the other continents on foot," suggested Hugh. He started singing, *Always Look on the Bright Side of Life.*

"Just fuck off," ordered Marty Flowers. "I want an action plan and a media package on my desk before end of day. My bosses are expecting results. The faster we can get out of here, the sooner we can get onto something new, and hopefully more lucrative."

Olivia turned off the recording and took another drink.

LSI? I thought that they were with DIF. Marty was lying again. That fucker. She took another swig. He said he was with the government, but LSI sounds like a private company.

So we're heading to a ship. And getting images of what? Of a damaged ship? Unless the ship has an aquatic sub, maybe?

But why me? Why not a chopper?

Draining the ocean? That's impossible. Isn't it?"

She took another swig and remembered when her grandfather first took her out when she was ten.

Couldn't even tie my shoelaces back then. I was at the helm, and he had me make a run. When I called a gybe and the boom almost hit him in the head because the sheeting wasn't pulled in, he let me know that it wasn't my fault, and he was right—that old fart.

And when I was eighteen. We got out of the way of that hurricane. He called it just right. The forecast said the other way, but he called it just right, and we kept on going just because we could. We went to Cancún.

How could anyone? How could anything take away an ocean? It's like taking away the world's snowflakes. Like a world without clouds, without a moon, or a sky without stars.

How could anyone even dream of such a thing?

Olivia was awakened by someone banging on her door.

"What do you want?" she asked.

"We have to get going," demanded Marty.

"Fine, but it's only 06:00."

"We're kind of in a hurry."

"You could have told me that last night," she said.

When she came out, the others were still eating, and the place was a revolting mess. After showering and walking into this, she felt unclean again.

She grabbed an assortment of food from the fridge. While munching, she listened to the weather report and rechecked the travel plan. The weather projections were getting worse.

After setting sail, she spent way too much time cleaning up. She really wished she had brought along a helper. It was galling to have to put up with a load of do-nothings.

That night, when she attempted to listen in on another of their work sessions, she discovered that the batteries had died. After replacing them, all she got from the device was talk about baseball scores and something about going to the capital. The lack of information was leaving her unable to sleep. There were too many urgent questions.

Did Marty get an update from the ship?

Was the military called?

Was she risking her ship and her life for bastards who were actively lying to protect people who are destroying the world?

She took another couple of gulps and stared at a bare bulkhead. She was alone with four armed men that she didn't trust, and one of them owed her a lot of money.

In the morning, the weather forecast on her VHF radio warned that the hurricane was moving in their direction. There was a possible category four coming their way.

Another bad one, she thought. *A good excuse to dump these losers.*

When Marty was in the head, Olivia approached one of his contractors. Earnie was looking at what was in the fridge.

"Who do you work for?" Olivia asked.

He looked back at the others and said, "Marty must have told you."

"Didn't really say. I'm just curious."

He dragged some lunch meat out of a bag and dropped it without resealing it.

"Well?" she asked.

"Lindsey Scientific International," he said and nervously stared at Brad.

Brad Lewis got up from his couch seat at the table and asked Earnie if he could help.

"She wants to know about the company."

"Climate change. We research ways to make the place a better place. Fix the environment, that sort of thing."

"You all work for LSI?"

Hugh walked over and told her that they were contracted to LSI to provide advice. "All scientific groups do that. They get the best and brightest," he told her. "Lots of hands working for the best solutions. You know that kind of thing."

"That kind of thing," Olivia repeated. "You might all consider seasickness pills and get to know where the head is. There's a storm coming." Marty was still in the head and had remained very quiet.

None of the men looked like technical people. They weren't like doctors, scientists, dentists, or lawyers. They were of a rougher sort. From that moment on, she knew that she could not trust any of them.

Olivia locked herself in her cabin while she unboxed her gun and made sure it was loaded. She kept drinking while she stripped her Glock pistol down and oiled it up.

Olivia paced as she called her husband. She tried to reach him throughout the day, but she just got an answering machine. She wiped her sweaty palms on her thighs. She covered her face and arms with suntan lotion as she continued to nervously pace around the cockpit.

After mooring at a remote inlet, she brought her dinner to her room. She checked to make sure her gun was where she had hidden it.

"Sunburnt," she said, as she stared at burnt legs. Cancer, she thought. That's when they leave you.

It's not like him, not to call back, she thought.

She took another drink and a lot more after that.

It's Evelyn Robinson, his accountant, she thought.

'That's all I need,' she remembered her husband telling her during her last call. His saying that to me was all because of her. Yeah, her and those too many missed buttons.

She went into her cabin with another whisky bottle and plopped onto the bed.

She remembered when Grandpa left her the boat. Her father was bitter. "And what the fuck would he have done with it? He'd just sell it, for God's sake. He doesn't know a fairlead from the back end of a boom vang."

A world without Sail would be like living without Grandpa. What about the dolphins, the cormorants, the albatross, or the flamingos? A world without sea turtles, humpback whales, or parrot fish. No more seafood. That can't be made real.

Olivia felt her face, and it felt hot. A baseball cap isn't enough, she thought and drank some more.

Someone started smashing at the door. It was hours after lights out. She let him keep on doing it.

"Mrs. Butler, wake up. We should talk."

What the fuck? He's not the boss of me, she thought.

Marty turned the handle of her door, which was supposed to be locked.

Olivia grabbed the gun that lay under her mattress and turned off the safety.

The door opened, and he said, "We need to hurry."

"Why did you destroy the ocean?" she asked and pointed the gun at him. "It's the ocean, for god's sake!"

"Wait. Calm down. It is not me. Ugh, an accident, I guess."

Olivia got up and shot him. She felt the recoil of her weapon as the man stumbled backwards towards the companionway. She heard the thud of his gun on the deck. Blood pumped out from his chest. His face looked shocked with disbelief.

She stepped over him and pointed her gun at Brad Lewis.

"You destroyed it all. Why?"

"Mrs. Butler, we—"

She stood solid and determined as her father had taught her. The bullet hit him in the forehead, just where she intended it to be. His face had a stunned look as his body twisted and fell. His head hit the table.

Earnie managed to get out. Hugh, who tried to reach for his gun, was shot in the side but managed to keep climbing up the companionway. It was dark outside, but the light from the galley shone into the cockpit.

Hugh dived overboard. Next to the wheel, Earnie pulled a gun out. From the steps, Olivia shot Earnie twice in the chest. He didn't get a shot off. His body stumbled overboard.

She heard Hugh swimming towards shore. She pulled a handheld light from the cockpit locker.

After shining the light on him, she asked, "Why did you lie to me? And why would you laugh?"

It took four shots before Hugh stopped swimming. A red spot appeared between his shoulders.

Olivia returned to the galley and placed her gun in the sink. She took a bite out of the sandwich in the fridge and put it back.

"Fucking Evelyn Robinson, take that," she said as she took another drink. She scratched herself as if she had an itch everywhere. After locking her door again, she stumbled into bed, dropped the bottle, and pulled into a tight little shivering ball as if she were going to fade away into sleep.

After getting rid of the bodies of Marty and Brad in open waters, Olivia gave up trying to talk to her husband. She realized that she didn't know him as well as she thought she did. He had hurt her, and he'd have to crawl a lot of miles for her to give in, even a little bit. She felt like spending the day unloading all the ammunition on the sea, but it was too disrespectful.

"Damn you, David Butler," she groaned. She kept her ammunition and offered the rest to Davy Jones.

She was wondering if she should move and rename her boat. Maybe go to the West Coast. She's never been. This girl still needed a lot of work on her, which she would have to pay for.

It wasn't just her anymore. It was her and a pile of soulless ghosts. Maybe she'd go to Louisiana to fix that. She hated what she thought others forced her to. She was definitely in the mood to let all the sails out.

She got stopped by a heady discovery. She found multiple copies of identification in the wallets and personal belongings of the recently departed. Marty Flowers' driver's license revealed that his name was actually Jonathan Williams. Brad Lewis was Bradley Stephens. The passport of Hugh Clarke identified him as Hugh Donahue. Earnie Saunders was really Earnie Furlong.

Identification cards associated them with LSI, DFI, DCI, the military, DHS, a couple of law firms, and the Coast Guard. She couldn't access their laptops, but one cellphone was unlocked. A message from Marty told him to make sure he convinced everyone that LSI did it. "I know you can do it," he said.

"Well, drop my drawers. Look at this shit."

An LSI brochure from Brad's suitcase said that the LSI corporation was testing a carbon system that they planned to install on ships around the world. The system was going to store carbon as solid blocks.

"It cleans the air to save the planet," the paper said. "It is going to heal the world."

"Lord Almighty!" said Olivia. "There's no way these barn fucks were carrying a damned black hole. Marty was a scammer and a damn liar, that's why. He was just trying to put these folks out of business."

She took off her shirt, palmed her hair back, and let the nipples flash in the sun.

Olivia kept course towards the LSI location for another two days. She had since thrown most of the passengers' gear overboard. She kept the satellite radio. In spite of her reticence from the day before, she made a call to her husband. Still, he didn't pick up.

She leaned on the wheel and took another sip. "Jonathan Williams—what a clown. He should have just told me that he made it all up."

With another taste, she thought about the guns that she found in their luggage. "Probably good that he didn't. By the looks of it, he would have tried to kill me earlier than he did. Anyway, who the fuck would be stupid enough to believe what any of these idiots had to say?"

In the middle of the afternoon of the next day, the sky on the horizon lit up with a mushroom cloud. She was stunned at what she was seeing.

Her boat accidentally veered directly into the wind. It lay in irons. The vessel was stalled and unable to catch the wind to come about or tack either way. As mountains of water and hurricane winds picked up, Olivia Butler said, "Well, isn't that fucking amazing?" She threw a half-filled bottle away.

She started the motor and angled off to sail into a hurricane. She thought of the ghosts and blessed herself. She kept turning the wheel, and she screamed, "Fuck it, boys. This is what we were made for."

Getting Out

Two years after General George Edwards passed, life in the land took a turn into hard times. Jedd Bozz's truck, for example, was on its last legs. The tires were almost done. It was missing a tailpipe and the alternator, and the electrical system were temperamental, to say the least.

As he raced his mud-spattered box truck into the yard, the wheels squealed. The steering wheel was loose. He veered to hit a thin, malnourished dog. The side bumper grazed it. The animal rolled and scampered away. He and his hired help chuckled as he backed up to the loading dock alongside two other trucks.

He recognized Dave Stewart, who was wearing dirty, oversized coveralls. He was waving. A couple of thin helpers stood behind him. Jedd got out and opened the back doors for them.

Dave scouted the inside with his flashlight. "Not much here this time," he said. He kicked someone and got a groan.

"This one can go," he yelled. A helper pulled him out.

"Nothing to this one—number one." Another helper dragged out a corpse.

Dave shone a light on a young man. His hands were dirty, and his pants were covered with mud.

"What happened to you? Fall in a mud puddle?" Dave asked. He put a yard ruler under the man's chin to get a response.

"Leave me alone," the young man moaned. His skin was grey, and there wasn't much muscle on him.

"If you're ready for work, stand up. If not, you're with the rest."

The young man got up. He was hunched at first but straightened and faced Dave. Outside in the sun, he hunched again. His eyes were sunken, and the skin was dry and flaky.

Jed thought that he looked so weak that Dave could have blown him over.

"How many fingers do you see?" Dave asked.

"Four."

"Good enough for me. Boys, lead this one to truck two. If this one gets some grub, he might last."

"If it were me, Dave, I would have left him," said Jed.

"All the rest to truck one, boys," ordered Dave.

There was another groan from the back, but Dave and Jed moved on.

The thin man was dropped on two other men. They moaned. One pushed him away, and the other kicked. The doors closed, and the box returned to darkness. The thin man kept crawling until he found a nonthreatening place to lean on.

"Where did everyone else go?" said a voice.

"The other truck."

"To bury them? But some were still breathing."

"Organs," said a voice in the back.

Somebody with a weak voice said, "That can't be possible. Somebody's got to tell—"

"Who? The feds? Who do you think is running this? We're fucked," said the man who kicked the thin man when he came into the truck.

"Me. I am getting out of here," said the thin man at the back.

"Bud, you don't know it, but you're already dying," said another voice on the far side of the truck.

I am not dead, and I am still here, thought the thin man. "Where did you all come from?" he asked.

"They are making collection runs, is what I heard. They are picking up men from across the South."

The thin man's name was Robert Edwards. The truck made another three stops. At the last stop, in order to fill up the box, everyone was forced to stand. Since he kept falling over, the men around him made room for him to sit down. One of them crouched and offered him an apple.

"And where did they send you?" the man in the red T-shirt asked him.

"I was gardening in a greenhouse until we got hit by the hurricane. I was moved to do the cleanup. They locked some of us in storage at the end of a contract and didn't come back for days. Didn't feed us. They just took me here."

"I can't say I'm surprised. They had me sorting garbage. I mean, really. 'Sorting to recycle,' they told me. My name is Collin." He went on with details about how he got there. Robert didn't hear the rest. He had fallen asleep again.

The truck stopped at a prison. The sign said that it was the Blackwater Correctional Institution. Armed guards led the men in a line inside.

"We are not criminals. You don't have the right," said a man who had a shirt that had most of the buttons torn off.

A guard placed a baton across the side of his head and said, "Shut the fuck up. Do you really think you are going to argue with us?"

The man cried, "No, no, no. Please," and fell to his knees.

The guard pushed the end of the baton against the man's forehead. "No problemo. Move your ass."

In the first room, registration was done. Personal information like social insurance number, driver's license, and health coverage, if they had it, was entered into a database. Mug shots were taken.

In the second room, the inmates were stripped. Most of everything they wore went into a single garbage can. Valuables such as watches, medals, rings, and money were tossed into a large bucket. Wallets with their ID were tossed into another. They were shaved bald, deloused, showered, and handed a pile of prison gear.

A large man of about three hundred and fifty pounds, after stepping out of the shower, demanded to see a lawyer. A guard smashed him on the back of the head. The man fell unconscious onto the floor. Two other men slipped and nearly fell behind him.

"Freddy, why did you go and do that? He's not even dressed. Now, he's going to have to be dragged out."

"Terry, you're such a weenie. How did you ever get in here? You just mind your mouth. Get the new guys to do it for you. Well, look at that, it's time for my break. I'm sure you'll set things right before I'm back." Before leaving, the guard yelled, "Move it!" he shoved the thin man against the wall, causing him to crumple to the floor.

To Robert, the guard sounded like his father.

"Robbie, forget all that socialist crap. Forget politics. I got you into the best law school. Just work your ass." The general was the only one who called him Robbie. He believed that his father kept baiting him so he'd feel small.

"*Yes, sir,*" he remembered saying.

"No more of that shit. Bad times are coming up. You need to toughen yourself. You have got to prepare yourself."

Didn't mean shit when everything blew up, did it? Robert thought. *First, the bomb. Then they closed the fucking school. Then things went to blazes. There was the mounting rent, the cost of everything, and the collapse of the goddamn banks. Then the country couldn't produce enough food, so they drafted the unemployed and sent them to private for-profit work camps. What kind of a fucking idea was that?*

A naked young Mexican man with a tattoo of skulls on his arm helped him up. After a shower, Robert was escorted to the infirmary.

Robert lay in an infirmary for the next two days with five other patients. One had fractures that were being treated. The other three seemed to be as emaciated as he felt. The people who treated them wore prison garb.

When the IV bag was changed, Robert asked, "You don't get paid either?"

"Shut the fuck up, or I'll give the bed to someone else."

From another room came some screaming and some smashing around.

"Lack of anaesthetics or a welcome committee?"

"Better get some rest. You will be on your back for two more days, and then you are back to work," the male nurse said.

A cube van took Robert and five others, who were in a weakened state, to work with a pharmaceutical company. Robert thought that the others looked like zombies as they plodded behind their mops. He was a few years older than the rest of the crew.

Besides keeping an office clean, Robert occasionally had a chance to feed, maintain, and move some animals around. Being near the macaque monkeys was a highlight of his day. It was a temporary reprieve from feeling helpless.

The grey and brown furred infants were really cute. He liked being close to the pregnant mothers. For the first time in a long time, he felt like he was near something nice.

Instead of prison garb, he wore white company clothes. It implied that his crew worked for a cleaning company. The company logo said DPI. Under their baggy leggings, they wore ankle bracelets.

At lunchtime, their boss passed out bowls. The inmates served themselves cold soup from a large thermos dispenser. When his boss leaned forward, Robert saw that under his low, V-neck, buttoned sweater was a gun holster. The only time the man talked was to remind them not to speak to anyone for any reason.

"The government deals harshly with this sort of thing," he said.

It was the first time since he was drafted to work in a greenhouse that he heard someone use the word government. He took it in like everything else. Everything felt like an aimless blur. It took him a week to feel like he wasn't going to fall over.

At night, he slept in a cell with four inmates. None of the others looked like criminals. They were younger than he was, and each of them looked clueless.

After lights out, Jeremy, who was a kid from Tennessee, began crying.

Collin, who was with him when he first arrived, loved to brag about racing. He told Jeremy to toughen up. "Everyone is going to step on you. You think you've got it bad. This is just the start of bad. Pull it together."

"What's wrong with him?" asked Stephen Miles.

"He worked in the kitchen. I heard that someone tried to cut him," said Collin. "That can happen to anyone. Got to toughen up and be careful. This isn't scout camp. What about you? I heard that you're from Mississippi."

Stephen told them that he had recently finished high school and was training to be a firefighter in Texas, and because of it, he was assigned to clean up after a hurricane. "I didn't like it," he said.

"What's bad about that?"

"Taking down high-risk buildings with no pay. Are you nuts? What do you think is wrong with that?"

"I'm going to get myself work in the garage," said Collin.

"That's not even legal," said Jeremy.

"You don't know that," said Collin.

"Who is going to trust getting their car repaired in a prison? Would you?" asked Jeremy.

"Maybe it's government work?"

"Do you know who is doing it?"

"I just heard them talking about it."

"Just like I thought, you're making it all up," said Jeremy.

"They got a lot of work. Some say too much work," said Collin.

"I am sure they do all sorts," said Jeremy. "I'm sure they're into a lot of bad shit if you dig deep enough."

"Around here, you have to be careful about what you're talking about. Why don't you all count sheep?" asked Robert. Some of us are trying to get some sleep."

He liked feeding Floppy. He named the brown-furred monkey that because her ear was torn, and it flopped. The first time he saw her, she was drugged up and flopped backwards in her cage. He thought that was funny until he realized that she was in pain. She was pregnant and was looking forward to the day when he'd see her with a baby. There were other young ones in a cage, but they didn't have mothers, which he found strange. It was part of his job to bottle-feed.

As the days progressed, all of the animals acquired more sores. Floppy seemed to recognize that he was there to feed her each day, up until something was done to her head. A week of tests also made her completely blind. From that day on, he refused to return to the feeding room. He did everything he could to mop floors and clean toilets instead. He couldn't bear his helplessness to do anything to prevent their pain. He also removed himself from young Jeremy. He understood what was happening to him was being done to the monkeys. Robert desperately needed to leave the lawless hellhole that his government put him in.

Within five weeks, Robert was reassigned to another line of work. His team provided landscaping work for institutional projects with schools, stadiums, and government properties. The crews worked at least twelve hours a day, including Saturdays. The label on Robert's shirt said DLI.

Looks like they change the middle letters for each kind of service they provide, he thought. *Wonder what they do for DXI?*

At lockup, he discovered that a new roomie showed up on Collin's bunk.

His name was Joel.

Robert noticed that Jeremy had another bruise on his arm.

"Do you think Collin managed to get to the garage?" asked Jeremy.

"Doubt it," said Robert. "They wouldn't have needed to move him."

"He was doing laundry. I noticed that people from his crew are still here," said Jeremy.

"Things happen in a prison," Joel said.

"What is that supposed to mean?"

"He left in a hurry, and his things are here. See his pictures. Looks like he likes to draw. Not bad, actually, if you like souped-up bikes and cars. I found some socks and small cereal boxes. Suggests to me that he wasn't planning on leaving. Like I said, things happen."

"What have they got you doing?" asked Robert.

"I am in a basement all day doing data entry."

"Typing, you mean?" said Robert.

"Yeah, basically."

"I don't see Collin doing that," Robert said.

"Almost none of the people I work with have been charged with anything. How can this be happening?" asked Jeremy.

"It's madness. Total madness," Robert said.

"People are going to make a run for it," Jeremy said.

"Maybe that's what happened to Collin," said Stephen. "Do you think he got away?"

"No," Robert said. "He wouldn't have gotten away. Jeremy, any luck with your request for a transfer?"

"Nobody cares," he replied.

Early in the morning, Robert and his crew were driven through the gates of someone's personal property. The smelly cube van dropped them off. Other crews were shuttled elsewhere.

While Robert was planting a tree, he watched his supervisor, Jeffrey Winters, bait a new thin kid. He refused to enter a kennel with large snarling dogs. The boy only moved once Winters removed his gun from his holster.

Robert approached his supervisor and told him that he needed the boy to help him to plant some trees.

"Plant what you can; we're not staying," Winter said as he wagged his gun before returning it to his holster. As you can see, Daniel is busy."

As he dug holes near the house, he thought of his father. It was next to a huge crater where General George Edwards died. He was told that it was a nuclear explosion that killed him.

The government declared that the bomb had saved the world from an attack. Why they believed that a meteor was attacking them sounded ludicrous. There were lots of rocks that fell out of the sky. Never did anyone claim they found a virus or something dangerous, or that any of them were connected with aliens. Judging from what he had witnessed since then, it suggested that the government had become completely insane.

I am sure he's thundering from his grave, he thought. He imagined his father sifting through the ruins of Manhattan. To learn that the higher-ups were going to make it worse would have been galling.

No idea what happened to my brothers, he thought. *Maybe they left the country. If my mother were alive, she'd be livid. Of all of us, Olivia would have been the first to get out. I am sure she's at sea with Grandpa's boat.*

The evil that's happening is beyond comprehension, he thought.

Robert was determined to make his escape eventually, but he needed to know more before he took the risk. A law in the South authorized law enforcement to shoot on sight anyone who escaped from the service program.

Robert shovelled wood chips around each of the planted trees. Winters yelled, "Stop daydreaming. Leave it. You're leaving now."

Robert rushed to the front of the house and saw Daniel climb into a black SUV.

"Somebody has money to burn," Robert mumbled.

The seats of the SUV were removed, and the crew was squeezed into the back. Daniel was the only one besides Winters that he recognized. The other four didn't look very capable. He hoped that he could keep away from them.

It took half an hour to get to the next site. It was another prison. The original building had been expanded fourfold. Fencing was being added. There were about two thousand soldiers doing drills. Temporary housing was built outside the fences for the troops.

The crew got out next to a long row of sod pallets.

"What's going on?" asked Danny.

"They have a lot of sidelines," said Robert.

"Who are they?"

"Don't know."

The pallets were aligned next to a perimeter wall of a large concrete and stone house. It had a large garage. There were six Humvees parked on a large circular driveway in front. A half dozen soldiers, who were chatting on the front porch, went inside.

A small excavator, along with other landscaping equipment, was left next to the main entrance gate.

Winters pointed to the property and ordered, "Start raking; there's a lot of sod to be laid," ordered Winters. "And watch yourselves. These are people that you don't want to mess with."

Robert whispered to Daniel, "Grab a rake and follow me." He grabbed his own rake, a sledge and some stakes. Both of them slipped through the open gate.

The dirt was dry and, for the most part, clay with stone. "Cruddy back fill shit," said Robert. He started raking small stones into piles for someone else to toss over the stone outside wall. He watched a soldier exit the front door with an automatic high-powered rifle. He was wearing army fatigues with tactical gear.

There's someone who values their privacy, Robert thought. "Good morning," Robert said as he raked.

The rifle was held with both hands at an angle across the soldier's chest. He swept the barrel of the gun towards Robert.

Fuck off, you too, thought Robert and moved to the side of the house. "Let them finish this," he told Daniel. Starting at the side, Robert showed Daniel how to rake. All around the property, where there was supposed to be a lawn, there was only dirt. Someone had already brought in a rototiller and taken out the weeds.

When they got to the backyard, there were another six more soldiers standing around. There was enough space for another house on each side without being cramped. At the back, there was room for another six with a road between. The land at the back was cleared of trees and was flat.

"Hold up there, bud," a soldier who was standing on the back deck said. "Don't want to get yourself killed, do you? Don't move until I get back."

The soldier returned and said, "OK. It's off. Go do your thing."

"I have some trees to plant. I'll need the owner to tell me where he wants them."

The soldier opened the back door and yelled, "Billy, go get Mr. Sullivan, please."

A man wearing jeans and a tie came out. "How many of them are there, boy?"

"Twelve, sir."

"Follow me then."

Jeffrey Winters, seeing Ricky Sullivan escorting one of his inmates, raced to catch up. Jeffrey tried to take ownership, but Ricky, for the most part, ignored him.

Robert marked the spots with the stakes.

"Take care of those. I don't want to have to get someone to do it again."

"Yes, sir, Mr. Sullivan.

"What's your name, son?"

"Robert Edwards, sir."

Staring at Jeffrey, he said, "Winters, make sure it's done right."

As Ricky Sullivan started to walk off, he hesitated. By the way, I have a guest this afternoon. Make sure there are no disturbances. Understood?" While he went back into the house, a soldier swept his rifle towards Robert.

"You heard the man," Winters said. Realizing that he couldn't see the others, he hurried back to the front.

When Robert returned with the mini-excavator. It had a small bucket and an attached trailer, which carried the trees, topsoil, wood chips, and fertilizer. He acquired the gear so that he would not have had to interrupt the owner's meeting.

Robert felt really uncomfortable when another dozen soldiers with high-powered rifles posted themselves along the stone fencing in the backyard. He felt more so with the addition of snipers on the roof.

The step-down deck behind the house was at chest level. There was a long oak table in the centre of the deck's octagonal shape.

They raked a house length away from the back of the house before starting to plant the trees. Robert managed to dig half of the holes with the excavator before he was interrupted. A private that wasn't in battle gear handed him and Daniel lunch bags and cups of coffee.

"I don't drink coffee," Daniel said. A soldier behind them told him to shut up and keep working. In spite of the soldier's bark, both sat down to eat.

"Hot sun and coffee are not a good combination," Robert muttered. He watched the private return to the barracks.

"What are you looking at?" asked Daniel as he nibbled on some sandwiches.

"Winters didn't bring our dog food today. Neither was it from Mr. Sullivan. It came from the army's canteen."

"Good sandwiches though," said Daniel.

"I'd prefer the taste of freedom," Robert said. "And all those guns around my head are bad for digestion. Winters is keeping away because he's afraid of Sullivan.

"What's the prison for?"

"It's for you and me and folks the government doesn't like. What I'd like to know is—where did they move the convicts to?"

A man dressed like a waiter started setting the deck table. Robert and Daniel got up and went back to work. Robert proceeded to climb onto the excavator, but was interrupted by a soldier who snapped his fingers and pointed to a shovel.

An armed soldier came out of the back door. Once he got confirmation from the posted sentries, he gave an all clear to those inside. Rick Sullivan escorted a man outside.

"Ricky, I'm impressed. I mean, truly."

"Patty, you know what we've accomplished. It's so good to see the project in the light of day." A scantily attired woman came out. "Penélope, this is Patty Monahan."

She grabbed his arm and led him to his chair. "Patty, if there is anything we can do for you—"

"Yes, of course, Penélope. Thank you very much," he said as he sat down.

"Penélope is one of our finest hosts," said Ricky.

"That is plain to see."

Robert waved Daniel over to help him dig the remaining holes.

As they left, he heard Patty Monahan say, "With your resources and my influence, there's nothing stopping us, is there?"

"No senator, I guess not," Ricky said as they clicked glasses.

"I have heard that DPI is doing well," said Patty. "Since I've talked to you, I've arranged some lucrative tenders for DCI."

Ricky looked at the soldier standing by the door and pointed to the yard.

He told the soldier who stood near Robert to tell them that they were done for the day. Robert pointed to the excavator, and the soldier told him to leave it. He lowered his rifle and moved it ahead to direct them to get moving.

"Until when?" asked Robert.

"Not my problem," the soldier said.

Jeffrey Winters was told that none of them were leaving until the job was done. In spite of Jeffrey's complaints, he was ordered to escort the workers to the prison and wait for an officer to give him further instructions.

"I hope it doesn't rain," Robert said.

"So what? You have an excavator," said Winters.

"Who were they?" asked Daniel.

"They make all of this possible."

"Shut up, Edwards. That kind of talk can get people killed," said Winters.

"Now Jeffrey knows what it's like not to have rights," Robert said. "The only thing I have ever heard him talk about was about him wanting to buy land north of here. There's as much of that happening as us being hit by a thunderbolt."

Once they reached the prison, a soldier let them in and locked the workers in cells. On the good side, there were only two to a cell. On the other side, the mattresses smelled of piss and mildew. Although it was only three in the afternoon, the prison didn't serve food nor have electricity.

x

When the sun came up the next morning, Winters and the crew were let out. A private handed each of them cups of coffee and meal bags.

Once the trees were planted, Robert asked the guard at the back to ask Mr. Sullivan to make an inspection.

The guard opened the door and yelled, "Mr. Sullivan, the kid is asking for an inspection."

Ricky Sullivan from the deck looked down at Robert, who was standing on the grass.

"Major Grimes has already done the inspection for me. The trees are fine. Winters will make sure they get a good watering when the lawn is done. You're General George Edwards's son, aren't you?"

"Yes, but how?"

"We have methods."

"You mean that General Edwards?" said Monahan. "The bomb and all that. So terribly inconvenient. He should have known that time waits for no man. Wasn't inconvenient for you, was it Ricky?"

"Patty, you never know when to keep your mouth shut. So boy, you're looking for a way out. What can you do?"

"I was studying to be a lawyer before the university shut down."

"What about the forces? Were you enlisted?"

"No. I didn't get the chance."

Patty Monahan had an arm around scantily clad Penélope. "Lawyers coming out of the woodwork. They are everywhere these days, aren't they? No, no, Ricky, we have seen enough of those. There's a special place for those."

When he went back in, Robert heard sounds of women laughing until something like broken glass hit the floor.

Ricky whispered something in the ear of his guard. The guard waved to a soldier to approach. After the soldier received his instructions, he escorted Robert off the property. Daniel was told to keep raking.

"So why am I the only one leaving?" Robert demanded. The soldier ignored him.

When Robert repeated the question to Winters, he was told that you did fine work here, but that you are needed elsewhere. It's all about priorities.

Before he stepped into the black SUV, he replied with, "If it's about priorities, then let Daniel plant the trees. Given a chance, he can do more than the rest."

A soldier drove him back to his prison. This time, he was chained and alone. He wondered if he would ever see any of the outside crews again.

I never expected to hear anyone tell me that the General was inconvenient and slow, Robert thought. *Or that his death could have been anything more than a terrible accident.* The rolling rural landscape looked more bland through tinted glass. *And I'm now completely invisible from the outside. So this is what it's like to be one of the disappeared.*

When Robert returned to the Blackwater Correctional Institution, he saw that most of the inmates were new. That was the same for the guards. The place had changed. The guards looked tense and meaner. The place seemed noisier. Perhaps that was because what was being said was more intimidating. The new inmates were bigger, in better shape, scar-laden, and had tattoos.

Robert was led to a different cell with different cellmates. They weren't drafted kids. They looked like hardened criminals.

"You saw Ricky Sullivan. How was he?"

"How do you know?"

"Robert, I'm Toni. This is Rodriguez, and this is Emilio. Nothing gets past us. If we want something, most of the time we get it. Capiche?"

"Yeah, I saw him. What do you want to know?"

"Who was he with?"

"Lots of soldiers."

"I asked you, who was he with?"

"Patty Monahan and some women. That's all I know. We're not bosom buddies."

"Too bad. Maybe you'll find some here. You never know." He lit a cigarette and blew a smoke ring. He lit another match and pretended to throw it at Robert.

"Hey, what are you doing?"

"Chill, Robbie. Just chill." He laughed. "For now."

"I thought so," said Rodriguez. "Fucking cocksuckers."

"Hope they burn in hell for burning those we cared about," said Emilio.

Rodriguez smashed the wall.

"Rodrigueze, did you get it?" asked Emilio.

Looking at his palm, Rodrigueze said, "I got that Patty right where I wanted him. We'll get back at him for what he's done to us." He used his hand to mimic his firing a gun.

At breakfast, Robert didn't see Danny or members of his crew. He also didn't see Jeremy or Stephen. The guards ordered everyone to return to their cells.

"I am not an inmate. Where's Jeffrey Winters?"

None of the guards would answer him. They just threateningly patted their batons.

What the fuck am I doing here with these losers, he thought.

Three of his cellmates were playing cards.

"What the fuck is going on?" Robert asked.

"What do you mean?" Rodriguez asked. "What do you think is supposed to go on?"

"I'm not a prisoner?"

"Sure looks like you are. You have the coveralls, the bars, and the shit food. What are you? The tooth fairy?"

"I was drafted."

"You are what they say you are, then, shithead," said Toni.

"What?"

"Are you making money for them?" said Toni.

"I was."

"I think they moved the others somewhere else."

"Where?"

"How should I know, and why would I care?" asked Toni.

"How could you stand living in a cramped space like this?"

"Nobody can," said Rodriguez.

"We are supposed to have access to the outside."

"Once upon a time."

"There must be someone I can talk with?"

"You have to buy your way out. You have to have something to offer."

"Some used to work in a machine shop."

"Not since we've been here."

"But you've only been here a couple of days."

"Robbie, if you're going to survive, you need to understand how things work. So fuck off."

"What happens here is what they tell you. If they want you to make money for them, you will do that. If they want you to rot, you will do that. If they want you to die, so be it."

"If I'm locked up all day in this little cell, I'll go nuts."

"Some do, and then they die. Don't try to go nuts," said Toni. "What did Ricky Sullivan want with Patty Monahan?"

"I told you, I don't know much. They seem to be in business together. He bragged about what they have already done and was bragging about a new project. Must have something to do with a lot of soldiers."

Sullivan is living in a house across from a prison. It's an hour and a half from here. The prison is going to be huge. It's being expanded to four times the original size. He has thousands of soldiers camped out next to it.

"You told me that you didn't know anything."

"I don't. That's all I know. Well, Sullivan did introduce Monahan to a woman. Penélope was her name."

The men sat on the top bunks. Toni kicked Robert's thigh hard. "Don't lie to me again. If you know something, don't think for me. Just tell me."

"By the way, what you saw was only a small part. We have seen three more of those camps. There's a lot of bad shit going on out there."

He put his cards down and said, "Time for a new game. Deal this bum in."

"There's one more thing," Robert said. "Monahan had my father killed."

Being confined to their cells only lasted two days. Robert spent the following days working in the laundry room. Emilio and Rodriguez worked in the kitchen, and Toni told them that they had him sewing.

In the next week at morning head count, he caught sight of his former bunkmates—Jeremy and Stephen Miles. They were dressed in company coveralls. Afterwards, he told Toni that he had noticed that some of the outside workers had returned. At lunch, Robert sat down with Jeremy and Stephen. His current roommates showed up.

Toni whispered something in the ear of someone sitting at the table. He and two others, without saying anything, left quickly. He, Rodriguez, and Emilio sat down in their place.

"Where have you been all this time, Stephen?" asked Robert.

"They have me cleaning up from the hurricane again."

"They're sending us out the day after tomorrow," said Jeremy.

"How many in your crew?" asked Toni.

"Just us and Davie and Diego."

"When you go out, is it the same boss man that shows up?"

"Yeah. Kenny Johnson is always there," said Stephen.

"Is he like these guards?"

"No, he doesn't work out. He doesn't talk much. He threatens, but if he pulled his gun out, he would probably shoot himself. He's a real fuck-up," said Stephen.

"Neither of you is wearing prison gear. Isn't that going to be a problem?" asked Robert.

"No way I'm going to let anyone steal it," said Stephen.

"I get your meaning. I see that they have got you working for DWI."

"What are you talking about?"

"That's the label on your pocket," said Robert.

"OK. I didn't notice. What they got you doing now?" asked Stephen.

"Landscaping for the most part. Right now I'm here waiting to get out."

"Here and there," Toni said. "Like him, we're just waiting to get out."

At lockup, Robert learned that his bunkmates were missing. At breakfast, he located Jeremy and Stephen and sat across from them.

Another person sat down beside Stephen.

"You must be Davie," Robert said.

"Get the fuck out of here, asshole," said Davie as he checked over his shoulder to look for the guards' reactions.

"What are you talking about?"

"Those assholes—it was you?" said Jeremy.

"You're not making any sense."

"They stole our coveralls and left in our place," said Stephen. "Toni fucking broke my finger." He showed Robert the cast.

"He threatened to cut them all off if we didn't go along with him," said Stephen. "Then he smashed my head against the wall."

"He poisoned us and then locked us up in our cell."

"Was that really going to work? I mean, isn't your boss going to know it's not you?"

"Kenny Johnson is a fuck-up. Without his gun, he's a nobody. Well, actually, even with it, he's a nobody."

"There's only the three of you here," said Robert.

"They persuaded Diego to go with them," said Stephen.

"Why didn't you run?"

"Why the fuck didn't you? You would be dead, and we wouldn't be having this stupid conversation, would we?" said Stephen.

"It's the fucking government, that's why," said Robert. "They know who we are, where we are, and probably where we're going.

"I feel like I've been asleep all this time. This is all fucking nuts. Done nothing wrong. Shouldn't be here. This is kidnapping. It's obvious. It's illegal."

"Robert, why don't you go tell that to the guards over there? asked Stephen. "The ones with the guns. No-one gives a shit; that's why."

"So, why did you bring those fucking losers to us?" said Jeremy.

"I didn't. They just followed."

"You're the fucking loser. Just stay away from us," said Davie.

Robert quickly tried to eat, but dropped a bread roll.

When he reached to pick it up, he heard, "Yeah, just keep away," said Stephen. "You're trouble. Stay away." He watched their feet scurry away.

In the evening, Robert learned that there were three new inmates in his cell. A man with a goatee without a moustache was reading on Robert's bunk.

"Hey, that's my bunk," said Robert.

"Yours is down here across from me. If you don't like that, leave." The other two laughed.

"Then give me my stuff," said Robert.

"You don't have any—stuff," said a man with a skull tattoo on his right forearm.

"The toilet paper at least."

"I didn't see any. What about you boys? Apparently, they didn't see any either."

Each body was given a roll that had to last a week.

"So what am I supposed to do?"

"I don't know. You'll make do. Just don't expect us to shake your hand."

He learned later that the one who took his bunk was Louis Byrne. The man across from him was Billy Carver. His curly hair was wild-looking, but he kept an ordered bunk. Like Toni, he was more ordered than his appearance. The heavy block of a man on the other top bunk was Cyd Wellings.

"We hope that we can all get along nicely," said Billy.

"But—," said Robert.

"Shut the fuck up. I'll ask the questions. Understand?"

Robert nodded.

"I've heard that you helped someone get out of here. I want to know how they did it."

"They did it on their own," said Robert.

"I don't want to hear shit." Billy showed him a knife.

"OK. What do you want to know?"

"How did they get out of here?"

"This place used to house people who worked on outside contracts. Recently, you lot showed up. Men from this prison took their clothes and pretended to be them. The organization for the groups managing outside work is not particularly well run. The supervisors that I have seen are not particularly bright."

"I want to know when another team comes in," said Louis. "Understand?" He cut the cover of a book that Robert had been reading. He threw him the book and, from under his pillow, threw him a roll of toilet paper.

A month passed. Robert continued to work in the laundry room. Another outside working crew did not show up. When Martin Perez of the Juan Sánchez faction beat him severely in the exercise yard, he was informed that Juan owned him. Billy Carver did not come to his aid.

The infirmary gave him stitches for his cheek and braced two cracked ribs, but didn't provide much help for a newly acquired limp.

Within a month, Robert started lifting weights. Juan Sánchez appeared and demanded that he get information from people. It meant making connections and getting white folk to talk. "You are going to be good friends with Todd Wilks, Ed Stewart, and Bob Oliver."

"What do you want to know?"

"Win their confidence and find out what you can for now. When I want more, I will ask."

Robert inferred that what made them special was associated with what they did.

Todd worked in the infirmary. Ed was a groundskeeper. Bob was a clerical worker.

Robert made initial connections in the library and church services for the most part. He managed to get Bob and Oliver to spot each other for weightlifting.

They forced Robert to blackmail Todd into passing them drugs from the infirmary. From Ed, the groundskeeper, they had Robert map the lay of the land beyond the prison wall.

Once Juan Sánchez learned what data Bob Oliver had access to, his thugs threatened him directly. Robert was forced to take enormous risks to get Sanchez what he wanted.

In the exercise yard, he saw one of Juan Sánchez's men push down young Danny, who was a former bunkmate.

"Mateo," yelled Robert.

"Stay out of it." He kicked Daniel hard in the ribs when he tried to stand up.

"What's the problem?" asked Robert.

Mateo punched Robert in the face.

"I asked what the problem was. He's just a kid."

Mateo threw another fist, but Robert blocked it. In the exercise yard, Robert had paid attention to how others fought and boxed. There were men in the Sánchez group who were dangerous, but he considered Mateo mostly a blowhard.

Robert had some success with his blocks. He moved in on the offensive, making some pointed swipes. It took a couple of attacks, but he was successful at smashing Mateo in the nose.

Mateo retreated at the first sign of blood.

Martin Perez stepped in and told Mateo to clean himself up. "Good form. I didn't think you had it in you."

Juan Sánchez stepped in and whispered something in Martin's ear.

"Boss, are you sure?"

Juan Sánchez took a swipe, but Robert blocked it. Juan leaned in and attempted to swipe his calf, but he managed to step away. Juan threw three good punches, and he managed to hit him hard in the shoulder. The circle of onlookers closed in. Juan aggressively threw punches to drive Robert back. He flipped over the back of someone who crouched down. He was kicked until he lost consciousness.

When Robert came to his senses, he wasn't wearing any clothes. He was encircled by well-tattooed, naked men who were squealing. He didn't recognize any of them.

Juan gave a wave for them to move in. There was laughter and cheers as they sodomized him. Afterwards, they beat him to a pulp.

When Robert awoke in the infirmary, most of his body was wrapped in bandages. Todd Wilks held a cup with a straw.

"Juan wants you to know that he owns you," said Todd. "You never, never touch any of his men without his say-so. He also told me to let you know that you will get a second chance. If you understand, then suck on the straw."

Robert sucked on the straw. It wasn't water.

Robert remained in the infirmary for another three months. He spent most of that time trying to escape what had been done to him.

Toni got out. Why can't I? he thought. *Because he got lucky, that's why.*

Robert, while hobbling around on crutches, was for the most part ignored. Billy Carver and Louis Byrne moved to different cells. Billy's replacements didn't bother him much, but snored, which Robert put up with, considering. Juan Sánchez's group hadn't bothered him because they were preoccupied with the arrival of a new Colombian gang. By the time his casts came off, Juan and his captains had been killed from poisoned stab wounds.

Robert had spent a month in the exercise yard undisturbed. Pushing the weights was the only place where he was able to push back on the threat of death. It was an illusion. It was a small thing, but it stopped him from thinking about how emotionally weak he had become. An occasional repetition of *what was happening wasn't righ*t—also helped. It allowed him to recognize that somewhere within him there was a shadowed bit of his former self.

Robert was undeterred until young Daniel showed up. Robert was sitting doing some bicep curls in the exercise yard outside.

"Mister Edwards, considering what you did for me, I hate to have to tell you, but they want you to do something."

"Who?"

"Don't know. I am just the messenger. They told me, that you have to kill someone."

"No way."

"It might be someone whom you will want to kill."

"Juan Sánchez is dead."

"You have to get yourself into solitary. From there, you just have to do what you are told."

"Tell them I said no."

"I was told that it will be worse for both of us compared to what put you in the infirmary."

"Who do they want dead?"

"I am not supposed to know, but I heard something. Patty Monahan is in there."

"That's not possible," Robert said.

"That's his name. I am sure of it."

"When is this supposed to happen?"

Daniel looked back.

Robert saw someone staring at them and looked away. "Fucking Billy Carver."

"Daniel, when is this supposed to happen?"

Daniel looked up at the guards on the wall and just said, "Good luck, Mister Edwards."

As Daniel walked away, Cyd Wellings stepped in front of Robert.

"No, that's true," he yelled. "Stop it."

"What are you talking about?" asked Robert.

"No, don't leave me alone, you fool," he said, and he punched Robert.

Robert put his fists up to protect his face.

Men yelled, "Fight, fight, fight."

Cyd put something in his hand. "Toni Alcázar," he said as he fell to the ground. There was a bloody knife wound on his side.

Robert stood stunned as he stared at the bloody knife in his hands. Guards rushed over and bashed him across the head. When he tried to get up, they cuffed him. Another bashed him across the head again.

"The world has gone fucking nuts," he murmured as he crumpled to the ground. Before the two guards managed to drag him inside, a string of explosions blew up the prison. A bomb also blew up a wall in the yard.

When Robert managed to sit, everything was blurry. He heard lots of people running in all sorts of directions. The discharge of weapons seemed to come from everywhere.

"You'd better come with me," he heard someone say as he got up and staggered towards where he was being pulled.

"What's happened?"

"The prison got bombed. Solitary is now just rubble."

"Toni must have connections."

"Who?"

"Nobody, I guess," said Robert.

Daniel pulled him into the ruins of the prison. The two sat down and leaned against the wall. They watched the remaining inmates run through broken fences and building ruins. Guards shot a few, but most didn't bother.

Robert heard a guard say, "It was military ordinance, I tell you. It is not safe. We've got to get out of here."

One officer who checked his phone told another, "They're on the march. It's really happening."

"Oh fuck. Time to go home, while we can."

Since most of the prison was in ruins, the guards on the outside wall moseyed either to the kitchen or their parked cars.

A pair of guards came out of the kitchen. One of them was eating a sandwich. "Fuck this. Let the chief take care of it." The other looked at the young men who leaned against a remaining wall. He had a coffee and a rifle hung over his shoulder. Looking at his friend, he grabbed the gun and swept the barrel towards the two men.

The one with the sandwich threw Robert a key and told them, "Go home, boys."

"And don't look back," said the other. The pair walked through the ruins to get to their cars.

Robert and Daniel made their way to the remains of the kitchen, raided the refrigerator, and made themselves some sandwiches.

While eating a chicken with tomato, Daniel asked, "Shouldn't we be running away?"

Robert looked back and saw that the sunset had begun. It was getting dark inside.

"My bones tell me that this is all wrong. Somebody drops missiles on a prison, and none of the brass or reporters show up to check it out. Not a single guard or government type of any kind stays. They all have phones and radios, you know. There's that, and maybe I am losing my mind."

A chain of massive explosions lit up the horizon.

"Daniel, I hate to tell you this, but soon they will all come running back." Although Robert was shaking nervously, he knew that for to-day at least, this was where he needed to be.

PART 3

The Return

There was something deep inside Khaled's throat, and a heavy, wet growth firmly embraced his face. That something thick pulled inside. He tried desperately to grab his face, but his arms wouldn't budge. He couldn't feel his hands or legs. There was no light. He wondered if he still had eyes.

They're trying to kill me. Not again.

Thick vines wrapped across his chest and tightened. He heard things puncturing him. As membranes sucked, squirted, and touched, the black place faded.

"Dad, I'm sorry," was the last thing he remembered.

Once Khaled re-awakened, some straps had loosened, but other vines slithered and gave more pricks and pulls. A feeding tube was withdrawn, followed by the breathing mask. The big bands around his chest tightened again. A thinner vine tried to slip into his mouth again. Small ones slapped his face.

"Stop. Stop it, you fucking bastards," he moaned.

Something pushed on his arms and legs. Everything alien retreated. Khaled slowly moved his arms. His hands confirmed that he still had hair, eyes, and a face. He could feel them. He was left alone, cold and naked, in a coffin-likes pace.

Khaled rolled onto his side and into a fetal position. He kept wiping his face and feeling his neck behind a thick beard. Khaled was tired and not particularly lucid. He hoped desperately that something else wasn't going to grab him.

From above his head, something knocked.

Khaled returned the knock.

"Anybody in there?" came a voice.

"Damn it," Khaled said. "What the fuck?"

"Are you going to sleep your life away?" his youngest brother said. In Earth years, he was about fifty. "It's getting noisy in there."

"Nikos," Khaled tried to say, but started gagging.

His brother knocked again.

"What's it to you?" Khaled said.

"We're leaving. Stay, if you like."

"Fuck off." Khaled hit the lid above again. "Get me out of here."

Nikos opened it. When Khaled rolled out onto the floor, something hit him. Still dizzy, he sat up and stared at a pair of boots and a pile of new clothes beside him. The workman-type slip-on suits were a mixture of brown colours and had thick dark green patches on the elbows, knees, and shoulders. Nikos tossed him a roll of string, which he used to tie up a ponytail for his long, shoulder-length, straight, black hair.

Khaled tried to remove the sleep from his eyes and adjust to the dim lighting. His other six brothers were trodding around the small transit room. It appeared to be about nine square meters.

Nikos was the thinnest and most light-footed of all of them. He showed his usual jester-like grin and asked, "And how was that?"

"Like dying, you mean?"

"Yeah."

"I'm never doing that again," Khaled said.

To put on his clothes, Khaled leaned back on his pod. A dozen of them rose to form a set of stairs against a bare wall. He tried not to vomit.

To remove the hairy growth on his face, Khaled moved his fingernails across.

The cuttings fell to the floor. The feeling of a bare jaw was something almost approaching normal.

Nikos pointed to the pair of boots near Khaled's feet.

Their brother Alex sat down next to Khaled. He slipped on his own pair of boots. The black hair was short but his beard was still thick, and bushy. Khaled knew he wasn't going to touch it. The wide barrel of a man carried more muscle than fat.

"Is Barrly going to have them follow us?" Khaled asked.

"Probably, but it won't be just us that they are after."

"Fucking Ovidia."

"Coming out of the transit pod was rough; I'll give you that," Alex said. "But it's a wonder to be alive. And not getting cut up is a good thing." He gave his brother a gentle jab in the ribs with his fist. "Just think about it—about what we escaped from."

"Tell that to Dad and Michalis," Khaled said. "I mean, about running out like that. And what about Ahmed and Jamal? And how do you explain it to our sisters?"

Dinos, who sat down to put on his boots, told him, "There wasn't time. Don't pretend that you know better, because you don't. The decision was made by everybody." He scratched a long thin neck.

Khaled stared at his drugged mother, who was lying on the floor next to Tarek. "Would she have gone along with any of this?" Khaled asked.

"Nobody asked me," said Nikos.

"You don't count. Your Momma's Nikos," teased Khaled. He blew him kisses.

"Khaled, kiss my ass," Nikos said.

"Where's the Ovidian scent spray?" Khaled asked.

"Good, something to keep you busy. You boys can stay here for your Ovidian sweeties, while I, for one, disappear from here," Alex said.

Khaled watched Elias desperately trying to pull open a large, rust-coloured door. He was on the far side of the room. The man was clean-shaven like him, but his brown hair, although short and curly, looked mangled. He was always pulling on something. With his sleeves rolled up, Khaled could see the long scar on his lower arm. He wore it with honour. He was always the first to remind everyone. An Ovidian had tried to cut his arm off. He survived, but it took a long time to heal.

"Elias, why isn't she awake?" Khaled asked.

"Back off. She's fine. Do you really want to wake her up here? Do you really want to say hello? No? I didn't think so."

"Both of you, wake yourselves up, and give the rest of us some space," Tarek said. He stood next to their mother, and he was accessing a control console.

"Looks like a dim-lit morgue to me," Nikos said.

"Maybe that's what it is," Khalid said.

"Don't get ahead of yourselves," Sami said. He had a long strong jaw and didn't hesitate to poke it into other people's business and sharing contrary opinions. Where Elias tended to pull, Sami pushed.

Dinos threw up. Some vines dropped from the ceiling and cleaned up the mess on the floor and Sami's boots.

"Sami, I warned you about not getting too close to your brother."

"Khaled, go suck it up," Dinos replied.

When the vines retreated, there wasn't a mark in the rock ceiling to suggest where they had come from.

Tarek enabled the local generator to power up, and the lights brightened.

"So Tarek is going to wake her up," Elias said with a snicker. Elias fell back as the locked door opened.

"Door's open," Tarek said with a smug look on his face.

Beyond the door was a dark, wide tunnel with a low ceiling. Without a word, Elias disappeared into it.

Khaled crouched down next to his mother. She didn't seem to be breathing. He looked back at Alex.

"She's fine. I double-checked her vitals," Alex replied.

"I let the girls know that Mom is alright," Tarek announced.

"This is not where Mom left from, is it?" Nikos asked. "And look at this place. It's ugly and small, and there's not even any furniture."

"According to the system's communication logs, this was created long after our parents left," said Tarek. "It looks like the Ovidians sent some of their own, because none of them called back."

"But these pods are too small for Ovidians," said Alex. "Don't know what they sent here, but whatever it was didn't survive. I found dust remains along the lid seals," Alex said.

"You mean we absorbed creature crisps. What does that mean?" Nikos said.

"Don't sweat it. The system sterilizes the interiors of the pods before transmitting," Tarek said.

"If we can find the other station, we will probably find Ovidian DNA in the remaining residue."

"So what was this station created for?"

"They might have had a good reason, but that was more than five centuries ago. A lot has been forgotten, just because the Ovidians lost interest."

"From what I heard from Dad, this model isn't nearly as good as the original," said Alex. "The face masks are of low quality, and the place isn't well designed. I'm surprised that we all survived."

"Alex, you and Dinos should know why the transits kept failing," said Antonis.

"Temporal distortion?" asked Dinos.

"But Antonis, how could they have overlooked something so obvious?" Alex asked.

"Alex, you're the historian. Check your memory stores."

"Antonis, can you bring back Elias," Tarek asked. "The borer is broken, and the way out was never finished. It is not worth waiting around to fix it. I am just going to call up a form skiff."

Before Antonis entered the tunnel, Elias came out. He confirmed that the way out was blocked.

"Cheap bastards, weren't they?" Sami said.

"What did you say?" asked Dinos.

"Bad parts, not much here, and bad design, and not much attention to detail," Elias said.

"Fellow stinkyboos, over here please," Tarek called. "It would be a shame for you to get run over or atomized by our ride out of here."

Once everyone collected around the control console, Tarek called up a large bubble. It enlarged to accommodate the nine of them standing up. The oldest—Tarek and Antonis held their mother with her arms around their shoulders. For Elias, who was the last to climb in, it was a tight and awkward fit.

"Alex, suck it in," moaned Elias.

"Keep it down; you're going to wake Mom up," said Dinos.

"Shit," moaned Sami.

Tarek put his palm on the inside of the ball and commanded the device to take them to the surface. The object lifted and angled upwards. It passed through rock as if matter was just a shadow. It moved through the rock slightly faster than a walking pace.

"Nikos, do you know how the Ovidians treated Mom and Dad when they first landed on their planet?" asked Alex.

"They floated in an aquarium to survive being squished by gravity."

"Not at first," Dinos said. "They tried to force them to inhale liquids in the gel vats. Of course, they nearly died. It wasn't until they received the integrated symbiotic augments that the damage was repaired. It was a terrible beginning."

"What if this isn't Earth and it's poisonous?" Khaled asked.

"Then you go first," Nikos said.

When the skiff ball rose out of the ground, absolute darkness gave way to shocking brilliance. Some roof peaks appeared through windswept dunes. One or two stories of high-rise towers rose above the ground. Everything was buried in snow.

"Khaled, you're first," said Nikos.

"Elias, what do you think?" asked Khaled.

Tarek opened a door, and Elias breathed in.

"Almost a quarter oxygen, lots of nitrogen, and a pinch of other gases," Elias reported. "This is definitely not Ovidia. Doesn't look like it is going to kill us."

"Mom and Dad didn't say anything about snow," Khaled muttered.

After each of them stumbled out, they sank deep into the snow.

"But it's fucking freezing," Nikos said. The wind was cold and gnawing.

"Does that mean we're not on Earth?" asked Sami.

"Why don't you wake up Mom and find out?" Dinos replied.

"Dinos, just shut it," Sami moaned. "Go bother Antonis. No, I didn't think so."

Everyone followed Tarek as he moved past Khaled and Nikos. They were all burly and heavy. The snow reached their knees for each step.

"We need snowshoes," Antonis said. "Elias, can you and Dinos come up with something before poor Nikos's dick freezes up?"

"Hats, mitts, and scarves too," added Sami.

Within twenty minutes, the pair called the others in for a family circle. Everyone grabbed hands. Elias and Dinos emitted design kernels from their hands into the others.

After breaking the circle, each person's internal augments, created shadow moulds for the snowshoes, and clothing. Packets acquired snow born vegetative matter and refuse particles and other packets reformed the material to match the shadows specifications.

Once Nikos put on his snowshoes, he jumped a couple of times, waved his arms, and then twirled around.

"Nikos, don't. The threads have to adapt. Your body has to adapt. The joints, remember?" Tarek said.

"Complain, complain, complain."

"Dad's not here if you break something, is he?" Sami said.

Tarek made a long hoverboard for their mother to lie on. It floated a couple of centimetres above the ground.

Elias made a thick blanket for her. Three scarves kept her secured. Alex and Elias guided the device from behind.

Khaled looked around. The blanket of snow reached the horizons. He sensed a lot of water far away to his right side. A long way ahead, he saw signs of life.

"Footprints," Khaled said and pointed.

"But, they're all small," Nikos said.

"Maybe the people are all dead," said Khaled.

"Maybe," said Antonis. "Maybe not. Keep a low profile."

"Mom needs shelter. I can sense a frozen river in front of us. Let's get beyond that and find a secure place for the night," Tarek suggested.

"Why not here?" Nikos asked.

"Too visible, and I want to set up on the mainland." He waved for everyone to move on. Everyone followed him on a march above the ghost city's remains and across a wide frozen river.

Khaled watched a four-legged animal chase a smaller animal across the snow covered field. Nikos, who was beside him, asked Elias, "You gave a gruesome description of the creatures our parents first met."

"I wouldn't say that none of them cared," Elias said.

"It was the *Sym-Set Ardlings* that saved them," Tarek added. "They provided the enhancements while no-one else was willing."

"Not really, Tarek. It really was the *Sym-Set Bralins* that took us under their wing," said Alex. "They were a strange bunch. Mom said that the collective was an outlier. By Ovidian standards, they were strange. Dad called them *'the Boneheads.'* He thought of them like people on drugs all the time. But it wasn't drugs they were addicted to; it was philosophy and metaphysics, and particularly when it came to deviations from linear thinking. Antonis could probably express it better."

Antonis was generally a man of few words. A bare stubble beard along the jaw shaded a half-measure moustache. He let go of his chin and repeated, "Call them Boneheads. The name suits them better than Bralins."

"It wasn't a single set of enhancements that enabled us to survive," said Tarek. "There was a long line of them. Ovidians introduced Dad to the technology. Over the centuries, we were able to develop alterations that made us strong, capable and able to outlast any of them."

"Except Barrly and Sym-Set Overbear," said Elias.

"Except Barrly," repeated Khaled.

"I'm more interested in knowing why this place isn't teeming with people," said Antonis. "Why didn't they rebuild?"

At the top of a rise on the mainland, Khaled stopped following the others. After he watched the others cross the river he sat down with his back against the peak of a rooftop and faced the place where they come from. The ridge of the roof was only three feet above the snow cover. Some large buildings stood a floor or two above the snowline but most of them looked damaged. Many of the flat roofs had caved in. The rows of peaked roofs looked endless. He saw some more light-coated, small creatures running along the dunes. He swivelled to his right and noticed that in the distance twisted, rusted metal girders hung bent and broken over the frozen waterway.

He remembered his mother told him that she used to live near an ocean of water. He couldn't see it, but had a good idea where it was supposed to be.

With his mitts in hand, he thought of adding colourful strands. Khaled thought about the threads. He didn't know how long it took them to get to this place, but when he left Ovidia, according to Elias, he was one hundred and twenty five earth years old. He remembered Jena meticulously adding threads to her sweater. It was a long time ago, but it was before their parents sent her away. And here he was, after everyone was forced to leave.

Tarek told him that Nadia complained that Jena was going to spoil everything to rescue Dad. What cruel irony.

And weren't they all so relieved when she changed her mind? Bastards, he thought. *Why didn't I talk to her? Maybe we would have stayed behind. Maybe coming here was wrong.*

The threads that she had chosen had a mix of shades of the second sun's night sky that we had seen. Then there were those purples and oranges she loved. Some wound, rolled, and flared through her sweater. She left before it was finished.

There were those strands that were never added. The main ones that were supposed to have been added never were, nor ever will.

He pulled the snow closer and wiped his eyes to gaze at the dark green frame lines within his wrists and the skin that was turning blue.

Digging In

Behind Alex and Elias, Dinos marched. He hurried to move alongside Alex and asked, "Did everyone really agree to leave when we did?"

"What do you mean?" Alex asked as he guided his mother's hoverboard over a rough patch of ice.

"Did anyone ask her?" Dinos asked as he pointed to her.

"No way she would have left. Everyone would have stayed," groaned Alex. "Dad, Jamal and Ahmed wouldn't have allowed it. Neither would Tarek nor me. Your mother would have led us to war, and no-one would have escaped."

"You don't know that," said Dinos.

"There were only a dozen pods. We had to leave within a day. The Ovidians were able to communicate with each other. And we wouldn't have been able to stop an entire hive."

"No, but maybe one at a time."

"Dinos, it is easy for you to complain about from a comfy, safe place after everything had been said and done," Elias inserted. "But some of us had to make tough calls."

"And things could have gone so terribly wrong," Alex continued.

"Besides, I didn't hear a peep from you when it could have mattered. Why are you bringing this up now?"

"Khaled brought it up. It got me wondering, is all."

The group reached a ravine, and Alex and Elias stopped moving the hoverboard.

"Dinos, Tarek wants you to help him set up." Alex pointed to him to the ravine. He waved for others to join him.

Dinos slipped around Alex, who had crouched to check his mother's vitals. After Dinos and Sami cleared snow from the ravine, the others built a quick, secure accommodation. Elias called up huge stone walls from the ground. Tarek created and laid out red clay-like stones for the flooring. Antonis stretched out a rooftop. Alex laid rock steps that followed the slope up through the roof.

Nikos laid out insulated blankets for everyone to sit on and created heat crystals around the floor for heating. Antonis brought their mother in and placed her next to a heat crystal.

While Tarek sourced nutrients and water from the earth for a meal, Sami and Nikos covered the structure with snow. Tarek stepped out to the roof. "Dinos, you look lost," he said. "Nikos and Sami, where are they?"

"Chasing after Khaled, I'd expect."

Antonis joined the others outside and asked Tarek, "We can't put off not waking up Mom. Well, can we?"

"Wishing won't make it so," Tarek replied.

"The air smells empty," Khaled muttered. "It lacks spice; it has no flair." Khaled slipped his mitts on. "Except these," he said. He admired the threads that gave them an added blaze of colour and personality.

He saw Nikos march towards the rivers edge and then wave at him. Sami trudged behind.

"They couldn't leave me alone. Not even for a little bit," he muttered.

He uncrossed his arms, got up, and stomped towards the river crossing.

Nikos waited for him in the middle of the river crossing. Once Khaled got got close, Nikos said, "I thought you were going to crawl back into that hole."

"Considered it, but I had to go for a piss."

"That'll do it every time," Nikos said.

"Everything is already set up, no thanks to you. What do you think you're doing?" Sami said.

Khaled shrugged his shoulders.

"They're going to wake up Mom," Sami said.

"Are you really in such a rush?" Nikos said.

"Why?" said Sami.

"I'll show you once we get to the mainland," Nikos said.

Once they reached an open area on the mainland, Sami looked at Nikos and said, "Well?"

Nikos waved, kept walking for a bit and then said, "I saw some large machines in the snow."

"They're buried?" asked Khaled.

"No, that's the thing. They're not." Nikos stopped and pointed to them.

Khaled focused with his enhanced vision. He made out at least three vehicles that were on or near a roadway. "They might be old, but the tracks on the roadway appear to be recent."

Nikos walked off towards the wrecks.

"And where are you going?" Sami asked.

"I am going to get a closer look. Go back if you want. Sami, bug off."

Khaled rushed to catch up.

Sami trudged slowly behind.

"So Nikos, what is this really about?"

"What do you mean?"

Khaled kept staring at him.

"I'm just fed up with being someone else."

"What are you talking about?"

"Mom's favourite—just because she gave me someone else's name. Why don't they all clear off?" Nikos rushed ahead.

"So change it. How about Bob? You like to bob up and down."

"If they would just go away," Nikos said.

"Nikos, this isn't a good idea."

"Why not?" asked Sami.

"Those vehicles are strongly enforced and a couple have been blasted apart by something."

"Weapons?" Nikos asked.

"Nikos hold on," Khaled said.

Nikos kept walking and waved for the others to follow.

Khaled took another step, but an explosion threw him back.

Sami yelled, "No!"

From the ground, Khaled heard Sami order, "Don't move." Khaled, in his delirium, took off a mitt to touch the blood on his face. He heard a rock wall rise behind him.

"Khaled, get over here, and now," Sami yelled. "And follow your footsteps."

Khaled touched his face and chest. The blood wasn't his.

"Hurry up," Sami hollered.

Khaled quickly rushed to get behind the short wall Sami erected.

Sami crouched next to Khaled and said, "Nikos is dead. From what I saw, the explosion started at his feet. Let's do a quick diag sweep."

Each of them generated a utility that mapped what lay a meter underground within a quarter of a kilometre radius.

Khaled got up to peek over the wall.

"Don't be stupid," cried Sami. "Just give it a minute for the report."

Khaled stood up and said, "Mines. The place is filled with mines." Where his brother used to be was a hole with a scattering of body parts.

Sami stood up and said, "This is not fair. What kind of people would do this?" wailed Khaled. His arms were crossed and he was visibly shaking.

"He was the only-one of us who was kept innocent," Khaled said. "He had nothing to do with us coming here. What am I going to do?"

"We are going to have to tell Mom."

The brothers like the creatures on Ovidia had acquired ways of communicating with each other over distances. Both, however, were shocked and confused.

"Khaled, if you don't tell them that we lost him, they are going to go looking for him. There is no way to prevent them from learning about it."

"Yeah, I suppose," Khaled muttered. He uncrossed his arms and, with Sami's help, began a retrieval of what was left of their baby brother.

Khaled created a little box and sank it below the surface of the snow. Sami sent out a utility that searched, collected, and dropped Nikos's remains into the box. They atomized loose pieces of clothes and the snowshoes.

From behind, the boys hesitatingly guided the levitated box towards the family campsite.

They sent out probes ahead, but no evidence of mines was found.

"Now we know why people don't live around here," said Sami. "And it's going to be like Dad used to say: 'When we choose to make our mark, step with a light footprint.'"

"...or we'll get crushed," Khaled added.

In the rock house, the brothers sat in a circle around their mother and some red-hot crystals. Tarek put a pillow under his mother's head. Everyone wore thick throw overs, similar to what they were sitting on. The dim light from the radiant crystals projected giant, moving shadows on the walls. Tarek distributed bowls of food and some herbal tea.

"You wake her up," said Tarek.

"Not a chance," Antonis said.

"Alex, it was you who drugged her," said Tarek.

"That was here. Dad did it on Ovidia. It was Sami who kidnapped her.

"Always blaming Dad," said Tarek.

Everyone stared at Sami.

"Antonis, you're a coward." Sami gave them a backhand wave and then said, "Fuck." He grabbed her arm and injected her wrist with a mild stimulant.

"No-one likes my cooking?" Antonis asked. "It could get messy. I'd suggest you finish up."

The rest quietly emptied their bowls with their fingers.

Ionna opened her eyes and blinked.

"What? What the hell?" Seeing everyone so close, she sat up. "What the hell?"

"It's fine, Mom. You're safe," Tarek said.

She looked around at the dimly lit rock cave and asked, "Why shouldn't I be, and where are we?" She looked at the coveralls and asked, "And for god's sake, why are we wearing these?" She picked up Tarek's empty bowl and tossed it up. It landed in her lap, and then she threw it against the wall. "Fares, where the hell are we? This isn't even goddamn Ovidia. Fuck. And where are the girls?"

Alex and Elias slowly backed away from Tarek.

"Antonis made something for you to eat," he said.

"And what about my other six sons?"

"Dad didn't come," said Tarek.

"What do you mean? That fucking asshole. Always thinking of himself. No, no—no. And why is it so fucking cold in here? Tell me that they're all coming." While staring at their faces, all she saw was despair. She got up, pulled at her curls, and said, "I have to walk. I have to walk. Nobody say anything."

She touched the blocks. "This can't be Earth. Well, at least not where I came from."

"Mom, I am pretty sure we're on Earth, but from what we've seen, it is covered with snow," said Tarek. "Really deep snow."

"Sami, Khaled, and Nikos are outside. Dad and the others aren't here," Antonis added.

"Are they still alive?"

Alex lied and said, "I'm sure they're fine."

Ionna placed her hands on the cold blocks to feel something.

"This was your father's idea, wasn't it?"

No-one looked at her.

"Why were the girls left?"

"There were many plans, and this is the one that got done," Tarek said.

"Spicy Doritos and bug poop," she said.

"What?" Tarek asked.

"Never mind."

"There's nothing we can do about the others," Tarek said.

"Antonis, what does 'really deep' mean?"

"Above rooftops, in some cases."

"Might have to do with general relativity," Elias said.

"You believe that time slowed for us?"

"And we have no idea how long the trip took for us to get here."

"Wormholes, time dilation—fuck, fuck, fuck. So if someone left to-day, they might not show up until all of us are dead. Elias, I don't want to hear any more of this. I'm old. I need some space. Can we go outside?"

Tarek handed her a bowl of algae mush and followed her with a bowl of tea.

The sun was starting to set when they got to the top of the hill above their house of stone. She looked at the footprints that led to buildings on the horizon.

"When we left, there were buildings and concrete everywhere," Ionna said. "I can sense water. It might be an ocean. Those towers on the horizon might be what was left of the Bronx or New York. They would have been rebuilt, maybe many times, so why am I looking at ruins? This is definitely not global warming."

"Super volcano maybe or an asteroid crash?" said Tarek.

"Good Lord. Well, welcome to America, boys. They say it's the land of opportunity."

Antonis elbowed Tarek to direct him to what he was looking at. Khaled and Sami were returning. He didn't see Nikos, but Khaled was pushing a box.

The rest had picked up the cue and returned below. Tarek put an arm around her to try to corral her with the others.

"Mom, we'd better step softly until we know what we're up against. What do you suggest that we do tomorrow?"

By the time Antonis had returned to his place next to a radiant crystal, he had assessed what the returned diagnostic packets told him. His little brother was dead. He spun his palm, which was a cue for his brothers to listen. He sent out communication packets to inform his brothers that Nikos was gone. He shared with them what he had seen and asked them to review the evidence for themselves.

He beckoned for his mother to sit. Once she sat next to him, he gave her his throw over and offered her more hot tea.

"The snowline must end at some point. What's south of us?" Antonis asked.

"There were a lot of cities—Philadelphia, Baltimore, the capital, Richmond, Charlotte, and Atlanta. This coast used to be brimming with people. I don't know how far away Ovidia is from here, but it has been a really long time since your father and I left. Many thousands of years, maybe."

"Maybe," he repeated.

Khaled entered the house with his head down. Ionna noticed that no-one looked at him.

"Nikos. Where's Nikos?" she asked.

When Sami came in, again she asked, "Where's Nikos?"

Sami looked for a place to slip into, but his brothers were seated too close to each other.

"It couldn't be helped," Khaled said. "There's nothing we could have done.

Alex got up and gave his brother a bowl of tea. "Take your time." He offered Khaled his seat.

Sami came in and he was invited into an expanded circle.

The brothers all sat down but Ionna stood up and began pacing.

"Mom, stay with us," Tarek said.

"But it's Nikos."

"Mom, please join us. It's the circle."

Crouching, she asked, "But how can I bear it? It's Nikos. This is too much. No." She sat down again.

No one spoke. The silence was gruelling.

Alex, Tarek and Antonis stared at Khaled.

Khaled bent towards the floor, with his hands tussling his hair.

Ionna was looking at the ground and her arms were tightly crossed. She sat up and glared around the circle at everyone but Sami and Khaled.

"He stepped into a field of land mines. There was nothing that could have been done to save him," Khaled said.

"Kill first suggests that this is a vicious place," Tarek said.

"I suggest that we go to a warmer climate," Sami said.

"There are all kinds in this world," she said.

"What's that mean?" Alex asked.

"There's a mix of good and bad everywhere."

"Mom. We know," Antonis said. "But Sym-Set Sari Khalil is here. We are still here."

Tears began to flow, and she got up again. She pointed outside and said, "Prospect Park—I think he would have liked it there. It's where I met your father. It was a quiet place, and it had a zoo." She chuckled.

"I agree with Antonis. This place isn't safe," Alex said. "We should leave this place as soon as possible."

"Was there any evidence of who did this?" she asked.

"We saw three damaged vehicles next to a roadway," Sami said. He pretended to ignore Tarek's stare.

"Tomorrow is his time. It will be in the morning. He needs to be buried in a special place. That's where we will exchange the living memories."

"We have much to grieve," Antonis said. "The road ahead is where we should grieve for the rest of us. It will be difficult, but I believe that it should be on a different day."

Everyone nodded in quiet agreement.

Ionna got up and headed to the exit.

Elias got up to follow and asked, "Mom, where are you going?"

"To be alone with my son," she said and left.

When Elias sat down, Sami said, "You realize that mapping out a huge underground city before tomorrow is going to be a huge challenge. And will Mom really remember something that happened to her over six centuries ago? And what if they built over it?"

'Our best is what we do.' "That is what Dad would have said if he were here."

Antonis realized that she now now lost two sons with the same name. Both times it happened, she wasn't awake. He was seriously worried about how she was going to handle the trauma. In spite of what his mother had told them, Antonis followed her outside.

Nikos was buried late the next day. In the ruins below the snow cover, Tarek and Antonis discovered signs and documents that were written in languages that their mother was familiar with. It was the final confirmation that they had indeed arrived on Earth. After locating the cemetery, Ionna was able to locate Prospect Park. Nikos was buried deep in the ground between what used to be a small forest and a lake. Standing at his grave site, everyone in the circle wrapped arms as they had done for centuries. Each of them not only voiced stories about him but also shared a selection of real memories.

On Ovidia, creatures stored information within themselves instead of external libraries. As part of their enhancements, Sym-Set Sari Khalil were provided with what was equivalent to a second brain for enhanced storage. When Ionna shared what she experienced of Nikos when he was alive, the images were real and personal.

Ionna and her husband, however, came to discover that the real old memories could get overwritten in the primary brain. To call them up from the backup felt dissociated—like it belonged to someone else. Ionna felt old.

Dear Lord, she wondered. *Could it be possible that I'll lose ownership of what I know of Fares and my girls?*

Something about Khaled's mitt made her feel dizzy, and she almost stumbled. She looked away and wrapped her arms tight as she remembered watching Jena sew.

Remnants

The family spent a second night in their secure stone house. The family agreed to move south to a warmer climate. The cold was too alien to what they were used to. They sought answers as to why the world had changed so much and how it had become so hostile.

While the others marched south Alex, along with Antonis, checked out the wrecks that Nikos had discovered. On Ovidia, the two dealt with threats to the family. Neither was averse to harassing or even killing when something had to be taken care of.

“A lot of blood was spilled here,” Antonis said.

The two walked along a roadway that had dozens of severely damaged military vehicles. The husks were stripped of anything usable.

Based on the varied wear of vehicles and their depth in the snow, Alex assessed that a series of small battles were fought here.

“None of the battles appear to have happened recently, but the tracks on the road are fresh,” Alex said. “This has happened since the last snowfall.” He wiped ice from his beard. “They came from the west.”

“They'll be back,” said Antonis.

“Most of them were stopped by small-capacity explosives, which suggested that the battles were fought mostly by soldiers," Alex observed. "Looks like it was just a series of small-scale regional conflicts." He looked back but didn't see his brother behind him. His footsteps led a long way across the field to the other side of a tank.

"As usual, I'm talking to the arse end of someone's intelligence. And aren't I the fool for expecting something different?" Alex bent down to look at the tracks and followed its route. He took a deep breath and muttered, "That being said, there's a promising chance that they'll come across our footprints before we get beyond the snow line. Won't that be heartening?"

The family marched south without interruption. Insulated blankets draped over a large lean-to shelter were used for accommodation. After hiking for a week and a half, they stopped at the lip of a wide, deep depression. Ionna attributed it to the remains of a series of nuclear bombs.

When Tarek asked how she felt about it, she replied, "With, profound disappointment. The stupid assholes weren't up to the job. Damn all of them. In the morning, let's get the hell away from this shithole."

She sat on the rim of the crater, looking away from it. The snow stretching from the slopes covered most of the devastation. Ruins of high-rise buildings towered on the horizons. The appearance of dark splotches snaked where wind-swept rolling dunes pulled snow away from some submerged roofs. Around what must have looked like the end of a lost world, each of her children stood in silence, holding in the pains of their secret guilt and the tragedies of overbearing losses.

Ionna, on her walk, had slowed down the others because she'd stumbled while sifting through centuries of saved history. Returning to the half-said and the unsaid had been tearing her up. Losing Fares was like having lost her hands. He was that to her. She used to be able to feel and touch. When the suns were too bright or overbearing, she could block them. With him, she would argue, break things, and manipulate pantomime, and he knew the real meaning. She was able to hit when she didn't mean it, beckon when she did, and hold on to him when she didn't know.

Tears came. "Fares, Nikos," she breathed out.

It was at this spot where she mourned her ten daughters, her husband, and her lost sons. Ionna understood that her daughters didn't have enough time to get to the space terminal. She couldn't understand why each of them declared ignorance about why her husband and two other sons weren't here. That 'Dad arranged it that way' didn't sit right. *Such bullshit.* She didn't want to be protected. She had lived through too much of it.

It was here on that night that Sym-Set Sari-Khalil shared their losses within the family circle. Everyone wrapped arms around a heat crystal, and they shared their stories. From their memory stores the souls came back to life.

In mid-morning, after they left the last of the line of craters, Ionna received a touch to her shoulder and then a hand clasp to her mitt. It was a smiling Antonis. Nodding, he let go and pointed to a restaurant sign. Her reshaped eagle-like eyes confirmed what he saw.

"When I lived in Brooklyn, I used to work at a bakery."

"And you used to manage a restaurant," Khaled added.

"That was across an ocean. That was a long way away from here. I see a restaurant down there. It is two miles west of here. The snow has been blown away from a cracked window. Yes, I'd like to go there."

"But—" said Alex.

Elias nudged his brother and said, "Sure, Mom, let's go."

Alex didn't reply. It looked like Antonis was going to insult him again. "Antonis, Elias—both of you, don't you recognize the danger that you are putting us in?"

"We'll keep it short," Elias said. "Besides, a building is more defensible than being in the open."

"But if we had already crossed beyond the snowline, we wouldn't have to worry about being tracked, would we?" Alex replied. He turned, but Antonis had gone. "And why would I expect anything more?" he muttered as he scratched at a thick beard.

Ionna looked at a clear, blue, sunny sky above and opened her arms to it.

"OK. Alex is right. We need to make the best use of our time. We might be stuck in our ways, but as a family, we have done a phenomenal number of things. In a short amount of time, we are going to have to get back to work. We're outsiders again, and it's not going to be easy. We need to know what we can bring to the table for this place.

"It's time for a business share. We've done it before. I'm sure we'll do it many times again. When we get to the restaurant, I will expect a business highlight from Ovidia in our next family share."

Everyone was caught off guard. While she marched ahead, the brothers mulled over what she was really asking.

"Mom's back on it," Dinos said. He was the first to follow her.

We had this summary sharing so many times before, Tarek thought. *And it happened when we had to confront something awful and new. Sym-Set Sari-Khalil had to stand up and realign itself, but I don't know if Mom was aware; it always happened when someone got hurt or died.*

Tarek noticed that Antonis was missing.

A food delivery service was what came to mind for Tarek. When he was young, they used to scout the wilderness for specialty food items for the Sym-Set that had adopted them. Ovidians were able to get what they wanted, but the delivery system was extremely slow.

It was just the five of us, remembered *Tarek. Zoe, Antonis, me, and Mom and Dad. It was such a long time ago.*

It was an excuse to leave the hive and explore the world beyond. We got as far as the Conobawn sea. The jungle was thick, colourful, and dangerous.

Tarek brushed his forearm which was almost bitten off. *Dad saved it. Mom said it was a miracle. There was almost nothing connecting it. Dad, with steely determination, sewed it back together in time for the augment to begin its attempt to heal. The same thing happened to Elias. Each one in the family had been bitten more than a couple of times by venomous plants and animals. Their augments could cure most things. He remembered it saving his sister Zoe from a jungle poison.*

No wonder I haven't thought much about those times, he thought. *It was amazing that any of us survived.*

Pulling a lightweight cart with four wheels through the jungle was daunting. The word got out about our service, and the demand within our part of the hive was overwhelming.

The delivery business enabled us to enhance what they had given us. Levitation and earth sifting—what a wonder that was. But the bartering of biome data for information access is what got us here.

My memory of the four of us filling up a cart is what I choose to share for his food delivery service.

Antonis marched away from the others and headed north. *Managing business connections is what I have always done,* he thought. *I guess that is what I still do.* But that being said, he remembered his young sister Annie asking him, "What does Father do?" It was before she passed. Annie was twelve.

"He's a shit disturber," Antonis told her. "Well, actually, a scent whisperer is closer to the truth."

It was true that Annie was twenty-five years younger than him, but he had come to know that her childish-sounding ramblings were just her way of teasing him. It was soon after their talk that she moved away.

"Humans communicate primarily with their voice and appendages," Antonis told her. "We also blush. Like the Ovidians, we also carry other creatures, like bacteria and microbes. The Ovidians live with more.

"They're walking fart machines," Annie said.

"I suppose," he replied. "An Ovidian is actually a composite of at least five species. Your father gave them nicknames.

"The first was the Butt. It had big bone-like antlers like a mountain goat that pointed back at the side of the head. The legs look elephantine but were functionally crab-like. They sometimes walked sideways.

"The second was the Milli. The millipede creature was integrated with its gut, and its many thick legs allowed it to rotate and spin. It provided most of the creature's support.

"The third were the Clappers. They looked like thick brown algae, but felt like thick leather when you touched them. The camouflage capability was almost as good as an octopus. The design changes on the creature's coat reflected their status, social cues, and mood. The coat changes when they were angry, sad, and contented.

"The fourth was the Tinker. It's a tapeworm-like creature that provided appendages on demand. The Butt lost its original eyes, but the tinker provided and shaped visual sensors, including eyes, anywhere on demand. Most importantly, it provided appendages for handling things.

"The fifth was the Frame. It was also like a tapeworm, but its contribution was immense. It provided structural reinforcement, enhanced memory storage, and was fully integrated with the other four species.

"Annie, why is this important to know?"

She shrugged her shoulders.

"The frame was part of us. It helped us heal and enabled us to stand and exist within the crushing atmosphere of this planet."

Antonis kept walking. He hadn't thought about her in a long time. It was cold, and he was glad. He removed his mitts to feel the gnawing sensation of the freezing. *And then Annie was forced to move across the sea against her will,* he thought.

He kept walking away from the others.

And then an Ovidian deliberately crushed her, he remembered. *There wasn't enough left to save.*

A memory of Dad and the Boneheads will be what they get, he decided. Antonis kept marching. He had to take care of business.

Alex stared at the back of Tarek's head and slowed his step. He let the rest move ahead. There weren't any footprints or obvious cues that he should be worried about. It's just that for some reason, he felt unusually vulnerable at this place.

I remember complaining about Tarek's teaching us about Ovidians, he thought. The man was two hundred years my senior, and I didn't want to have anything to do with him. Tanya, Jamal, and Elias were the only ones I listened to.

It's so strange to look back. I spent so much of my life doing just that—studying the ways of Ovidians.

"A philologist?" asked Tanya shortly before she left.

"It's historical linguistics. I am studying their words and etymologies in this hemisphere."

He remembered her giving him a stunned look.

"But they don't have a written language," she said.

"No, but there are variations of their language that are tracked within archived memories. Communication varies slightly in some hives and biomes, and I've noticed changes over time."

"So you're collecting and documenting scents from memories. How are you tracking that?" she asked. "And how are you able to recognize the patterns?"

"Elias and Antonis invented technical aids to make it possible. I was actually spending most of my time with Ovidians and in less crowded hives."

"OK. So how did you convince them?"

"Bribery. Gave them specialty foods. Things they couldn't refuse."

I miss that laugh of hers, Alex thought. *More than anything.*

I look back and wonder how truly useful the work was. An Ovidian would have been more suited to the research, but it wasn't something that they were interested in doing. I found that hard to believe. It was a front for my main studies as an *Archivist Interpreter.* Who was it that created the Space Program? Why did it fall out of favour? Those are questions that I was trying to solve. Unfortunately, to get answers, I might have sometimes asked some of the wrong characters.

A memory of Tarek teaching about the Ovidians—that's what they'll like.

Like Dinos, I loved building things, thought Elias. Dad spent so much time developing scent communication devices, weapons, and system infusion. Alex and Antonis came up with application ideas, and when Dinos was around, we made it happen.

A memory of Dad with his Ovidian communication system is what I'll give them.

Dad always puttered with ways for us to make that return trip, thought Dinos. *He was always convinced that his ideas were possible in spite of what Elias kept telling him.*

With Alex's help, I spent much of my time researching astrobiology. I found evidence that we were not the only aliens that were brought to Ovidia. We were actually the fourth. The Ovidians just couldn't figure out how to keep the other ones alive. And when we got our augments, the big fellas had no idea that we would outlast them all.

An image of Dad working in a lab as a research scientist is what I'm going to choose.

Sami rushed to check out the broken window of the restaurant before the others. The cold of this place was so different from the tropical jungle-like Ovidia that they were used to.

He remembered tramping through the hive with Khaled. Ovidians don't take criticism well. A caustic remark about the ugly flower display on Bely's back had Khaled zooming up a wall. Never seen him climb so fast. The Ovidian tried to smash him. *It probably would have torn him apart if he hadn't reached the ceiling, he thought. Boy, that really got Khaled going.*

The best business thing we did, I'd say, was probably the psychoanalyst services that Dad provided. By learning how to keep alive, it might be said that he came to understand the Ovidians better than they knew themselves.

Ovidians emitted deep sounds from the sides of their chest. Their mix of wavelengths, illuminations, and odours was unrecognizable to humans without aides. Besides the outward displays on their coats, they marked territory with pheromones and excretions. Whether they were outdoors or in the hive, they didn't use toilets. It really stunk, but I guess we got used to it.

In order to communicate with our hosts, Dad built a kit of devices, which I helped to build and maintain. He wore speakers under his armpits, frequency emitters at the side of his neck, and odour boxes at his wrists. To replicate the choreography of sounds from elephantine and millipede foot dragging, he added sensors to the sides and back of his shoes. With that kit, we were able to have serious conversations with Ovidians. Dad moved beyond just talking with them.

Dad learned that sometimes the integration of the five species was misaligned. When they provided scents, vibrations, or illuminations, cross-messaging might happen. If entities within an Ovidian weren't consistent, they might get ostracized or maybe even punished. The misalignment might even slander the rest of the five members in its Sym-Set group. It was up to us to make tools that could help determine why the creature's subspecies weren't wholly integrated.

The popularity of the service almost got us all killed. To survive, we had to make the service less visible, so we could deal only with members that we could trust.

I am still amazed that Dad had the foresight to make sure our augments didn't come with additional subintelligences.

The memory I choose to share is a memory of Dad communicating with Bely. The Ovidian wasn't misaligned. He suffered from a digestive reaction. Dad was more than the sum of his ideas.

Khaled stared at the rest, who were caught up in their own thoughts. Ahead of him were long streaks of dark rooftops emerging from the drifting snow.

When I wasn't helping Mom with her pharmaceutical experiments and biome research, Dad had me monitor the Ovidian distribution system, Khaled thought. *He wasn't convinced that the Ovidians would continue to support us, and obviously, he was right. When things went wrong, it happened quicker than we were able to deal with it.*

Sym-Set Overdrive showed up and tried to take over our operations. They eventually came up with a plan to lock up my dad and my brothers.

Nori, who was one of their disciples, stepped in and proceeded to suffocate me in order to rip out my augments. That one wasn't much of a brain whiz.

Thanks to Antonis, only my arm was crushed. He got me out. Unfortunately, it got me going. If it hadn't happened, Michalis would probably be walking with me to-day.

I'll send out a memory of distribution research.

What have I done? Ionna wondered. *The memories of this place don't feel like mine. It's like they belong to a soul long gone. Ovidia is what I have lived. My children are my memory.*

Running businesses was what I got good at, she thought, and it made her smile. *And trying not to be successful or too conspicuous in a land of giant bugs was unmercifully hard.*

When the family reached the restaurant, Sami smashed the window so that each of them could slip down inside. Once inside, the family sat around a table on rusty chairs. Ionna carried a tray of cups and bowls from the kitchen. Alex brought in some heat crystals. Dinos prepared some tea from melted snow and nutrients he collected from outside.

"You have come a long way since you worked in a kitchen," Tarek said.

"I am definitely not the person that I was then. You pick up a few things after living more than seven centuries.

"Where's Antonis?" Ionna asked.

Everyone shrugged.

Dinos poured his mother some tea.

Ionna looked at Tarek and circled the table.

"What did Dad do when he was here?" Khaled asked.

"He fixed things. If he were here, he would have fixed the window, chairs, and holes in the ceiling. He wanted to complete a degree in medicine in this country, but it didn't happen. A lot didn't happen."

Your father made a connection with an Ovidian by drawing pictures. The Ovidians had arm-like appendages, but eyes were not their primary mechanism for interacting with the world. The one who worked with Fares grew a set specially for their conversations.

"Once your father figured out how Ovidians communicated, he was able to use that to his advantage. Even after we absorbed elements of the Tinker and the Frame, we were confined to wheelchairs for a long time.

"In the early times, Antonis, Tarek, Nadia, and Zoe continued to support your father's augment research. Their work broadened into other medical research and space program testing.

"When we arrived, the space program operations were only marginally active. It wasn't a good look for the ones who ran the department. I neither trusted nor liked anyone connected with that organization. Looking back on it, I find that it was ludicrous that they needed our help to support the transponder devices."

"It was my impression that Ovidians gave up sending their own to Earth because they didn't trust their own technology and weren't willing to take risks," Tarek said. "They couldn't bear that a being might wake up on a strange world with the loss of a subspecies and become a useless cripple. Forcing a Sym-Set to mercy kill was also something that they wouldn't authorize."

"Didn't bother the team that built the original system, did it?" his mother said. "Those twits were just a bunch of useless weenies. Boys, do you miss that sweet tropical smell of Ovidian shit?"

"I do," Khaled replied. "It reminds me of home."

"Time to move on," Ionna said. She noticed that Antonis was still missing.

The family gathered around in a standing circle and held arms around a heat crystal.

"He's here," said Tarek.

Antonis slipped through the window and rushed to join the circle. Each shared a comment after providing a stored memory.

Tarek said, "Small things can be used as leverage for something more important."

Antonis opined, "Technology on its own won't save us."

Alex added, "Find a niche and use it as cover to get the answers you are really looking for."

Elias said, "Great engineering comes from vision that is capable, experienced, consistent, and well-weathered."

Dinos said, "Determination can reveal great secrets."

Sami suggested that, "Blind business expansion in a hostile environment can lead to ruin."

"Organize escape plans well in advance," said Khaled.

After they all sat down, Sami asked his mother why she didn't share a memory.

"Sami, I'm your mother. You know what I do."

As everyone laughed, Antonis stared at Alex and drew his finger across his throat and soundlessly said, 'Dust.'

"Alert beacons," muttered Alex. He seriously didn't believe that Antonis could have turned a military vehicle to dust.

Dinos poured his mother some more tea.

Ionna put both hands around her cup, stared at it, and asked, "So where do we go from here?"

"Somewhere warm," Sami replied.

Elias caressed the scar on his arm.

Before Ionna attempted to crawl out the window, she asked Sami, "Are you coming?"

Within two days of leaving the restaurant, the family managed to get beyond the snowline.

Life on the Farm

Khaled maintained a strong grip on the dashboard and the side door. His mother drove hard. The sun was setting beyond the top of the treeline. He knew that as long as the remaining light shone, she was going to keep moving. He and Sami bounced about wildly in the cab.

"These are very uncomfortable machines," Sami said.

"She's driving too fast," said Khaled.

"More potholes than road, that's why," Ionna said. She almost hit her head on the cab's ceiling as she bumped off the seat. The military troop carrier didn't have seat belts.

"Where are we going in such a hurry?" Khaled asked.

"To the nearest city," his mother replied. "We should be able to find work and a place to disappear in. At the moment, it's difficult to assess what kind of world we've landed on."

"Mom, was letting them go a good idea?" Sami asked. "The army is going to come after us."

"They were sleeping in the back. They'll remember Alex pulling them out and making them run," Ionna said. "They can't blame us for taking the truck if they didn't hear us drive off, now can they?"

"But are soldiers with guns going to care what anybody thinks?" asked Sami.

"We'll defend ourselves when we have to. Sami, just leave it at that."

"One of them tried to shoot Alex. We're lucky that there were only three of them," Khaled said.

A couple of hours ago, Khaled had seen his mother narrowly miss a deer. Its determination not to move out of the way didn't cause her to slow down.

"Maybe we should talk to people before we surround ourselves with something we have difficulty getting out of," Khaled said.

Nobody answered him.

The truck raced around a corner. Before Ionna was able to counter-swerve, or anyone had a chance to swear, the truck flew through the air. The left front fender crumpled as it smashed into the far lip of a crater in the road. The truck did a front flip, bounced, and rolled over a line of trees. The truck lay upside down as it slipped back towards the ground. When it stopped, the hood almost touched the ground.

Khaled noticed that there was blood on his hand. He didn't know where it was coming from, but he managed to force his door open. As he dragged his limp brother out, he noticed that his head was bleeding. He placed Sami on the far side of the road, and Antonis and Alex dropped his other three brothers next to him. They had hauled them out from the back of the truck. Both were bleeding, and Alex was having difficulty walking.

Alex rushed back to the truck and tore the door off. Their mother was almost impaled by the steering wheel, but a protective bubble saved her. Alex managed to slide her out.

"So why didn't they make those for the rest of us?" Sami groaned.

Khaled got up and stumbled around while trying to figure out how badly he was hurt. Besides a broken wrist and collarbone, he had a dripping head wound.

He knelt beside his brother and had his augment draw material from the nearby forest floor. Another augment configured and dried the organic material so that it could be used for slings and bandages.

By the time Antonis and Alex sat down, only Dinos had not awoken. Tarek asked everyone to hold hands as he said, "Sym-Set Sari-Khalil." Everyone repeated it. From a diagnostic report, Khaled learned that he had more breaks and wounds than he was aware of. Their mother had shoulder and rib fractures. The head trauma to Dinos and Sami was more serious than his. The group laid hands to assist their augments to realign and heal what was difficult to fix. Each healing session weakened them all.

"We are going to have to leave," Alex said. "It's not going to be safe to stay here. We need to continue this in a protected place."

"A couple of kilometres back, I saw a turnoff. It's better than going ahead," Ionna said. "Sami and Dinos were the priority. Alex is right. It will be difficult, but I suggest we hoof it for another few kilometres."

"OK, Sami, it's time," said Khaled.

"What?" he asked.

Khaled pointed to the truck and asked, "No complaints?"

Sami gave him an innocent stare.

"Alex, just leave it," Ionna said.

Khaled picked up Sami and gave him a wood cane to lean on.

Alex stared at Elias, hoping for some support.

"But we could have fixed it," Elias said.

"And look at you," said Tarek. "You can barely walk, and the arm with the scar is in a sling."

"The military made the problem. If they see the mess, maybe they'll have an incentive to fix what they've destroyed."

Tarek waved for the others to keep up as he and his mother marched ahead towards the turnoff to the side road.

The first time that Elias and the others would have a neighbourly conversation with an Earthling was four days after leaving the bombed roadway. The trail that they followed was as poorly maintained as the roadway. Some of the green forest's branches intertwined overhead, which made the route look like spooky dark tunnels.

"We need to find a safe place to stay, before the military picks us up," Elias said.

Khaled points to the forest.

"People—We need to live and talk with real people to learn anything," Alex said. "Elias, you go with Khaled, and maybe some day we'll come back for you."

"Up your nose," Elias said and showed him his knuckles.

Early in the afternoon, a small electric-powered trailer approached them from behind. The group stood in an open patch that warmed them with sunlight. Elias told the others to back off the road, but he beckoned his mother to come near. When the vehicle got close, he waved and stepped in front of the light vehicle.

When the driver stopped, his eyes darted from person to person. His hands started shaking.

"Could you give us some directions?" Elias asked.

"¿Qué tal?"

Alex looked at his mother.

"Buenos días. ¿Hablo inglés?"

"¿Inglés? Si, hablo español."

"¿Dónde estoy?"

"America." The stranger said and pointed ahead. "Charlotte."

"Gracias," she said and put a palm towards the sun. "Hasta luego," she added and waved as he passed.

The man gave a big nervous smile and revved up the engine.

Elias stepped away, and the man raced past.

"He doesn't speak English, and he's heading towards Charlotte, is what I got," Alex said.

"Pretty much," Ionna said. "When the ice covered the United States, the people moved south. It looks like what remains became part of Mexico. Eventually, they changed the name to America. I was winging it back there. Since I don't really know the language, I don't know how we are going to fit in."

"That man was scrawny, unnaturally pale, and really nervous. Was he sick?" asked Alex. "I think he was going to try to run me over."

"No, he didn't look sick. Generally, that's what humans look like," his mother said. "He was nervous because we don't look like them, and he felt threatened."

"You and Dad?"

"Elias, yes, like that. You can imagine what Ovidia would have done to a thin body like that," Ionna said.

"Will our bodies adapt, or will we always be like this?" Dinos asked.

"Don't know, but I like the way I am," Elias said.

"Good, because no-one else does," Khaled said.

"Don't act like a fool."

"Khaled, fook off," Sami said.

"Wear a scarf, and don't show them your knees is what I got from this," Alex said.

Khaled pulled off a pine cone from a tree and stared at it as he walked. "Mom, are there other things here that can kill us?" he asked.

"Yes. Ask before you do something."

That's just her saying, Don't act like a fool, Elias thought and kept grinning for more than a couple of steps.

Later in the day, Alex and the other seven approached a farmhouse. He noticed that a man in suspenders was digging a hole for a fence. The three posts that he had already put in were made of wood.

"Not very efficient," Alex muttered. Both he and his mother tightened their scarves. Alex had his scarf tied like a tie, which hung loose in front. He still walked with a limp.

The others stayed back while Ionna and Alex approached the man to get permission to camp out for the night. The man picked up a shovel, took a step back, and rested on it.

"Buenos días," Ionna said. "Mi español no es bueno."

He twisted a palm in the air and asked, "¿Qué puedo hacer por ti?"

She bent her neck to rest on a pair of hands to suggest sleep and then pointed to an open field. Next, she pointed to the sun and traced a line to the horizon.

Alex pointed to himself and his brother, Dinos, and offered to help build his fence. He pretended to dig.

The man gave a perplexed look.

Alex rolled up both sleeves, showed his strong arms, smiled, and said, "America."

The man laughed and said, "Si, America."

Alex gave his name. The man told him that his name was Miguel. The man drew a line where the holes were being dug.

"Dinos," Alex called as he waved him over.

Alex gently motioned for the man to move away from the new fence line.

A shadow form flashed a couple of times. Within two minutes, a new metal post emerged from the ground. It was at the height that the man requested. Alex put a palm on it and then raised it a quarter of a meter higher and looked at Miguel quizzically. The stunned man came closer and raised his hand a half meter higher. Dinos caused the post to grow to the raised height.

Alex drew a finger along the line and the other side and then pointed to the others.

"Si, bueno," said Miguel and nodded to Ionna.

Ionna offered her thanks and led the others to the next field.

In pantomime, Alex asked the farmer if he should rip out the posts that were already put in, and the man responded with a swipe. "Si," he replied.

With his bare arms, Alex pulled out two of the posts.

"You're sweating," Dinos said.

"You can do this one."

"Me? No. I wouldn't dream of it. You are the one who offered."

"What a lazy fart," Alex replied as he pulled out the corner post.

"I'll set one there," Dino said. At the corner of the fence line, he added a new thin metal replacement post. He flashed a hand and smiled.

The farmer replied with "Si, si. Eso es realmente bueno."

"Bueno," Dinos repeated.

"Si. Si," Alex said sarcastically.

When the first fence line was finished, Miguel yelled, "Increíble."

“Si. Increíble,” Alex repeated.

Alex drew a finger around the pasture.

“Si. Mañana.”

“What?” Alex asked.

Miguel mimicked the sleeping and the sun-setting pantomime that his mother had displayed earlier.

“Si. Mañana,” Alex said.

Miguel took them around to show them his livestock and the rest of the farm. The land was rolling, hilly, and rocky. Miguel had a large acreage. Most of the land was forested, but there were large expanses of open land that permitted the livestock to run free. The long runs of fencing were old and decrepit.

Tarek was in a rush to get out of the stone house that the family had just built. He was stressed. Elias almost bumped into him when he stepped out of it.

“You too?” he asked.

“Mom is fidgety,” Tarek replied. “She wants long wood-like planks above the clay plate flooring. It’s not practical, and we’re going to do it again somewhere else.” Tarek laughed. ‘But they go with décor.’ He kept walking towards the barn at the back of the property.

“At least, we’ve got ourselves a place. We’re earning the trust of the locals. But something else is bothering you; what is it?” Elias asked.

“Everything was dangerous on Ovidia. Under our feet, over our heads, the wall and what was coming for us. The threat was immediate and coming at us all the time. The crushing weight is what showed us our limits. Everything here is too light, way too open and sterile. Look at the farm, the roadways, and the stone house. Other than the military, I have no idea what the dangers are. My bones are telling me that puttering with nonsense is going to get us killed.”

“And I thought that it was just Sami,” Elias said. “You’ve just explained why I was more comfortable walking than in the truck.”

“Elias, you’re demented,” said Tarek.

Alex snuck up on them from behind. Before Tarek could get a word in, Alex added, "Next time she's driving, we'll squeeze you in the back with a load of noxious stinkyboos. By the way Miguel Winters wants to talk to you."

"The farmer?"

"Yeah. He's worried about something. I think you should talk to him."

Tarek noticed that Miguel, was standing next to the barn.

Tarek left his brothers and waved to the farmer. He pulled on his horseshoe shaped moustache.

"Hello Miguel, I am Tarek," He pointed to himself.

"Hola, Tarek," Miguel replied. He said something and made a pantomime of running legs and pointed to where their new building was.

"Deer in the pen?"

"Casa," said Miguel, and he made the sign of a pitched roof.

"The deer are supposed to be there, and there's a house there," Alex said.

Tarek placed a palm facing the ground and made a small rock. He put his hand over the rock, and it disintegrated to dust. Tarek pointed to the building, and he said, "Mañana."

Miguel said, "No, no," and then pointed to a place farther back on his property.

Tarek smiled, nodded, and similarly pointed to the back of his property.

Miguel pointed to himself, and Tarek nodded.

Miguel waved a palm and smiled. He patted Alex's shoulders a couple of times.

Tarek made a puppet talking sign with his hand and said, "Mañana," and pointed to the woods behind the barn.

Miguel nodded to Tarek. Since his was wife was calling for him, he abruptly left.

Tarek joined his brothers, Alex and Elias, who were standing in the forest behind the barn.

"Alex, what do you think of his operation?" Tarek asked.

"He is selling livestock," Alex said. "It's a modest enterprise. He could seriously use some extra hands."

"He doesn't bring much to market because he's only got a small trailer," said

Elias. It's parked in front of the barn.

"He needs more fencing, and I know that he could use help supporting the farm," Tarek said.

"And his house is in rough shape," said Alex. "The biggest limitation for being more productive, is getting access to a low cost feed."

"We need more information about the weather and the water supply," said Elias.

"Besides deer, he also raises some chickens, cows, goats, and pigs for his own use," Alex said.

"Does he have a dog?" Elias asked.

"One and a cat. I saw them." Alex said. "Why?"

"Dad used to have a dog. Mom told me that she had a cat. I was just curious."

"Maybe we don't need to go to Charlotte," said Elias. "Maybe we can help this fella out. He asked us to make a shed for him in the back. If he gets a new truck, he'll need a large garage. So why don't we build a place for ourselves under it? Tarek, you can study how this world works, and Mother can dicker with design schemes all she wants."

"To turn his operation around, we'll need to enhance the food supply," Tarek added. "This isn't Ovidia, and there are a lot of unknowns. And how much of a threat is the military?"

"Tarek, suck up the attitude and let's just get on with it," Alex said.

"OK then, find out if Miguel is selling to locals, a reseller, or directly to a market," Tarek said. "And find out if venison is popular in Charlotte. I'll sell the idea to Mom. Miguel's wife will be the one who will need the most convincing."

"Her name is Sofia," Alex said.

"And what about Antonis?" asked Elias.

"He won't like staying here," Tarek said. "He will head off to the city no matter what we do. He was never one who liked being confined."

"Tarek, you were pretty restless yourself. Is staying here really what you want to do?"

"It's about being smart, and not necessarily about how we feel. We'll only find a niche once we get to know the locals and the society that they live in. I'll manage as long as I can keep busy."

The next morning, Ionna headed to the Winters' house to meet Miguel's wife, Sofia. As she crossed the yard, she noticed that Alex and Miguel had a difference of opinion. Dinos pulled on his ear as a hint for Alex to steady his tone. Alex, who was lumberjack-like, didn't have Antonis's subtler touch.

There wasn't much need to dance when you're doing business with a giant water buffalo creature like an Ovidian, Ionna thought. *But he's got to learn to work it out on his own.* She hurried to see Sofia.

By the time she got to the veranda, she heard Miguel acquiesce. Alex's vine-like crosshatched wire mesh was going to be laid out rather than what was in the barn.

After knocking on the door, she heard Mrs. Winters chastise someone. When the door opened, Sofia stepped away and refused to look directly at Ionna. Her hands were fidgety. Mrs. Winters ordered the children to stay away from the door.

Ionna asked if they could talk. Sofia came out and shut the door behind her. Ionna suggested they sit on the porch, but the woman just asked what she wanted. Ionna introduced herself. She told her that she was here with her seven sons, and all of them had a thyroid condition that they inherited from her.

"¿Dónde está tu esposo?" She asked. Ionna, in broken phrases and pantomimes, told her that her husband had passed away. They were all sorrowful for his loss. She told Sofia that Fares had suffered a long, painful illness.

Ionna told her that they hoped to go to the city eventually. She asked if there was anything that she should know about the place before making a visit.

Sofia implied that Charlotte was not a good place to visit or be near. She told her to speak to her husband about it.

"How do they do magic?" she asked in Spanish.

"It's not magic. It's a new invention."

"Could they teach Miguel?"

Ionna shrugged and opened her hands. Ionna told her that she needed to make clothes for her sons. She was good with thread. The boys are so large that it is difficult to get something to fit from the shops. She asked if she perhaps had some pictures and material samples.

"Quizás," she replied. Sofia looked at the door.

Ionna knew from experience that when a group of children weren't making noise, they were probably up to something. "Si," she said and nodded.

Sofia opened the door and peeked in. She looked horrified. She raced inside and yelled, "Andrés, no!"

The boy, who was about three years old, was drawing on a wall.

A small dog beside him started yapping.

Next, Mrs. Winters made a mad dash into what looked like a kitchen. "Juan, no!" she yelled. She came back with a young boy in her arms. A young girl who was a couple of years younger followed them out. She was eating a cookie.

"Te lo dije—no," Sofia said. Ionna took that to mean that the boy was getting grief for standing on the kitchen counter and raiding a wall cabinet.

Ionna waved goodbye and closed the door.

By the end of the second day on the Winters' farm, Ionna had acquired a safe place to live and a framework for operating another business. She had acquired permission to create another stone building on a far remote corner of the Winters' property. Ionna's family lived four levels below it. Their entrance was behind Miguel's storage building.

In return, Miguel was going to receive enough money from the sale of logs to buy himself a new truck. The large storage building and garage above ground above the Ovidian's household were made for his use.

After the construction was done, Miguel brought over some clothing samples and advertising materials. Ionna passed them on to Elias and Dinos, who sat in the commons on the first floor. "We need a new line of clothes. Torch everything else," she said and squeezed her nose."

"Elias, it's your boots," mocked Sami.

"So if you're not building monitoring systems then—"

"Yeah, property security…I'm on it. My design is almost done. Relax."

For furniture, Ionna got Khaled to volunteer to add hanging chair and hammock slings throughout the house. It was similar to what they used on Ovidia.

When Tarek returned with Antonis, she handed them bowls of tea. Antonis, after accepting the tea, stared at Tarek, who brushed his nose and looked around. "OK, Mom, what's up?"

She asked both of them to add thick insulated carpets throughout the house.

"What?" Tarek asked. "But what about plants?"

"Plants, stinkyboos, and all the rest, you mean. No, I don't think so. Earthlings wouldn't feel comfortable."

"But it's for us?" Tarek complained.

"Please," she asked. "The Winters wouldn't understand."

Alex came in and headed downstairs. Before she heard another complaint, she hurried after him. She followed with a pair of bowls and a teapot in hand. Alex stopped on the second floor, where the bedrooms were. Ionna waved the teapot and beckoned for him to follow. She kept walking down to the workroom in the basement.

She invited Alex to sit down in a sling chair beside her. There was a small high table between them where she put the teapot and bowls.

"Definitely Khaled's work," Alex said as he poured her a bowl of tea. "Quick and not very practical."

"It's better than having to put it on the floor, don't you think?" She threw him an apple that she had hidden in her pocket. She retrieved an apple from another pocket for herself.

"OK, Mom. What is it that you want?"

"Just a cup of tea. Nice to sit and have a chat, isn't it?"

"Yes, Mom, of course. So what's on your list?"

"You mean like, plumbing, power, and central heating?"

"What's wrong with heat crystals?"

"Just considering options, that's all."

Alex bit into his apple.

The other five brothers tramped downstairs. Tarek was leading.

"Well, look at that, everyone's here."

"Except Antonis. I believe that he's out scouting around," said Tarek.

"And that's going to be for how long—days, years, or maybe decades? Does anyone know?" asked Alex.

"You know, Antonis. He'll be back when he has something to say," Sami replied.

"Khaled made everyone a place to sit," said Ionna. "Make yourself comfortable. Aren't they lovely?" Ionna asked.

Sami was going to say something but stopped once he heard the pound of Elias's boot.

"If you're here for tea, you've got to get more bowls from upstairs," Alex complained.

"So what did you find out, Alex?" Tarek asked.

"Mom wants furniture," Alex said. "Tables, chairs, couches, and stuff."

"I said, no such—"

"Besides, Miguel has invited us for supper," Alex said. "He wants to introduce us to his family."

"No, that is not going to happen," Ionna said. "He didn't ask his wife, Sofia. She's afraid of us. But I wouldn't worry about it. She'll come round once we give her something she wants."

"Which is?" Dinos asked.

"If we listen long enough, she'll tell us."

Alex took a stretch on his chair and yawned. "Well, besides that, Miguel took me for a drive around the neighbourhood. I got to meet some neighbours who also sell livestock in Charlotte. Goats and alpacas mostly. The cleared properties are widely scattered. Most of the land that I saw was undeveloped. There are a lot of small properties that don't seem to do much, but Miguel told me that most are self-sufficient.

"One thing I got was that everyone is afraid of the government. It's not only the military to the north but the soldiers and police in Charlotte as well."

"If the locals don't trust them, it'll be worse for outsiders," Ionna said.

"On the plus side, only a sixth of Miguel's land is cleared, so it's possible to grow his business. He has been selling to a single wholesaler, and complains that he has been taken advantage of. He was told that if he could bring more, he should be able to get a better price."

"Well, boys, it looks like we might get ourselves into the ranching business," Ionna said. "Personally, I prefer alpaca or sheep to deer, but we have to start somewhere. Maybe we'll get the people down the road to work for us. Besides luring him with money, at some point, he will need a new house. From what I have seen and heard from Sofia, they are definitely in need of an upgrade."

Within the two months that the newcomers were permitted to stay on the farm property, Miguel had benefited greatly. Besides making money from the land clearances, all of his fencing was replaced, and the pens were doubled in size. Ionna's sons helped maintain the farm and made extensive repairs. Sofia, however, continued to complain that she didn't feel safe with so many huge, threatening-looking foreigners.

Alex left the house because he thought he heard Miguel arguing. The farmer and Tarek were standing in front of a feed drying rack. A large ten-foot-wide vat stood in front of them. It was waist-high.

"Hola, Miguel," Alex called.

Miguel said something quickly. Alex, in Spanish, told him to slow down and that he was still learning.

"Tarek, it's not working. You forced my deer to eat this, and you have made them sick. I can't have you hurt my deer. You understand, don't you?"

Tarek looked at Alex and grabbed some of the dry seaweed-like feed and moved it through his fingers. "In texture and nutrition, it's just like what they eat. I don't know what's wrong."

"If one is sick, it will affect the rest of the herd."

"I'm getting close. I just need more time."

"You told me two months," Miguel said.

"I need another two months," Tarek replied.

"Tarek, I agree with Miguel," Alex said as he shook his hands in the air. "What he says makes perfect sense. We can't take chances with the herd."

"Alex, what are you doing?" asked Tarek.

"Miguel, how about you sell six of your deer to him?" Alex asked. "He will make his own pen and will treat the deer as he sees fit. You are right; testing shouldn't be done on your herd. And if he can't manufacture a healthy new food for the deer within another two months, then we'll give up on it and find a better way to make money."

"My deer?"

"Miguel, I know it's a sacrifice, but it will be worth the risk."

Miguel, who was looking at Alex, said, "Sami said something about helping me move my house back." Tarek, who was behind him, shook his head in disagreement.

"We'll build you a large wagon for your new truck," Alex said.

My new truck?"

"Of course. With more feed you'll need it, won't you?"

"But—"

"The house, you mean? Yes, I am sure that when the time is right, we can look at that and lots of things."

Miguel showed him four fingers. Alex showed him five and, without looking back, marched back into the stone house.

Two months came and went. Tarek discovered a way to create a vat-based supply system, but it wasn't then. He kept delaying for another four months. Only one of the deer survived.

Although Sofia was uncomfortable with the newcomers, she wasn't able to prevent eight-year-old Juan and six-year-old Elena from talking to Alex when they fed the animals.

Miguel had shown Ionna's sons how to access electronic systems. The only broadcasting channels available were state-sponsored and tended to be boring.

Ionna learned that although they lived in a country called America much of it was a collective of competing, warring feudal states. The main centres of power resided much farther south, in Monterrey and Mexico City. The area around

Charlotte was a northern backwater.

Recent news from Charlotte explained why Sofia was behaving more distraught than usual. Residents outside of Charlotte's city walls were warned to prepare themselves against invaders from the north and the west, and there was nothing in the broadcasts to suggest that a local militia would be available for their support.

Charlotte

Elias and Dinos accompanied Miguel on a drive to a market in Charlotte. With money from the sale of livestock, they were going to buy a bigger truck. The city was an hour's drive away from the farm. It was five months after Tarek introduced the new feed source.

Miguel told them that the farm lay next to the Blue Ridge Mountains. After passing over some foothills, the land changed from forests to flat farmland.

Elias heard Dinos complain from the trailer, "Definitely need a bigger truck." Dinos even crouched down was taller than most of the deer in the trailer. He was a foot taller than his brother and a lot thinner.

"My children felt the same way," Miguel said.

"But the deer weren't crowding them."

"Maybe not," Miguel said. "Where's Antonis? I haven't seen him for months."

"He was never one to sit still," Elias said. "He's wandering around. Charlotte, maybe, or possibly Mexico City. My mother says that he keeps in touch, but he never tells her much."

"Out there, it's a dangerous place for newcomers. He might tell her more when he gets settled. Or if he finds a good woman, she'll force him to have more to say."

Elias laughed.

"Old self-centred Poppa Antonis," Dinos said as he laughed. "Could you imagine him with another twelve Antonises around his neck? Wouldn't that be perfect?"

"Or probably get himself killed," Elias said.

"What are you looking forward to seeing in Charlotte?" asked Miguel.

"Just the simple things," Elias said. "How do they live, eat, and get things in this world? In this part of the world, I mean."

"And Dinos, what about you?"

"I'd like to see how the city runs and maybe take a ride on a train."

"Never been on a train?"

"Uh, not this one," Dinos said.

"There have been concerning warnings on the news," Elias said.

"We've heard. Sofia is very worried. It's not a time for sightseeing, but we do have to do some shopping. We'll have to be careful."

"Have the soldiers from the north bothered you?" Elias asked.

"Not recently."

"So, they have."

"It was three years ago, and it was bad. They took almost everything we had. Sofia was pregnant. She escaped with Elena and Juan into the forest. It was a scary time for us. I don't know why they didn't come back. You people looked so strong. I thought of that when I first met you."

"Have you had problems in Charlotte?"

"There are places to avoid. We do our shopping, go to church, and drop off the deer. I don't go looking for trouble, so I don't expect any. Elias, if they ask for your papers, let me take care of it. You should not do any talking. They'll know that you are not from here."

Elias, who was dressed similarly to Miguel, snapped his suspenders and repeated, 'shopping, church, deer; no trouble.'

"Elias, let me do the talking," Miguel said.

Miguel told Elias that Charlotte had been rebuilt many times. When they got close, he pointed to the walls around it.

"Although the security in the city is tight, there are sections of the wall that were never finished," Miguel said. "Some of it is falling apart. Everyone uses trains to get inside. The few remaining streets that have not been built over are blocked. I have heard that few of the buildings have views of what's outside."

Elias noticed that none of the farms near the city wall had planted any crops. The houses had broken windows and doors. The smell in the air was lifeless. The fortifications looked weak and cheap.

Miguel followed a road that circled around the city wall to get to the livestock exchange. While offloading the livestock, Elias asked, "So if you don't trust this place, why do business here?"

"These are desperate times. It's a risk to go farther," Miguel said. After receiving a receipt on his electronic reader for his deer, he headed into the office. Elias and Dinos followed.

Miguel waved his reader over the office's receiving device that was next to a figurine. The man on the other side had a round body, a scruffy face, a short, greasy head of hair, and thick hands. He sat in a chair, grinned, and stroked his chin. "Halo, Miguel," he said.

Miguel looked at his reader to confirm the transaction.

"What's this?" he groaned. "But that's a fraction of what we agreed to online. What's going on here?"

"Times are hard. We all have to bear what we can in these trying times."

"How did this compare to the last time you were in or even a year ago?" asked Elias.

"This is fifteen percent less than what we agreed. And that amount was less than a year ago."

"Miguel, do you know this man?" asked Elias.

"Hugo Carrillo," the man said. How do you not know me?"

Elias put a hand around a statue that was on the counter.

"Pietro," said Elias. It was the name that was printed on the label for the statue.

"Our proud and righteous ruler," Hugo said, and he chuckled.

Elias crushed the metal statue. "To some perhaps."

"In this day and age, one can afford to be flexible. Isn't that so, Hugo?" Elias tossed it into a garbage can, leaned over, and said, "Do I need to discuss this with someone, Hugo? Where I come from, a deal is a deal." He drummed his glove-covered fingers on the counter. Dinos leaned with his elbows on the counter. With two unusually blocky men staring at him, the man behind the desk got up out of his chair.

Looking at the garbage can, Hugo stared at the receipt again. "Fine. Fine. Just give me a minute. He made a change on an electronic device and stepped towards Miguel.

Miguel checked his reader and confirmed that his account was credited. "Muchas gracias," he said.

Elias pulled Hugo to him. He took a glove off and put a big hand on the side of his face, and then held his chin. "This time we just had a misunderstanding," he told him. "Next time I won't let it go." He poked his finger on his forehead to push him away. "Have a nice siesta, Mister Carrillo."

As they headed out of the office, Dinos put his gloved hand near his face.

"Relax," Elias replied.

In the parking lot, Miguel wiped his brow. "They are all thieves," he said. "It gets worse each time I come. It's not just here. It's the whole place. There are three places to sell, but they're owned by the same company."

"You need to be more careful," Dinos added.

"Elias, they carry weapons," said Miguel.

"I understand what both of you are saying. But if you are going to scale the business up, you'll need to get a reliable price. If we can't do serious business in Charlotte, we should look elsewhere; maybe even Mexico City."

It was still early in the morning, and Dinos found the sun bright. Concrete rubble circled the city wall for a couple of kilometres in all directions. It was the remains of demolished buildings. Tall wild grasses and weeds grew within the cracks. There weren't any trees, just a lot of leftover stumps. He heard dogs barking, but he didn't see them.

From the earnings of the livestock sale, Miguel was going to buy a new truck. Dinos remained in order to mind the Miguel's electric vehicle.

Within half an hour, six carloads stopped near the city entrance. All of the occupants brought packs and luggage to the train station. Five of the carloads had large families.

Looks like what is coming is serious, Dinos thought.

Within that time, only two people came out, and they were armed. The two soldiers dressed in black marched towards Carrillo's office.

Dinos rushed into the sales office to warn them. Elias was doing most of the talking. He took a glove off and shook the salesman's hand.

"You don't have time. There is an emergency we have to respond to," Dinos said. He prompted them to get the keys and waved for them to hurry.

Once outside, Elias gently slapped Miguel on the back. "A new truck. No more sitting in the trailer for Elana and Juan."

"And Andrés," Miguel added.

"And your new business is looking up. Sofia will be proud."

"Don't get ahead of yourselves, boys," Dinos said. "Carrillo called in the police. If we don't get out of here now, we're going to find ourselves in a mess of trouble."

"Fine, fine," Dinos said as he drove the Miguel's electric vehicle into the yard. The truck has ramps for driving it into the truck box. Dinos drove the front end of the vehicle into the cube van. Elias and Dinos manage to haul the trailer up and over the front end.

After locking the cube van's door, Miguel drove out to the city ring. Elias was adamant that he wanted to see what was inside the city. Both Dinos and Miguel complained that it obviously wasn't the right time.

"Miguel, we know there's trouble coming," Elias said. "For the near term, it will probably be more unsafe than it is now. You did say that Sofia wanted you to stock up. And since there are families coming here for protection, I would like to know what the city has to offer. Aren't you curious? And Carrillo cheated us; we didn't cheat him. He just gave us what was promised."

Miguel thought about it for a bit and, without answering, headed towards the entrance of the train station. "Don't stand out, and let me do the talking," he said.

When Dinos and Elias obtained their train tickets, their likenesses were recorded, and they provided fake addresses that Miguel gave them. After acquiring the tickets, Miguel told them not to look like they were travelling with someone else. There were only two officers on the station platform who were vetting travellers. Both of them were busy interacting with passengers who had luggage.

The three managed to take the train downtown to the shopping district. Miguel pointed to soldiers marching in parade formations in the streets leading to a central square.

Miguel pointed to a tunnel that had a shopping cart icon on it. He led them to an indoor market, where he led them to the fruit section of a grocery store. Miguel took out a pair of small, thirty-centimetre canes from an inside pocket in his jacket. He clicked the top of one of them and then hit the other end on the floor. It reformed into a tall two-wheeled shopping cart. He gave the other to Elias along with a card.

"The card is my son's name," Miguel said. "You might want to bring a few things back." As he dropped grapefruit into his cart, he swiped them with his card. The remaining credit total showed up after each swipe. He did the same with oranges, pineapples, and bananas.

Elias picked up a grapefruit.

"Not that one," Miguel said. "It's bad. You have to squeeze it to feel if it's good." He squeezed one and handed it to him. "That one is better."

Elias took off his glove and squeezed each of them for a comparison. He then playfully squeezed the back of Miguel's neck and said, "This is a good one."

“Elias, go suck an orange,” Miguel said, and they both laughed.

Dinos asked him why he took green bananas rather than yellow ones.

“The green ones last longer. If you wanted to eat it now, you would buy a yellow one.”

“You don’t eat much fruit from where you come from?” asked Miguel.

“Mom does the shopping,” Dinos said.

After they finished grocery shopping, they asked people in other stores what they thought about outsiders wanting to move into the city. They were told that there were rumours that there were accommodations for outsiders in the military barracks, but all of them were convinced that it was a lie. The warnings were consistent. ‘Don’t bother,’ they said. The advertisement was just an attempt to extort desperate people from their money. If there were any jobs available for outsiders, it would only be as a soldier. Miguel noticed that Elias was nervously scratching a scar on his arm.

At Dino’s prompting, they headed into a tunnel that led to a train station. They were stopped by three men in uniform. They were prompted to show their papers. Miguel pulled out his papers. He told them that he could vouch for others.

“They have their papers, but they left them in my truck,” he said. “We are on our way there now.”

The officer looked up at him and said, “We received a complaint about you. We would like you to follow us to the station.”

“Who made the complaint? What was it about?”

“Are you resisting arrest?”

“What’s the charge?” Dinos asked.

“An officer, behind the one talking, gave Dinos an electric shock.”

“We don’t take kindly to strangers,” said the one behind.

The officer in front gave Miguel an electric shock. Miguel fell to the floor as Dinos did.

Elias grabbed a leg from each of the fallen and swung them behind him. He threw his gloves off. He squeezed the officer’s hand, forcing him to drop his weapon. He picked the man up and threw him at the other two. When each of them tried to get up, he picked up two of them and blocked their heads. For the other, he just kicked him, which smashed him hard against the tunnel wall. Elias stamped on each of the weapons, causing them to break up. He picked up his friends and tried to get them walking.

They shuffled back the way they came with their thin five-foot shopping carts. "Don't worry about getting a ticket. They only collect at the entrance gate at the wall."

"Are you OK, Dinos?" Elias asked.

"Just winded," he replied. "I'm fine."

"Hugo Carrillo must have labelled you as undocumented foreigners," Miguel groaned.

"What does that mean?" asked Dinos.

"It can mean anything they want it to. The government is corrupt. If you get arrested, you might not even get a hearing. We have to be careful."

They accessed the train station through a different tunnel. When they entered the train platform, there was a police officer standing on their left side.

"Don't say anything," said Miguel. "You might not see their weapons, but they're armed, and this is a public place."

Elias looked to the right and saw another three other armed officers marching towards them.

"They are carrying weapons too," Dinos said. "Elias, don't do something foolish."

"Miguel, go home to your family. Stay safe," said Elias. "We can take care of ourselves," said Elias. He stopped in order to let Miguel go alone to the open door of the train.

"That's them," he heard someone say.

Both brothers kept their heads down and walked to an open door to a car on their left.

"Gentlemen, where are you going in such a hurry?" asked an officer who approached them from behind.

Dinos stopped and said, "Home. Can we help you?"

The three officers on their right, who were running, caught up to them. They had firearms drawn.

The officer who came from behind moved in front to block their access to the train. "We have footage of the pair of you resisting an arrest," he said.

"An arrest for what?" Elias asked.

"Show me your papers, please."

"Sorry, we left them in the truck," said Dinos.

"That won't do. You will have to come with us. The officers took their gloves off, threw them away, and placed them in handcuffs.

"What are we being charged with?" Elias asked.

"I hate to repeat myself. Don't cause me any trouble. If I feel so inclined, I'll trigger the remote, and both of you will lose your hands. Bloody freaks." He gave a wave to the others to take them away.

One of the officers grabbed a box of patisseries from the cart. Another kicked it over, spilling the contents across the platform. Before Dinos could complain, another officer smashed the side of his head with a baton.

Elias and his brother were escorted into the back of a police van. Officers grabbed their hands and handcuffed them to a security bar inside.

In English, Dinos told him that it looked like Miguel got away.

"It means that we have a long walk back ahead of us."

A guard next to Elias told the guard by the door, "The news says that troops are moving from Cincinnati to Richmond. Do you think they're coming here?"

"They might just be kicking out more of their civilians. There's not much to eat up there."

The other guard said, "If they are pushing them down here, we'll be ready for them. Maybe those foreigners are like these two toads." He poked Dinos with his nightstick and laughed.

At the police station, Elias and his brother were thrown into a cell with twenty people. The place reeked of urine and feces.

"Hello. What's this? Ugly or what?" said a man with a cactus on his t-shirt, and he attempted to shove Elias. Elias grabbed his hand before he touched him. When he tightened his grip, the others heard the man scream and something break.

Dinos threw a fat fella into two hefty men with bad teeth that stood behind him. Dinos smashed two others to the floor, who also tried to step in. One at the back, who originally wanted to advance, moved back to the wall.

Dinos put his hands up. Elias raised his palms, beckoning everyone to do the same. When most of the others did the same, he said, "That is what I want to see. People who like to get along."

Elias saw his brother pointing to a tall, thin guy who was sitting on the floor. The man had a bloody nose and a gash on the side of the head.

"Mister, what's your name? I'm Dinos."

"Ricardo."

"I saw you come in with your family. What happened?"

"They took all of our money, separated me from my family, and threw me in here."

"Undocumented migrant, right?"

He nodded.

"Did they offer a place for you if you joined the military?"

"No. They just sent me here."

"What about you, cactus?" Elias asked. "Did they offer you a job with the army?"

"Anyone willing to join up with these people has to be insane. The new bodies are just set up as shooting targets for the other side. I have no wish to commit suicide for these idiots."

"So who is going to obliterate this place, the northerners or the folks to the west?"

"I would bet money on the Northerners. They are good at distracting and keeping the city focused. The westerners will talk, but the northerners will sweep down in the end."

"Maybe, but Monterrey only allows what is in their best interest," said guy who wore a red baseball cap. "That's where the real power lies. If it doesn't like something, it will step in."

"I'm Elias . So why are you here?"

"I'm Fredrick. I came here to find my sister, but they told me that she moved. Like you, they called me an undocumented migrant, took my money, my car, and all I owned, and threw me in here."

"They are definitely not nice people," Elias said. "That can't be good for business."

"In my opinion, this place is rotten to the core."

"So what's the purpose of using this place as a clearance centre?" asked Dinos. "Putting people in jails is expensive. You have to feed them and watch over them.

"Indentured servants or cannon fodder, is my guess," Fredrick said. "Women and children could be sold for other purposes."

"I really, really don't like this place," Elias said. "Next time we go shopping, let's go somewhere else."

Elias and his brother were booked four hours after they were thrown in jail. Elias was escorted into an inquisition room afterwards. He was charged with aggravated assault, resisting arrest, and sedition. A guard grabbed his hand, undid a cuff, and locked it to a bar that was fastened to the table.

Two guards sat across the table from him.

"How did you come to the conclusion that I was being seditious?"

"The state has no tolerance for violence. Particularly against the state."

"Which has nothing to do with me."

"Blockhead, don't interrupt Barry." He smashed his nightstick on the table.

"Tony, run the video." He showed a clip of Elias slamming three police officers in the tunnel.

"I hope they are well and fine," said Elias.

"You can ask them next time you see them."

"Where are you from? Obviously, you're not from around here."

"I travel. I am looking for a nice sunny beach. Where would you recommend?"

"A smart asshole, hey. Keep your mouth shut until you're asked something."

"Barry, this guy is a monster. Look at the size of his hands, his neck, and that jaw. I bet if you smashed it with an iron rod, he wouldn't even feel it. And that arm. There's green in it. Maybe he's radioactive."

"I just want to leave. What do I need to do to get out of here?"

"Sunny beach, my ass. You are from the blast zone, aren't you? Damn," said Barry.

"You two are delusional. I was just shopping, and you folks carry on like lunatics."

Barry whacked Elias on the side of his head with his nightstick. "I told you. Only open your mouth when we ask you to."

"Where are they sending me?"

"Wherever the higher-ups decide. If they have work for you, they might keep you."

"If not?"

"Barry threatened to hit him again, and Elias put up an arm to block. "Tony, bring in the next one. I would like to get out of here."

Elias awoke, after lights out in the cell, to someone's screams. Ricardo, who was a tall, thin man, was calling for help. A bald man gave backup shouts. Five others were moaning. One was coughing up blood in the communal bucket.

Dinos was woken up too. "It can't be the food," he said. "I know that at least two of them, like me, haven't eaten."

Elias shivered and moved away when he noticed that two men who lay next to him on the floor were bleeding from their mouths. He beckoned for his brother to stand. There were two others who looked in that state. A few more were squatting and looked pale.

"Hell, this is bad, Dinos."

A female guard trudged in and said. "Alright, alright. Keep it down." She turned on the main lights. "Jesus," she said. "What on Earth is this? Oh my god, it's here too."

She ran back from where she came from.

The woman returned with two more guards.

"My god, what is going on?" asked Sergeant Murphy.

"A plague?" asked the female guard.

"There are only a few of us left, Sergeant; what are we going to do?" asked the other male guard.

"The hospital?" asked the female guard.

"I'll make some calls," Sergeant Murphy said. "Now, everyone, out of here.

About twenty minutes later, someone outside hammered a brace on the other side of the door.

"Dinos, time to leave."

"What do you mean?"

"The Sargent wasn't calling for a doctor. We are locked up until a cleanup team moves in."

"She used the phrase 'here too.' That means that what's happening here was brought from somewhere else."

Elias kicked the man below him, and he didn't move. He did that to the man beside him, and he didn't either.

"Damn this," Elias said, and he tore open the metal door.

"But shouldn't they be quarantined?"

"This is a shoot first, ask questions later kind of place. I'm leaving."

Dinos helped him kick the entrance door down.

To get outside the police station, the men tossed three officers around. None of them looked well. They managed to get outside, and only one officer followed them. He fired from the front door, but he didn't chase them.

"That was unusual," said Elias.

"Must be really bad inside."

In a parking lot, Elias forced a driver to stop. He got in the front, and Dinos got in the back.

"You're going to the train," Elias said. He kept his thick, powerful hand at the back of the man's neck.

"What are you going to do with me?" the sheepish man asked.

"Just do as you're told, please."

"Mister, those are drones. They are going to blow us up."

"Dozens of them," Dinos said.

He leaned out a side window and focused on the centre of the swarm. Dinos turned one of them into an attractor. It drew the others to it. The metal fused together, and the mass fell out of the sky. Only two managed to escape the trap. Dinos managed to destroy one, but the other climbed out of sight.

The train station was only a short drive from the police station. The man nervously looked into Elias's eyes as he backed out of the car.

"You didn't crash the thing. Didn't make a fuss. Normally, I'd pay you something, but the bastards stole our wallets. Shoo. Get out of here."

"Elias, come on. They know where we're going."

They hurried up the stairs to the station platform. The train had yet to arrive. Policemen on the platform noticed that they were coming out of the stairwell.

"Follow my lead. I am winging this," Elias said. He bent down to one knee so he could touch the concrete. He knew that others didn't need to do this, but he needed to focus his attention. He was trying to set the boots of two of the policemen on fire. At first, he just got some sparks, and then a sizzle. The three officers kept marching towards him.

"You there!" yelled one of them.

Elias focused on one man, and his right boot lit up. He focused on the next man, and his left boot lit up.

The third man took out a firearm. Dinos dissolved the gun. The man's hands disappeared with it.

People started screaming and running towards the tunnels and stairwells.

Elias generated another remote program that wrapped the two officers near him in a silk-like cocoon. The wraps stopped the fire from burning the boots.

Dinos tried to wrap the handless man's stumps in the same way, but his attempts were clumsy. "Elias, help," he yelled.

In the meantime, he heard another policeman from the middle of the platform yell, "Stop them."

"Dinos take care of that," Elias ordered. He rushed over to try and stop the blood from pouring out from the man's stumps.

"It would be so much easier to make gauze bandages if we were on the ground," Elias muttered. It took a great deal of his attention to generate enough material to stop the bleeding entirely.

The officer Elias was trying to save was barely in his twenties. "He didn't mean to," Elias said as he tried to fix his wrapping mistakes. The man suffered cardiac arrest.

"No, no. No," Elias groaned.

He generated a small object to try to get his heart going. "Damn, I know almost nothing about these weak creatures. Damn it."

"Elias," Dinos yelled again.

Two more officers had drawn their firearms, and Dinos did the same as he had done to the other. Both had lost their hands.

Elias gave a quick last look at the young man and said, "Sorry, but we've run out of time." As he hurried over to the two other fallen officers, he noticed that everyone had run away. There was only his brother and five immobile police officers on the platform.

The train that came from uptown was crowded. Dinos and Elias pushed their way in. Men and women kept bumping into them.

"Give me space," Elias growled.

"Easy," said Dinos.

"I can't stand this. It's like being buried underground under a mountain of stinkyboos."

"Just keep it together until we get off."

"We should have waited this out under the station until this blew over," Elias said.

"I don't think it would have. We just need to get out of here, and as fast as possible."

Elias looked down and saw a young boy looking up at him. He was being smashed against his leg by the crowd. Elias tried to look away, but he was met with a circle of faces.

"What are you?" asked the boy.

"Vegetarian," he said. It was a word he picked up from watching state media programming.

The boy kept staring.

"Vegetables are good for you. They make you big and strong."

The boy kept quietly looking up.

"Elias, you're not helping," said his brother.

When the train arrived at its last stop, there were lines of armed soldiers waiting for them. The brothers followed the crowd out. A blaze of rifle fire brought down running passengers. The fire came from the far end of the platform. Soldiers fired from behind a thickly armed military device. It had a turret with a high-powered gun on it.

Dinos raised a large slab of stone, which flung the vehicle on its side. Elias generated a rifle in the middle to be an attractor. The other rifles were pulled to the high-powered magnet. With all of the metal each soldier carried, they were all brought together. Elias dissolved all of the metal and generated a large wrap around them.

He didn't want to know how many of those men were going to die. He just knew that he still was breathing and needed to get away. He saw the little boy from the train. He was being pulled away to the exit. He was beckoning him to follow.

The kid isn't afraid of vegetables, Elias thought. Elias pointed to the way out for his brother.

Outside in the parking lot, Dinos stopped a driver who was unlocking a van. Elias told the man to put his seat back as far as it could go and then ordered him to leave. Elias got in, but it still was a difficult fit.

"Are you sure you can do this?"

"I watched Miguel."

Dinos stared at him.

"So you can do better?"

"Come on. Get on with it."

"Yeah, learn as we go," muttered Elias.

His driving was bearable, but braking was another matter. When he was going to hit something, he picked up speed and raced around and between ongoing traffic. Braking too hard almost caused him to sideswipe a donkey, a tractor, and an oil tanker. He headed into a side road that was well-treed and had hilly ground. He drove into a driveway of what looked ruined from a past battle. He stopped at a rocky hill.

Within the hill, they created deep caverns., and drove the car into it. They built a swinging rock door and initiated a rockfall to bury the door. Dinos created a machine to collect and keep piling dirt over the rock. It dissolved when its job was done.

Elias sent an encrypted message informing Alex of what had happened. It said, 'It is not safe for us to return. We will remain in hiding. The city is unsafe. It is infested with plague, and they are expecting a war. Stay safe.'

Elias had crouched in a corner.

I went there to learn about those people, he thought. *And I just killed them. I should have known better. It shouldn't have been necessary.*

He noticed that Dinos was keeping busy. *Food and water. Good for him,* he thought.

Elias buried his hands in his face and shook.

We've lived so long. And is killing all that we have to offer this damn godforsaken world? Mom, I hope you will be able to forgive us.

Disarray

Yellow leaves with a tinge of orange floated on the surface of a half a dozen vats. The water pools were set up in a line by the side of the Ovidian's underground house. A tall pile of Miguel's timbers lay behind.

"Something is wrong. I can sense it," Alex said.

Ionna stood across from him on a vat near the entrance to their house. They were bent over with their arms up to the elbows in the greenish water. Stone sides encircled a deep pool.

She poured more nutrients into the water. "Where do you see your interests taking you?"

"What?"

"In this world, if we find a bit of peace and security, what would you like to do? Return to astrobiology, linguistics, farming, behavioural science? Or maybe knocking heads?"

Alex laughed. "Too many listen to Antonis."

"Of everything that I have seen so far, children have amazed me the most," he added. "It's not just Andrés, Elena, and Juan. It's also the pup and the young fawns. They're the opposite of grizzles, vraks, or kibos."

"I suppose anything that won't kill you could be a plus," his mother said.

"I didn't mean it like that. It's just so different. Maybe it's ordinary here, but if that is what it is, I would like to have a part of that."

Miguel waved at them.

"Tarek has bad news. Just look at him," Alex said.

When Tarek and Miguel joined them, Miguel didn't greet them with a wisecrack. He just took off his hat.

"Miguel told me that Elias and Dinos were arrested in Charlotte," Tarek said.

"The man at the market—Carrillo is his name—tried to cheat us," Miguel said. "He called the police. They stopped us after our shopping. If there was just one policeman, a few pesos would fix small misunderstandings. There were too many of them."

"Why weren't you picked with the others?" asked Ionna.

"I had papers. Elias told me to leave. And I had my family to consider. There were a lot of people in uniform. The army was marching through the centre of town. Our government must be getting very nervous. So far there hasn't been much fighting. I believe it is because the government has been paying bribes. Something must have happened.

"I don't know what will become of Elias and Dinos. Maybe they will be forced to join the army. And what am I to do?" asked Miguel. "I can no longer sell to Carrillo. I don't know if I will ever be able to sell to anyone."

"Earlier, you told me that Elias got you a fair price to-day," Tarek said. "We will make sure that the next time we will get you an even better price. Have faith."

Alex patted him on the back. "And just like you've told me, Miguel, Buck up."

Miguel put his hat back on.

"When Elias is ready, he will let us know what is happening," said Alex. He passed his hand across the surface of the tank.

Ionna pulled a kelp-like plant from the water.

"Seaweed?" asked Miguel.

The plants will be tree-sized. They are also stocked with fish.

Alex grabbed and showed them a thirty-centimetre-long trout. He let it jump out of his hands.

"I am sure that Sofia and the children could use a taste of trout," said Miguel.

"Ionna is convinced that there might be a market for other foods where we might be the only supplier. From the microbes in the vats, we can create anything. Much of food is about presentation and texture."

"Seafood?" asked Miguel.

Alex patted Miguel on the back again and said, "Miguel, what has happened on your trip was intense. But you made a good profit, and with that new truck of yours, we will be able to do so much more." He grabbed his hand in his and said, "I promise you that we will keep you and your family safe. The next time we go into town, I am sure we will be able to double your return."

"But increasing the herd takes time. We're not growing rabbits," Miguel said.

"With what you have here, we can become much more productive. Maybe even in time, maybe rabbits."

"I will hold you to that," said Miguel.

"One thing, though—what's a rabbit?" asked Alex.

Miguel slapped him on the shoulder and laughed.

He heard Alex ask the question again to the others as Miguel was walking away. That time, Alex noticed that he didn't smile.

After Miguel left, Khaled and Sami showed up.

"Sofia was livid about something, and Miguel looked stressed," Khaled said.

"Getting a visit from the police is the last thing that anyone wants," Alex said.

The day after Miguel returned, Alex stepped outside, in front of the farm. He stretched his arms to a flaring yellow sunrise that illuminated long wisps of clouds with bands of orange. It filtered through the trees in front of him. He stomped through the damp morning mist and found his mother feeding the fawns. She was wearing a long green Irish-looking sweater. It looked like it was made of wool, but was mostly composed of an algae base. Her mitts were in her pockets.

"Antonis is still missing," Alex said.

"He talks to me," she said. "His instincts have always been good."

"But it's dangerous."

"So can doing nothing." She saw Sofia running towards them. "Something is wrong," Ionna said. She tightened her scarf and quickly put her mitts back on.

"It's Miguel. You have to take him to the hospital," she cried. "Do it, please."

Once inside the house, Elena started screaming at her mother. Andrés was on the floor and crying. Juan had taken a bowl of something out from the fridge and was eating it with his fingers. A bottle of milk had shattered across the kitchen floor. Alex patted the boy on the back, tussled his hair, and carried him out of the kitchen. His mother while lambasting him for the mess and pointed to where his room was. While Mrs. Winters ordered the other two to their rooms, Ionna quickly cleaned up the spilled milk.

Alex followed Mrs. Winters into the master bedroom. He noticed that Miguel's body had turned yellow. He saw that he had thrown up a number of times into a bucket, and missed at least once. There was some blood in it.

Ionna touched the farmer's chest with her gloved hand and ran a diagnostic. "Every part of him was reacting to something," she said. Through telepathy, Alex heard her say, "It isn't a virus that is killing him. It is something more insidious."

Ionna took a sample of Miguel's blood, using a syringe that Sofia had acquired. It was normally used for inoculating fawns.

"Mrs. Winters, if you don't mind, we'll have Sami analyze it," Alex said.

Alex heard Ionna send out a telepathic broadcast to her children. "I don't know what this is, but it's bad," she said. "From this moment on, everyone isolates. I mean, everyone. We will assume that it is contagious. Until we learn more, everyone should stay in separate rooms. And that includes each of the Winter's children."

"I am going," Miguel's wife said.

"Sofia, this is not a cold. This is extremely dangerous, and your children need you." Ionna sent other messages addressed to Tarek and Khaled. She told them that it was very likely that Sofia was infected and that she saw her touching the older children.

Tarek rushed into the house and tried to distract Sofia, while Alex was wrapping her husband up in blankets.

Khaled followed and, in another telepathic message, volunteered to protect Andrés.

Alex picked Miguel up in his arms and hurried to his truck."

Sofia screamed something from the door, but Tarek managed to convince her to return inside.

Ionna climbed in on the passenger side.

"Mom, no, you're not coming. It's too dangerous."

"Too late, I'm here. Let's go."

Alex stared at her and then at the sick man between them. "Are you going to stay in the truck?" he asked.

"OK. As long as you keep me informed."

Reluctantly, he let her stay and drove on.

A few minutes after leaving, Alex and his mother received a memory message from Sami. His message said, "The state broadcast has issued an alert for their capture, and it gave their names and showed their faces. It says that they are wanted for murder, and are armed and dangerous."

He also added, "Not too many look like them—just us. Each one of us is now marked."

Alex replied with, "Stay covered, and don't forget the gloves. See if you can get more information from the other broadcasts." He stared at his mother, but she ignored him.

When he got close to town, Alex received confirmation from his brothers that they were alive and in hiding. The earthling that Alex considered to be a friend, who was so vigorously alive yesterday, was now barely breathing.

Follow-up memory exchanges with Elias confirmed that what Miguel was suffering from was likely the same as what he had seen in prison.

The hospital was located outside the city walls. Alex was able to drive into the parking lot without being accosted by security.

Alex stepped out of the truck and proceeded to drag Miguel out.

"Alex, he's fading fast," she told him.

"I owe him, Mom."

"Just hurry back. Don't give me excuses."

Alex carried the body away.

Ionna ran after him. "Stop," she yelled. She put a pair of glasses on him and gave him a toque. "And do up that scarf," she ordered.

Alex stoically carried Miguel into the emergency room. There were long lines leading to the emergency room admissions, and the waiting room was swamped. Alex propped Miguel up in a chair.

Everyone in the waiting room seemed to have been suffering from the same ailment. Three people had fallen over in their chairs. Another two souls were lying in the hallway. The few hospital staff that he saw wore face masks.

Alex took a place in line.

Someone at his left in the nearby waiting room said, "Jose, that's one of them, isn't it?" Two soldiers stood in front of a woman in a chair in front of an alcove. One of the soldiers stared at him.

Jose pulled a rifle off his shoulder and nodded to his partner. "Mister, stop right there."

"What can I do for you, officer?"

Patients stumbled out of the way. Most of the line in front of Alex moved towards Jose's side of the room.

"Hey, stay away," Jose whined to patients who were moving towards him.

A man who stumbled towards Jose threw up. What came out was mostly blood.

Shocked, Jose accidentally fired and hit Alex in the shoulder. Alex kept moving to get away, but the man kept firing. He shot the man who threw up on him. He kept firing as he moved the muzzle back towards Alex. As Alex lay dying, he touched Miguel's wallet and vaporized it.

Jose, why the hell did you do that? That was crazy.

"He was escaping," he said.

"Jose, you shot him."

Another man who was waiting in line threw up.

"Luis, look around. I don't think any of us are going to make it out of here to-night."

The last thing that Alex was able to do was voice a single word to his mother —LEAVE!

"Mom, I know you want to go in, but hold off. Give us a couple of minutes," said Elias.

"But it could be too late."

"Mom—two minutes."

She got up and walked around the parking lot. There were dozens of vehicles there. She noticed that most of the cars weren't empty. They were filled with the dead.

"Mom," Elias said.

"How about now?"

"Alex is gone. He was shot. What was done can't be fixed."

"How do you know?"

"Miguel's heart is still beating. You left a diag construct in him. I was able to use the location as a relay for another routine to locate Alex. After finding him, I was able to clone and generate another diag utility within him. From that device, Dinos was able to use the relay point to generate another device that was able to generate an external search of the room. The place is filled with patients who seem to be suffering from what Miguel has."

"Think of the others. You can't take the risk."

"I just—"

"Mom, is killing the shooter going to bring him back?" Elias said.

"What is going on is severely under-reported," Dinos interrupted.

"The disease will kill the shooter," Elias said. "Leave him. Just get out of there."

It was still early in the morning, and the sky was still clear. She sat in the truck staring at the hospital door. She watched five more carloads of the sick being dropped off. They all looked jaundiced.

As she drove around the city wall, there were very few vehicles moving, but there were dead and dying people sprawled everywhere.

Why don't we see soldiers? she wondered. "Because they're inside the city," she told herself. "Dear Mother of God."

Ionna drove into the driveway, and Sami greeted her. He tried to give her a hug, but she backed away. "Miguel and Alex are dead," she told him.

He let her tell him the details before telling her, "We lost two of the children since you were away—Elana and Juan."

"Good Lord," she said.

"Their mother is still alive, but she's fading."

"And what of Andrés?"

"Khaled has kept him isolated. So far, he's not affected."

"Charlotte is crumbling," she told him, and then forwarded a telepathic notification to Tarek inside that neither Alex nor Miguel would be returning home.

She entered the common room on the first subfloor and found Tarek pacing back and forth. He attempted to give her a hug, but again she backed away.

Local state programming media were confirming that there was widespread sickness throughout Charlotte. A government spokesperson promised that they were on the verge of a permanent cure. The spokesperson blamed governments to the north and west for sending in a bioweapon.

"Nice to hear the news, but it's kind of late."

Tarek offered her tea, and she sat down.

"What are the other broadcasts saying about this infection?"

"The state to the west blamed the city for accidentally releasing the virus on their own people. They accused them of reusing banned munitions from the Neuron War. The state to the northwest agreed with that position and called for executions for all city politicians. The northerners believe that infections are expanding to cities in the south. Politicians in each of the three states are actively stoking fires for their people to bear arms."

"That just means that everyone is terrified, doesn't have a clue, and is getting desperate," Ionna said. She got up to look for something to eat.

Khaled entered the room from downstairs.

"Where's Andrés?"

"He and Barfy are taking a nap. He'll be alright. It will be good to have Elias and Dinos back with us."

Ionna was going to say something about Alex, but he nodded and just said, "I know."

"Mom, you mentioned that they don't have a clue, but there's a reason for that," Khaled said.

She grabbed a couple of algae cookies and rolled her hand a couple of times to make him come to the point.

"We've drawn blood from Miguel, Sofia, the children and ourselves and done tests. The military didn't have anything to do with the disease. We are the source of the problem."

"What?"

"It was created in a lab on Ovidia. Earthlings got the infection from us," Khaled said. "What was in Miguel was similar to what is in our bloodstream. The technology that enabled us to survive the harsh Ovidian environment also included a genetic weapon."

"If we touch someone, initially their internals will break down," Sami said.

"One could come up with something to protect organs, but the disease would continue to destroy everything else with our DNA markers. Our enhancements create subtle oils on our skin. Skin-to-skin touch generates an exchange of a biological agent."

"The agent will infect, if it comes in contact with human DNA," Tarek said. "It doesn't affect deer, dogs or cats."

"Some of the Ovidians we first met were afraid of us," Ionna said. It's not surprising that they wanted to kill us off, but that someone had the daring to try this was very unusual in those times."

"We can hug each other, but doing so will kill an earthling within a day," Sami said. "Infected earthlings can also pass the plague on through touch."

"That means that until we develop a cure, Andrés won't be able to touch anyone."

Ionna sat down and stared intently at a blank wall as she chewed on a cookie.

"What are you thinking, Mom?" asked Tarek.

"Around us, they are all running around madly and terrified that they're going to get infected. The big question is, what are the powerful cities to the south going to do? They won't be providing welcome wagons."

Dinos and Elias drove away from their bunker early the next morning. Twenty minutes later, Dinos heard a soaring sound from the sky high above the van. "Elias," he yelled, "Jump."

A huge remaining crater bore witness to the futility of that request. It may have lasted a fraction of a second, but every remaining Ovidian sensed Elias's death cry.

The night after the next, the horizon lit up through the trees. Thunderous bombings decimated the walled city and some surrounding settlements.

Before the end of the day, Sofia succumbed to her illness, and Andrés became an orphan.

Departures

Khaled felt his long hair and took a deep breath before choosing to go ahead. He tromped into Andrés's bedroom at noon. The boy was sitting on his bed. His arms were wrapped around a thirty-centimetre-long floppy green frog. His blankets, pillow, and clothes were scattered across the floor.

Khaled's farm overalls were supported with suspenders. His winter coat was left unbuttoned,and gloves covered his huge hands. He put a toque back on and a transparent face mask over it.

Seeing the Ovidian scared him. He moved back towards the wall. With a yawn, he rubbed his red eyes again.

"Andrés, you are supposed to be dressed."

"No."

"Let me help you, and I'll show you something."

"No."

Khaled levitated one of the boy's books up a couple of centimetres.

"Are you sure?"

Andrés went to the book and checked to see if there were strings attached.

Andrés reached for the book.

"Well?" Khaled asked.

The boy stared up at him.

"Why the mask?" you ask. "It's so none of us gets sick like your mom and dad."

"Since everyone else has one, you won't need it. Besides, at the moment I don't have one that's your size. But don't worry. You are safe with us, and we are going to protect you." Khaled pointed to the boy's church clothes that were on the floor.

Khaled was able to help fasten the boy's shoes, but he couldn't do up the boy's small buttons. He had to patiently tell him how to do it. When Andrés relented to put on his mitts, he got the frog back.

Khaled yelled, "Andrés Winters is ready. We're coming out."

Khaled had the boy sit in a small chair. He slowly levitated him outside. They meandered around the yard until they got to a place past the barn near the property line.

Six crosses stood beyond two holes in the ground. Two coffins rested on a table that was placed in front. Jars of wildflowers were set at each side.

Ionna, Sami, and Tarek, like Khaled, wore full face masks and thick gloves. The first three wore wide-brim hats, which shadowed their faces. Andrés's chair was raised to hover slightly over the table.

A small furry brown and white terrier by Tarek's feet sniffed and barked.

"Barfy," screamed Andrés. Tarek picked up the dog and put it on the boy's lap.

Andrés stared quizzically at Ionna and at the coffins. She put a hand on the coffin beside her and said, "Your mother." She put a hand on the other and said, "Elena and Juan."

"Papá?" the boy asked.

Sami pointed to the horizon and, with his hands and sounds, mimicked an explosion blast. "Charlotte," he said. "With Alex, Elias, and Dinos."

"And Antonis," Khaled said.

"Khaled, we don't know."

"But he went there—Hugo Carrillo. Alex told me. It was after Elias—"

"Oh no. He wouldn't," Ionna said.

Sami glared at Khaled. His hands formed a threatening fist.

Khaled hunched and nervously stepped from side to side.

"Enough," Ionna said. She pointed to the sky and blessed herself. The others did the same.

Ionna gave a reading from the Spanish Bible.

Each of them said a few words about the departed.

"Papá and Barfy liked Alex," said Andrés.

Khaled, who was looking at him, smiled.

Sami dropped an unfinished radio that Dinos was building. Khaled added a rusty shovel that Elias used. Ionna lowered a scarf Alex had given her.

Ionna closed both caskets.

Andrés offered his frog to Tarek.

"Juan and Elan," Khaled asked.

The boy nodded.

Tarek gave it to his mother, who put it in the children's casket.

They put a picture of Andrés's father with Andrés's mother.

Ionna threw a wildflower into the hole.

After burying the bodies, everyone helped plant wildflower seeds over top of the plot. Ionna called the dog, and it jumped off the chair. Andrés crawled off the chair and ran after it into the house.

"That was fooken bizarre," said Sami.

"Yeah, she shouldn't have let him run like that without mittens," said Khaled.

"No, but why bury wood and things?" It's such a waste."

"Local customs—like Alex's scarf."

"How about the Ovidians having to eat the pets of their deceased relatives?"

"No, I didn't like that one," said Khaled. "Almost died thanks to you. Tarek's making something. You can stay if you like. Smells like food."

Khaled wore a knapsack and pulled a floating transparent bubble up the stairs into the family living room. Andrés was in it.

"Khaled, and where do you plan to go?"

"Somewhere where there aren't people. I am going to do what I can to discover a cure."

"How is that going to work out? You will never be able to touch him, and there's no way you can tell just by looking at someone if they're infected."

"He can't stay here. It's going to be too dangerous. War is coming. If we were able to accomplish miracles on Ovidia, why not here?"

"Andrés, did you pack a stuffed animal?" asked Ionna.

The boy showed her a stuffed bat. He wore a thick winter jacket and had a fleece hat and gloves.

Tarek brought him a stuffed bright orange knapsack. "These people, they keep so much. All those books, and the music, for example."

"You are just upset because you couldn't bring your father's medal," his mother said.

"Khaled, things might settle down. I'll keep you posted," Ionna said.

Khaled nodded.

Tarek, with his gloved hands, helped the little boy put the knapsack on.

"I don't want to go," said Andrés. "Where are we going?"

"We are going to try out your hoverball," said Khaled. "We're going to play in the snow."

"Can Missie come?"

"The cat? No, not this time. We're going on a journey. She's staying because she needs to catch mice."

Khaled and Andrés followed the road north for two days. The round, crystal-like enclosure was a third of a meter higher than Andrés when he stood with his hat on. Although Khaled enabled it to hover above the ground, the boy was able to walk within it, similar to a hamster on a treadmill. Clips on his boots gave the impression that the bottom of his feet was stepping flatly. If he wanted to sit, a cloth fold-out chair could be pulled out. There were air holes on both sides and another for exchanging things. The boy's mitts were fastened to strings that were sewn to his jacket. The sole purpose of the enclosure was to prevent accidental touching.

"Where is it?" the boy asked.

"I am not sure. The last time I was here was in the winter. See, the trees are smaller and thinner. That means it can't be too far. Probably the day after tomorrow. Your father told me that he took you camping; is that true?"

"In the woods, behind the barn. With Missie and Barfy."

"Your dog and cat were with you?" Khaled asked.

"Barfy barked at the wolves and coyotes."

"Did you see one?" Khaled asked.

"Missie brought me a mouse. Father told me that Barfy wanted to go home. I got him some water, and then he had to pee."

They approached an intersection. Khaled told Andrés to hush. The trail followed a gentle slope towards the top of a hill. Khaled heard sounds of clanking metal approaching.

Khaled hurried into the woods. He pulled the bubble ball behind a deadfall and then forced the rocks to shift in order to create a crevasse. He quickly lowered the bubble and dropped in behind it.

Two troop carriers drove over the top of the hill and stopped a few lengths before the intersection.

"Everyone out. We'll start the burn from that side road," an officer commanded. "Have the rest park on the other side and muster here," he yelled.

Damn it, I'm probably on the wrong side of the road, Khaled realized.

Khaled sent out a small remote camera device that looked like a mouse to relay what was going on above. He was nervous because he was still able to see the sky. It wasn't much of a hiding place.

The mouse relayed a video of half a dozen soldiers carrying flamethrowers. They snapped to attention in front of their officer.

"Private McCauley, start a burn on the far side of the road."

When he heard that, Khaled quickly pulled himself out of the hole.

"The rest of you, in line of sight to the right, space every fifty meters," said the officer. "When done, move your full line to the right and repeat the burn with that spacing for the next section. Repeat four times and then report back to me. Understood?"

Khaled commanded sharp stone spikes to lunge out of the ground. They rose a meter and a half. The six soldiers who were in line were impaled.

Private McCauley, who had leapt away, fired his flamethrower at Khaled's location. The camera Khaled was relying on had melted. The log that he hid behind provided temporary protection.

He didn't know where the soldier was, so he had a block rise out of the road a couple of meters from the fallen soldiers. He made it shake in order to draw the man's attention. As the man turned, so did the flame. Khaled stood up. Once he caught sight of the man, a hole opened under him. The soldier banged his elbow, and the weapon flew away. Khaled forced the large rocks to close in on him. He made sure that the stone pikes turned to dust.

After pulling the hoverball out of the hole, Khaled, with Andrés in tow, hurried away through the thinning treeline. He had no idea what was on the other side of the hill and had no wish to find out. Once they reached the next trail, they followed it north. Khaled kept moving through the night. He didn't stop until he saw the trees behind them light up.

Didn't take long to find the bodies, he thought. *And such madness.* He sent the others a flying device. It was a routine that Dinos gave him. It would only travel a few miles, but he hoped that it would get close enough for the message to get relayed. He was telling the others that "The northerners are burning the forests. Protect yourselves. Soldiers are moving in."

Monterrey

Ionna stepped away from the entrance door of the house of stone. Everything she saw was black and ashen. Miguel's piles of logs behind the vats were burned. The surrounding trees were bare. She found dead fish floating in two of the six vats. From another she pulled a fish out.

"Stubborn and wily," she said as it jumped out of her grip.

After feeding the vats and composting the dead, she grabbed a feed bag and milk bottles. She marched off to help what was left of the remaining livestock.

On a trail to the open area, she found Tarek bottle-feeding a fawn. He fed her next to a fallen doe.

She saw tears in his eyes.

"It's a miracle she survived," he said. There were six dead deer on the trail behind him.

"Using fire as a weapon was horrific," she said. "The people who live here are the same as in the north and the west. They're probably all related. It was hateful and ignorant."

"The northerners probably don't know how to feed themselves," Tarek said.

"We'll have to take precautions," Ionna said. She walked past him. "I can see deer feeding beyond the gate," she added.

"Most of the livestock seems to have survived the worst of it," he said. It's good that we released the ones in the pens in time."

"That's hopeful. By the way, did you know that Sami found Barfy?"

"No. Where?"

"He was in Andrés's room. And when he lit the barn up, Missie came running out. They're both in the basement lab with him."

"And what could go wrong?" Tarek said and laughed.

Ionna quickly left. She marched off towards the open gate before she started to cry.

Ionna heard the sound of helicopter-like vehicles. The deer were skittish. It had been five days since the fires were started. She and Tarek were on the farm's open, unforested area. They were dropping bales of feed. She sent a telepathic message to her sons to run for cover. Without foliage, the burnt trees didn't offer much overhead protection. Looking back, Ionna saw their long line of tracks in the ash.

A vehicle landed in the field behind them. Rotors were attached on each side. Another helicopter-like vehicle landed in front of the property. The slope blocked her view.

"Shit," she muttered.

Another vehicle flew overhead.

Five soldiers came running from behind her in the field. Another three with high-powered automatic weapons rushed over the hill.

From overhead, someone shot at her. It missed her by a foot. Ionna was prepared to destroy the vehicle, but a package in the dirt exploded and caused her to stumble. A cocoon netting enveloped her before she hit the ground. She saw the same thing happen to Tarek. When the soldiers from the open field got closer, someone caused her netting to electrify. Ionna was able to survive it.

"Don't Tarek, there are too many," she warned. "Let's choose a better moment."

Ionna heard a voice from an officer's mike. The soldier reported that they had torched the house.

"Simpletons," Ionna muttered.

She watched soldiers attach a line to Tarek's cocoon netting.

The overhead craft launched missiles. It blew the stone house apart. She heard the officer's mike say, "There was only one signature inside, and it was no longer an issue."

"You brainless idiot, stand down and disengage," the officer yelled. "Are you sure?"

"Roger that," was the reply.

Ionna froze. It wasn't the netting or the electrocution. It was Sami. Another of her sons was murdered. "My Sami," she droned.

It wasn't that he was just stubborn and being a prick. He was pointing somewhere else. Sometimes he was right. He was so dogged—that was my boy. Her hatred of these people wouldn't allow her to cry.

The officer walked past her and yelled, "Don't take all day; hook the line and take her up. Not tomorrow. Now," the officer yelled.

She looked up at him. *Fucking bastards, I'm going to kill you all,* she thought.

A soldier hooked a line to her cocoon netting. The officer climbed on board. Someone inside made sure she was being pulled in fast. Five soldiers climbed in, and the helicopter-like vehicle took off.

She was dangling from a cord, which was hauling her upwards headfirst. The netting did not block her vision.

All I have to do is touch them, she thought. *A finger on their wrist or a caress across their face, and everyone that they know and love will choke on their own vomit within a day.*

But damned if I'm going to lose another one, she thought as she looked at her son, who was dangling below her.

The three vehicles headed south through the clouds. The two in front escorted the one with the prisoners.

As Ionna was brought into the vehicle, she pretended to be groggy. While moaning, she asked why they were being taken.

"Reconnaissance reported that there were people and livestock here," said a

Black man. "And just look at you. You're just the same as the murderers. The higher-ups in Monterrey want to see you."

So someone besides the states from the north and the west is going to get involved. And it's because they were searching for livestock. What a mess! Ionna thought.

"So why murder my son?" she asked. "Why didn't you capture him?"

"Don't answer that, Corporal Brickle. They're more trouble than they're worth," said a soldier with a gnarly, orange moustache.

"Yes, Sergeant Barnes," replied the corporal.

Ionna relaxed when she saw Tarek being dragged in. *He's still breathing,* she thought.

Once inside, his netting dissolved. He stood and focused on the machines that flew in front of them.

The soldier sitting at her left raised his rifle. Ionna sent out a packet. It generated a heart attack. Sergeant Barnes who sat across from her, and the soldier beside him raised their rifles. She also caused them to fall forward.

Tarek sent out a packet that enabled the rotors to buckle and be drawn inwards. Both choppers spun erratically as they fell.

Someone beside her shot Tarek in the chest. The top half of his body separated from the lower half. Both parts tumbled out of the vehicle.

From her frozen disbelief spilled the word "Tarek." Something smashed her head. Ionna lost consciousness.

Ionna couldn't see when she awoke. She couldn't move. They had tied and wrapped her like a mummy. A leather bag of some sort was secured over her head. Something like thick leather bands secured her. One was pulled tight across her eyes. Her hands and ankles were shackled.

She waited and listened.

"Colonel Bennett, ETA in fifty-five minutes, sir," the pilot said.

"Continue as planned," the colonel said.

Oh, Tarek, Ionna thought. She watched the look on his face as he fell away again—as his life left him. When he was small, she saw it. They were resting in a hammock in the foliage, away from the Ovidian's stamping feet. *He was leaning next to me*, she remembered. *He could barely walk.* A grizzle, a python-like thing, stretched into a strike pose.

I called it grizzle because when I cut it, it was like what spits out of a frying pan. Its insides burned and spattered. I kept slashing that thing until I thought that every memory of it was gone.

Tarek was there, filled with crying, yet he had a stunned look of amazement.

Was that what I saw in my boy that fell, or was it me? She felt the shackles on her ankles as she pulled.

"Colonel, I would like to request leave for a couple of days. It's my aunt," said Corporal Brickle. "She needs surgery."

"Corporal, this is not a nursery. The drills are mandatory, and so is your attendance at the parade and the hoisting of colours."

"But, sir, she has no-one."

"Request denied. Make arrangements after your next mission. This is the military. Suck it in."

Ionna could sense the boy's heartbeat racing. She pulled at her bindings. She knew that she could easily break them, but she hesitated.

Did Khaled survive the fire, or is he too among the dead? she wondered. *Could it be true that when I am gone there will be no-one?*

Poor Andrés. We tried. Ionna pushed subtly against her bindings.

But Juan and Elena, were like my Nikos and Theo in Greece. She felt that she was drowning in an ocean of someone's tears, again.

She called up an image of Nadia. It was when she had to send her away. Ionna imagined all of her girls screaming at her, *'Why did you send us away? Did you not trust us?'*

Ionna broke the shackle that bound her wrists. She asked, "How many in Monterrey? I've never been there."

"Shut up," said a soldier behind her.

"Fifteen million," said the pilot.

Not hundreds, not thousands, but millions, is what he said. Poor, wonderful

Andrés, Juan, and Elena. And even Sofia. And Monica, Ossie, Andy Li, and even Charlie. Fares, defending your children cost you everything. I think that you will understand.

Ionna did not have to move to generate an automated routine. She cooked up a recipe that would change metal to something that looked like sand. She willed it to attack the frame of the chopper.

"Sorry, boys, but you're amongst the damned. You carry the plague. Corporal, your aunt wouldn't forgive us." Ionna's bindings and netting disappeared.

As the vehicle shook and began to crack, the Colonel yelled, "Parachutes."

"Tarek, wait for me," she whispered.

As the metal turned, the wind blew away the dust. Everything else fell. Not one of the soldiers had a parachute.

As Ionna tumbled through the clouds, she screamed "γαμώ." She heard nothing because she was falling faster than the speed of sound.

In our wildest dreams, could we have ever imagined?—

From her lips came, "Fares, you are such a malaka...yamoto!—opa."

With outstretched limbs, she soared like a bird seeking a nest. In reality, her hands closed around empty, nonexistent, broken wine glasses, and she once again was alone. Like when she floated after an accident in Greece.

Before the moment blackness came, she heard a faint, "No, Mom. No." It was Antonis wailing.

Winter Blooms

An encampment of troops blocked Khaled and Andrés from continuing north. Soldiers were camped out on both sides of the road. Rather than go around, Khaled created an underground bunker. He decided to wait them out and acquire intelligence before moving across a cold, unprotected wasteland.

Khaled didn't have much experience raising or even talking with young children. He really didn't know much about them at all. He had only taken an interest in Nikos and Alya when they got older. With so many others around, it was easy to make himself scarce. The Ovidian young, for comparison, were sent away to nurseries at a young age. The males never got involved.

He watched Miguel interact with his children as he did with the livestock and their offspring. He was moved by the concern that Elena and Juan shared with their pets.

One good thing about the Ovidians—they won't eat you until your parents are dead, he thought. *Nori, of the Sym-Set Overdrive, threatened to when he tried to kill me. What a twit. He was just farting out his tinkers.*

Andrés sat in his bubble looking, at pictures in his book. Looking at the boy reading made Khaled think of Alex. *If the fool didn't die, he would have been sitting here,* he thought. *He was so much better at this sort of thing.*

The man was like an uncle to Khaled. He had another two hundred and forty years on him. Even if someone else offered to take the boy, he knew that for old Alex's sake, he had to be the one to step up. Now that he thought about it, he realized that he really loved the old fart.

"Gotta go," Andrés said.

"But you just went. Are you not feeling well?"

"Gotta go.

Khaled let him out of the bubble.

The boy refused to go back in. Khaled waited until he fell asleep before putting him back.

The bubble thing was very much a work in progress. How to fasten the heat crystal without burning the boy or damaging the bubble was a real challenge. Making the fold-out chair work as a flat bed needed fixing.

The boys' dislike of the bubble was not going to get any better. He didn't think that he would ever stop asking to go home. He was surprised that today he didn't ask about where the snow was.

Khaled learned that the only way he could keep Andrés from making noise was to talk to him. Khaled really resented that Barfy wasn't here.

The question Khaled resented the most was 'Where are we going?'

'We are going to save you from me,' was the answer he feared the most. Another answer that he considered was, 'Actually, we are going to return to Prospect Park and find a cure.' It was flowery and almost hopeful-sounding, but 'I might be the only one to save the world from us' would not mean much to a three-year-old.

Khaled fell asleep against a rock wall. He awoke to find a little hand dangling in front of his face. He immediately backed up and touched his face shield. "God,"

he moaned.

Andrés's cot swung. He woke up and attempted to stand. The bubble rolled back and bounced from rock to rock. "Damn it," Khaled said as he banged his foot on a rock. He heard noises from the surface. He put a hand over his mouth and tried to lower the sound of the boy's cries. Andrés stopped crying when Khaled offered to let him out again.

Khaled made him something to eat, but he wouldn't hand him the bowl until he repeated 'glove, glove, glove,' as he repeatedly opened and closed his own gloved hand in front of Andrés's face.

Khaled sent a couple of clumsily made mouse cameras to map the lay of the land on the surface. The initial versions were not very convincing-looking. It wasn't until he saw the real thing scurrying around in the cave that he was able to create better replicas.

He managed to get a rodent-looking device to bring him back a fleece coat. Once he acquired the fleece, he was able to replicate the material. He made a copy of the stuffed animal that Andrés's sister used to carry.

In time, he was able to build a stuffed action item that would do things for Andrés. The boy called it MonkEE. Voice commands made it do things. If he wanted to sit, the *Chair* command would open the chair. *Walk* would fold it back. For the *Book Out* command, the device would pull it out of his bag and give it to him. When he said *MonkEE,* it would sit on his lap if he was sitting; otherwise, it would keep hopping by his feet.

Khaled had heard a cry from Sami. There might have been something from Tarek and his mother, but he wasn't sure.

Being so close to the soldiers is what it is, he thought. *Sending something back when I get to Brooklyn will sort it out.*

Conversations that the mouse camera picked up let him know that they were from the north—well, actually, the northwest. He surmised that people kept away from the coast because of a risk of getting radiation poisoning.

Some day I am going to build a detector, Khaled thought. If he couldn't make it, he was determined to locate one and steal it.

He learned that the soldiers were determined to claim all lands north of Charlotte. The bodies, of the dead or living, were to be tossed into mobile incinerators. People in the snow-lands were desperate to move south. Officers in the camp had serious doubts about the notion. Just because there were no infected people in an area didn't mean that new people weren't going to catch what the others had; I seemed to be a common sentiment.

After spending two days hiding and listening, he overheard the officers receive confirmation that all land from where they were to Charlotte had been cleared of occupants. They were also told to expect to soon meet up with truck loads of settlers.

He overheard an old officer say, "Incompetent morons. The military hasn't finalized settlement plans for anybody. This is developing into a horrific mess. There is an invasion from the west, and the civilians are going to get wasted. What a pitiless mess."

When Khaled climbed up to the surface the next morning, his cameras confirmed what he was witnessing. The military had moved on. Beyond the top of the hill, there was no sign of anyone else moving.

"Andrés, tell MonkEE that we're going on another trip. We're going to play in the snow."

After getting out of the bunker, the pair followed the trail north for a couple of hours. As the evergreen forest noticeably thinned, the wind became abrasive and biting cold.

After walking for another half a day, Khaled saw a few children ahead. A younger boy argued with two others. Three very young children sat on the ground next to some small trees.

"What should we tell MonkEE?" asked Khaled. "Do they look sick?"

The boy got up from his seat.

"Be careful," he said.

The pair marched on, but Khaled pulled the ball to his left side, away from the line of children. When he got near, the two older boys stepped onto the road.

"Tomás, look at that. Your sister could use one of those, couldn't she?"

"Zaine Maxwell, you're such a toad. Carmen's way too big."

Zaine and the boy next to him flashed knives at their sides.

Khaled stared at the boy beside Zaine. The boy looked a little older. "What's your name?" Khaled asked.

"Tomás Flores, Mister."

"Tomás, are you sure you want to threaten strangers in these parts? Do you really think that is a good idea?"

He pointed to the children who were sitting in a row and said, "They are not doing so well."

"I can see that," Khaled said. "Girls, you look really cold." The three young girls were just a couple of years older than Andrés. "Why are you here?"

"Where we were, it was real bad," said Tomás Flores. "No food. People were hurting. My father heard that there was a safe place out here. A soldier shot my dad. We got no place to go."

"What about you?" Khaled asked the young boy with an oversized furry hat.

"I am Diego Lopez. Gabriela is with me. She's my sister. We came with Tomás, his sisters, and his parents because we got no-one.

"Tomás, where are your parents?"

"I don't know," Tomás Flores said. "Soldiers started firing. We was told to run, and we've been running since."

"When did that happen?"

"Yesterday, sir."

"Did the soldiers start firing because they thought someone was sick?"

"We don't know, sir," said Zaine. The boy looked at the ground and shifted his feet.

The girls were coughing and had the sniffles. It was dark around their eyes.

"Looks like the girls are sick. By the look of all of you, it has been a while since you have eaten. Tomás Flores, what do you want to do?"

"We would like some place to stay. Sir, we would be most obliged if you could help us get something to eat."

"Andrés and I might be willing to help, but there are a couple of rules no-one crosses. What do you think that is, Zaine?"

"Don't rightly know, sir."

"No hurting and no touching. If you don't touch someone, you won't get the plague."

"You have a ponytail," said Carmen who was the youngest.

"Not even someone's hair. No touching at all. Do you hear me? You might catch something else, but it won't be a just a bad cough. It could be something worse. If that happens, you are on your own. Do you understand?

"And no-one touches Andrés. Does everyone understand? Does everyone agree?"

Each of the children nodded both times. When Khaled and Andrés walked across a field towards a rocky hill, the rest followed.

Diego Lopez ran alongside to look at the bubble. "Does that mean I can touch it?"

"And if you accidentally touch his hand? Do you think it would be worth it?"

"No, I guess not."

Khaled created a deep space under the entrance into the rock face of the rolling hill.

"Oh, wow," screamed Diego Lopez. "Can you teach me how to do that?"

"No."

"You're some kind of hombre," said Tomás Flores.

After allocating places for each of them, he sealed the entrance.

"Whoa. I don't like that, mister," said Zaine Maxwell.

"Do you want the soldiers to find you?"

"No, but if someone touches me. It's crazy."

Relax. It will take a while for me to configure some lights, and I have some housekeeping to do."

"El esta loco," said Gabriela Lopez.

Considering that he had to make soup, thick bedding, heating, lighting, and arrangements for washing facilities for the girls who likely had pneumonia, yes, Khaled felt that he was crazy. He was convinced that he had taken on more than he could bear. He had to create a private toilet section, nightshirts, and a curtain. He also had to figure out how to wash and dry all of the clothes.

At one point, Zaine stood up and threatened to kick Tomás Flores. After threatening to kick him out, Khaled had him undress and ordered him to dunk his head into a small tub of freezing cold water.

"You are not coming out of there until all the dirt is sponged away," Khaled threatened. "That includes washing your hair."

When Zaine came out of the tub wearing a nightshirt, Khaled told him, "Next time, if you are good, I'll heat the water for you."

"Gracias, sénior," Zaine chattered.

Khaled learned early from his mother, a fundamental thing about feeding earthlings was to never tell them what they were eating. *'Just say that it is some little thing that was thrown together from leftovers,' he remember her say. 'That the texture was familiar was all that they needed to know. Tell them once, and they will never trust you to cook again.'*

With what he fried over the heat stone and mixed with greens, each of the children begged for seconds. That included Andrés.

When Khaled brought the children into the cave, he wasn't optimistic that Carmen Flores, who was the youngest, would get better. Her temperature was high, and she was extremely thin. It took another three days for her and her sister to recover.

At breakfast, he confirmed to everyone that none of them had the plague. "Once the girls are able, we're going to continue on our walk north," he said. "Is everybody fine with that?"

"Why do we have to do that? This place is just great," said Zaine.

"His ponytail is gone," young Carmen said.

"That's right. El hombre se lo cortó," said Gabriela.

"Why Mister?" asked Zaine.

"My brother had short hair," Khaled said.

"Who?"

"He's gone. He was like a father to me."

"Who?" Zaine repeated.

"His name was Alex. He was a real hombre. He wasn't somebody anyone would want to cross. Besides Andrés knew him."

"Sí, él era un hombre de verdad," said Andrés.

"El esta loco," said Carmen Lopez.

Khaled stood up. "Everyone will have work to do," he said. "You don't just want to lie around and grow fat, do you? We have a city to build?"

"In the frozen lands?"

"Yes."

Zaine went to smash hands with Tomás Flores.

"No," screamed Khaled.

"But you told us that we are not infected."

"The rule does not change. If an infected person touches anyone in the group, you will not know. It will continue like this until I create a cure."

"But—"

"No means no. Do you understand? I am serious. You're risking your life and everyone's."

"Si," he replied.

When the group crossed the snow line, Khaled told Andrés, "You can tell MonkEE that we are starting our snow adventure."

"Snow," Andrés repeated.

"Hey, hey," Khaled repeated and raised a fist into the air. He glared at the others until they did the same.

"Hey, hey," repeated Andrés and raised MonkEE's hand.

The snow was soft, and it was filling up the children's boots. It took a while to fit six children with custom-made snowshoes. It took twice as long to convince them how to use them. The oldest tended to run too fast, and the youngest tended to tromp back and forth around the same spot. Levitating them ever so slightly induced them to keep moving.

When he came to the first huge crater, he explained that they were to stay away from it.

"What made these explosions was poisonous. What is left in the ground is radioactive, and it kills. This is why people have moved away. Where we are going should be far enough away, so don't worry."

He considered bringing them to the restaurant where his mother led them, but decided not to. *The place has Mom's memories, not theirs,* he decided.

He did, however, stop at the first place the family camped out. It looked the same as when he left it. Although he was surrounded with children, for him the place felt empty.

Khaled marched the troop out to a patch of snow and sat down.

"Why are we here?" asked Billy Tomes.

"Good enough as any, don't you think?"

"Does anyone live in those high-rise towers?" asked Zaine Maxwell.

"I don't know for sure. I don't see any repairs, but it's possible."

The children started rolling around. Andrés joined in after Khaled let him out of the bubble.

Diego Lopez asked, "Are we waiting for somebody?"

"There is a city under us. It's called Brooklyn, and I want to take you there."

"Is there someone there?" Diego asked.

"I don't know."

Andrés trod over to where Diego was sitting.

"What do you want to do?" asked Diego.

"I want to build a garden," Khaled said. "Andrés, what do you want to do?"

"Barfy, Missie, and deer."

Khaled discovered that scattered throughout the New York underground, desperate people were surviving. He counted two hundred and seventy-six people. Only twelve of them were children. Most fed themselves through a combination of scavenging, hunting, and fishing. A parasitic armed group of forty-five kept everyone under control.

Within the first year, Khaled, with the help of his seven orphans, turned the Prospect Park ruins into a domed arboretum. He had planned to harvest enough food for three hundred people. Within nine months, the small militia moved and demanded to take over his operation. Within five days of the hostile takeover nine of the leaders of the paramilitary mysteriously disappeared.

Four months later, a new paramilitary group formed, and Khaled agreed to discuss their demands. He looked each and every one of the group in the eye and shook their hands. Within a day everyone of them was dead. The plague was passed on to eleven innocents, but Khaled managed to convince everyone else to self-isolate.

Within five years, Khaled managed to motivate the community to build domed enclosures for food production near the water. He turned Prospect Park back into an arboretum that included forests, a pond, and a waterfall. He made it to isolate himself from humanity. He continued to move outside the dome, mostly to connect with the children while wearing a thick hazmat suit. Andrés consistently reminded him that he looked stupid in it.

A group of twenty-five migrants from the west joined the colony. Carmen, who was the youngest of his group, died from the tuberculosis infection that they brought. Zaine left with three from the group. They had intended to locate stragglers. Despite warnings to stay protected, Zaine never returned.

In the years that followed, Tomás, Diego, and later Andrés helped build high-rise tenements within Brooklyn.

Estrella and Gabriela, from a young age, helped their stepfather enhance his messy tropical domed prison. When near him, they wore hazmat suits like his, so they couldn't touch him. The glass dome of exotic gardens was filled with wild, often poisonous, and nasty, untamed, orphaned creatures.

"But why did you make the jungle so dangerous?" everyone asked.

None of them understood what he meant by "It's just a little taste of home."

The girls, and later Andrés, eventually helped with Khaled's medical studies, and particularly his ongoing search for a cure for the plague.

Within twenty years of settling in the park, the colony grew into a town of fifteen thousand people. Gabriela bore six children, and Estrella had four. Diego had three, and Tomás had two.

When Andrés turned twenty-six his wife gave birth to a second son. At the christening, Khaled admitted to Andrés's that he was totally unprepared for acting like a parent for seven children but bragged incessantly that he was making an effort to be a much better granddad.

A couple of weeks later, Khaled received an electronic message. Strong governments managed to maintain order within South America. Network-wide text and audio communications were re-enabled. The message was from his brother, Antonis. He confirmed that he was still alive. Although Antonis had avoided the destruction of Charlotte, he was captured by the army and taken to Monterrey, where he learned that Tarek and their mother had been killed. He managed to escape and leave the country.

"Sami sends his fooken condolences."

"And what the hell does that mean?" Khaled asked.

"That you're not here with us."

"But he got bombed. How did?—"

"Lost a leg and an arm—nothing serious."

"Bring them along. I need something to test on. I've got some promising ideas for a cure."

"All this time and no cure, sonny, you are a slacker. Show us the lay of the land, and we'll pop over tomorrow."

"Are you close?"

"Me? No. Australia. We're in Australia. Sami is flying. The bird is one of mine. Cheers."

"Sure, why not?" Khaled said. "Careful. As usual, customs is a bugger."

Khaled looked outside through the glass. He was looking at the streetscape beyond. There was a cobblestone street that had a fountain. Shops lined the street on the first level. People lived on the four stories above. Estrella sat in front of the shop, breastfeeding a newborn. She was having a drink in front of a bakery with Andrés's wife. She was doing the same thing. It was Estrella's three-year-old daughter, Carmen, that he was looking at. She was waving at him. She could see him when no-one else could. It scared him.

Before she was born, Khaled talked to her and told her stories in his mind. He did it while her mother and he were working. The loss of Estrella's sister Carmen affected him deeply.

I should have persuaded her to give her a different name. Maria is her baptismal name. Maybe I should call her Maria, he thought.

He supplied the baby with memory images and descriptions. Before she was born, she replied. She did it more than once. After she was born, the baby would turn to look at him if he was nearby. Khaled talked to her in his mind. In turn, he'd feel a response of questioning curiosity.

Carmen was now three years old.

Khaled's isolation enabled him to develop a new talent. It was something that he didn't want his brothers to know about and definitely not any earthlings. It would serve no-one to learn that someone could read minds, and maybe influence thoughts, which could be a dangerous thing. Especially if used by people who could live a very long time. It was something that he didn't think there was any serious way of controlling or be honest about.

People won't have trust. For good reason, it will make them afraid, he thought. And for *Lord's sake, she's only three.*

What scared him even more was that he believed that she probably soon would be able to initiate a telepathic call.

Is it possible I taught her something new? He wondered. *Have I infected her? Could this, in the long run, become something worse than the plague?*

Khaled sat down next to an alligator that had just eaten and looked it over for any new wounds.

"Hello, Carmen, he told her in his mind. You be nice to your baby sister. Soon she will be old enough to play with you. You just need to be patient."

"A puppy," she asked him.

"Were you talking to Andrés?"

"Barfy," she said.

"Puppies are hard to find; I will see what I can do," he said. He waved and walked away towards his office. The alligator gave a big yawn.

Does Andrés still miss his dog? wondered Khaled. As he watched his adult son work with test tubes in his office on the other side of the glass, he realized how little he understood him.

Antonis's visit had to be postponed. They were turned back in American airspace by American aircraft. Antonis did manage to tell Khaled about where he last heard from their mother. He was being tortured by the Monterrey military. He managed to escape, but it took another eight days. He returned to the farm, hoping to retrieve a memento of some kind, and discovered that Sami was still alive. "He was in a very bad way," Antonis said.

"Fook. Don't believe him," Sami told him. "It was the dog and cat that saved me. They were as trapped as I was, and they would have starved. It was enough to make me try. I enabled some space and retrieved some water. Managed to stop my bleeding. Wrapped my wounds, and somehow put myself back together. Seemed that every time I was ready to give up, a couple of times the cat would keep licking my face. I am sure that Andrés missed them."

Antonis's trip was rescheduled for nine months after the first attempt to land. Fortunately, there was a lull in military hostilities. Antonis's aircraft had vertical takeoff and landing capabilities. It landed on a vacant field in the southern part of the island. The brothers rode arrived at the Prospect Park dome in a truck that had caterpillar tracks.

Instead of wearing a hazmat suit, his brothers wore aircraft helmets and flight suits. Once inside the dome, Antonis and Sami removed their protective gear.

Khaled noticed that Sami's chin still looked fractured after all these years. The rough and ready scruff of a beard did not disguise the loss of much of his chin. Although cosmetically it looked like his right arm and leg had grown back, they were reinforced with a metal mechanical bracing that Khaled had never seen before. When Antonis introduced his brother, he put his hand below the shoulder blades, which made Sami straighten up. If he looked down, Antonis would touch the same spot with two fingers, causing him to straighten up again.

Antonis, like Khalid, looked more human-like. Sami looked less so.

"Sami is more than glad to help. We've learned a lot since we last saw you."

My son, I'm losing him. Andrés is dying.

"Is it the plague?"

"I don't know what it is, but it's serious," Khaled said.

Part 4

The Crossing

Eight of Ionna's daughters sliced their way through the dense Ovidian jungle. Other than a change of clothes, supplies, and weapons, none brought any possessions of significance.

Nadia slowed to watch Tanya and Dina blast the lush growth ahead. Cutting and climbing over the thick growth was one thing; surviving what it concealed was another.

"Do we have enough time to get to the launch?" asked Jena, who marched behind with Zoe.

"It's a long way off," said Nadia. "Probably not. Surviving the jungle might be the easy part."

"Barrly wants us dead. Everyone, keep up. We're not going to give him the chance," said Zoe.

"You sure?" Jena teased.

"Yes, I am sure, and so are Natalie and the boys. He wants us torn apart, dissected, bottled, and put on medical display so they can tinker with your bits," said Zoe. "Is that clear enough?"

"Just swimming," Dina yelled as she kept carving a path for them through the jungle.

Jena marched ahead and asked, “Is this really the best way to get there?” She swiped the head off a Gowanda lizard that hid behind leaves near Nadia’s leg.

Nadia jumped back. And yelled, “Fuck.”

“Don’t mention it,” Jena said.

“Yes, it’s where we’re going,” challenged Nadia.

“And what if there’s no wind?” Jena wondered.

“The storms are cyclical. You can count on it,” said Zoe.

“And if it doesn’t?”

“Dicey.”

“Nadia almost lost her leg back there. You mean like that kind of dicey?” Jena asked.

“Ladies, focus and work the situation, and we’ll get through it,” Zoe said.

“Maria and Thea, keep up. We can’t see you from here,” yelled Nadia.

A minute later, Thea tramped out from behind some foliage. Maria followed.

“A stenchant croc almost took Maria,” Thea said. “Alya stopped it. It was twelve meters long and testy.”

Tanya stopped cutting in front and yelled back, “Didn’t kill it, did you?”

“Move off,” cried Thea.

“You first,” yelled Tanya.

“Next time, we’ll have you come and give her a nice kiss,” said Thea.

Zoe was the oldest of all of them. She had survived for five hundred and eighty-five years on the planet. She did what she wanted, and much of the time, the rest let her. Although Nadia was just ten years younger, they all deferred to Momma Zoe. Zoe acquired a chance to work with a Sym-Set across the sea when she was in her late twenties and took it. Nadia was told that it would be safer for her to move and that she needed to protect her overly cerebral sister. When all of the girls ended up joining them, it became obvious that their parents had forced them to move away to avoid any future possibility of incest.

Nadia, Jena, and Thea were the most aggressive of the lot. Nadia, like Antonis, tended to follow her own way. She travelled, took risks, and preferred the outdoors. Although Nadia preferred to coax rather than give orders, she wasn’t one to shy away from taking a harsher tone. Alya, who survived seventy-one years on the planet, was the youngest sister.

Jena and Alya moved up to keep clearing. The rest passed Tanya and Dina, who were bent over, trying to catch their breath.

A half hour later, the group stopped at a river. When Mamma Zoe reached the shoreline, Alya approached her.

"Have you heard from Natalie?" she asked.

"No, but I have confidence that we will see her on the mainland."

"You should know by now that she's unreliable," Alya complained.

"Well, aren't you bleak this morning? Alya, take a breath," Zoe suggested.

"So are we going to follow the river to the coast?" Dina asked.

"Would take too long. Don't want Ellie to worry, do we?" said Thea.

"Kibos are here, so stay out of the water. Would make a real mess of your boots," said Tanya.

"And don't forget the little purple wigglers," said Mamma Zoe. "They don't let anything go."

"OK," said Jena. "I'll make some blocks. Maria is going to need some help."

"My balance is fine. Let's get this over with.

Jena enabled a line of flat blocks to appear across the river. The tops rose just a centimetre above the surface and were spaced a meter apart.

Sophisticated demand scripts were stored in each of the augmented memory stores of the Sym-Set Sari-Khalil. A script or series of scripts created a central nanocell generator pod, which was usually projected into the ground. Each pod was configured to acquire from limitless energy stores distributed within the surrounding cells of dense substances. Predesigned satellite pods are replicated for each levitated pad. Once authorized, each satellite pod sifted, accumulated, and powered the creation of each levitated object.

The main weakness of depending on a raised walkway is that the created object has to remain close to a dense liquid or ground material and the controlling satellite pod. Not keeping a foot squarely on a levitated pad might cause the object to teeter, which could make it dissolve or sink.

Maria managed to cross without falling, but Alya stumbled in the middle. She held her breath, hoping the stone wouldn't disappear.

A meter-long orange creature with red and pink stripes and six legs raced across the water. The creature lunged at her. While Thea attempted to steady her with a levitating push, Zoe levitated it slightly and gave the wild thing a nudge. The kibos spun and rolled. Jena stunned it.

"God Almighty," Alya moaned. She steadied herself with her own skills and ordered everyone to shove off and leave her alone.

After everyone crossed, Jena brought along the stunned Kibos that she had tied up. Nadia disintegrated the rock outcrops that she created. The group's break was cut short when Nadia told them that the wind direction was changing. They quickly cooked the kibos and a mix of veggies. The meal was short-lived. When the thick brown dust clouds moved in, everyone rushed into the jungle for cover.

Although the storm was of hurricane proportions, the protection provided by the thick, dense vegetation was formidable. The women needed their face masks and infrared goggles to survive the poisonous air. During the storm, the predators tended to stay in place and were less nippy.

When Nadia reached the seashore, the wind had subsided. After removing her face mask and goggles she caught sight of Ellie walking by some tall plants and flagged her down.

When the sisters got close, Alya asked Ellie if she had forgotten where the sailboat was.

"You can try to swim across if you want. I'll watch," Ellie quipped.

"We don't have time for this," said Zoe.

"How long before the conobawns take her? What do you think?" Dina jibed.

"Around here, it would be the kibos," Ellie warned. She waved for everyone to follow.

She took them to a small inlet that led to the sea.

"Ellie, did you miss us?" asked Alya.

"Take a leap," she replied.

"Sym-Set Sari-Khalil," yelled Nadia. The others raised their fists and cheered.

With thick, well-anchored plants at their backs, the group of nine sat facing the sea and ate wrapped leftovers. An open sky was filling with billowing brown and pinkish clouds. The wind was picking up.

"It's sixty kilometres to the other side," said Ellie.

"Can it get us there?" asked Maria.

"What do you think?" Ellie taunted.

"Of course it will," Nadia said.

"Why the fins?"

"Since the boat has to remain high in the water to avoid the foliage, it doesn't have a keel. It has a wide, flat bottom with extended fins on the sides. We really depend on them when the boat is heeling."

"Heeling?"

"When a boat is forced to lean to one side. It is something I try to avoid in these waters. The fins could get torn off or dragged under. Without a reliable keel, we might flip."

"Let's not do that," said Maria.

The lines on the shore cleats were untied, and the boat fenders were secured onboard. The crew stepped aboard.

"To accommodate the powerful winds, the sails are small. We have to be diligent. What is coming up will be a lot worse than the last blast that passed through here," said Ellie. "The blowing sand will be pounding and blinding. I gave each of you a digital bracelet. I want to see everyone's arms up and with it on and active. If we lose someone, it is the only way we will be able to track where they went."

Everyone's arms went up, and each wristband had a small flashing light.

Ellie and Tanya controlled the sheet lines. Nadia and Maria used their augment skills to push on the port side. Jena and Thea controlled the starboard side.

Zoe, Dina, and Alya bided their time resting in the centre of the boat until they were needed.

"Ellie, are you sure your boat is going to get us across?" Alya droned.

"If it doesn't, I am sure that you will be the first to tell me."

"Give her some credit," said Thea. Looking at Ellie, she asked, "You tested it, right?"

"Have faith, girl."

"Shit," fretted Thea.

"What?" Dina asked.

"What's that?" pleaded Thea. She pointed to something in the pinkish water.

Many milky-looking tentacles, half a meter wide, wound slowly below the surface. "They are conobawns," said Ellie. "You will find them everywhere. They are carnivorous plants that can reach and grab. They usually keep down when there are storms. They come up to find prey when it is calm and sunny."

"Damn, is it clearing or picking up?" Dina pondered.

The sky looked indeterminate.

"The sea is acidic," said Ellie. "Keep your hands out of it."

The wind became notably stronger when they got a kilometre out. An hour and a half later, half the crew were doing everything they could to stop the boat from capsizing. The other half did their best to keep bailing, hoping that they weren't sinking. In another hour, the sandstorm got so bad that no-one could see more than a hand in front of their face. The four on the outside wore face masks and goggles. The goggles, unfortunately, weren't much help in determining where the waterline was.

The boat hit something suddenly, and it rocked chaotically. There was a steep heel to the port side. Maria and Nadia flipped out.

As Nadia descended into the burning murk, all that came to mind was *Antonis, fuck off.*

Below the surface, as Nadia helplessly felt herself succumbing to the encroaching darkness, she remembered what she was leaving behind.

It took a long time, but we did it. Our place felt like a real home.

Ovidian adults identified themselves with a Sym-Set of six adults. Their mates and children lived elsewhere. The young ones were raised by a lower caste of females. Parents only visited occasionally, which tended to be formal and disciplinary. What a cold arrangement.

Me, Zoe, and Natalie, who worked with different Sym-Sets, were the first to live together in the evenings. What spunk, she thought.

The Sym-Sets we worked for were lower castes. The creatures acquired things. Engineered worms, for example, brought rare minerals to the surface. An engineered fungus filtered poisons from rivers. Amphibians collected resins from underwater plants.

Since our friendlies only treated us like smart pets, we didn't have any rights. Took us a few decades before we were allowed to leave at night. It took more than a century and a half before I had enough sisters to live with to identify as a stable Sym-Set, and that was after two sisters were poisoned, one was eaten, and two were murdered. That was a pisser, wasn't it?

There were ten of us left. Ovidians limited a Sym-Set to six. But not the Sym-Set Sari-Khalil girls. No way.

Mother told me that her first two boys didn't survive. An Ovidian trampled on their first daughter out of spite and contempt. Fifty years later, they killed three more of her toddlers. Fuck 'em, she thought. *This place made us steely, and some of us, on occasion, took matters into our own hands.*

Acid gnawed at her face and limbs. Acid was slipping in through the mask. She bounced from a tentacle and smashed into another. *She remembered herself repeating Antonis's "Fucking right."*

Zoe was nearest to Nadia when she tumbled overboard. She kept staring at the bracelet as Nadia splashed into the water. She homed in on the signal and kept attached to her sister's signal as the boat sailed farther away.

Jena and Thea helped Ellie right the boat. The hurricane winds continued to pummel the boat.

"I have Nadia," Zoe yelled. Dina moved alongside to support Zoe.

Alya shuffled to the port side and desperately searched for Maria's digital signature. The visibility was terrible. Thea shuffled over to help.

Dina held Zoe's shoulder to sense what she had already done and seen. Zoe had managed to drag Nadia's shoulders to the surface. Dina levitated her to the surface. Both pulled her in as the wind whipped her body around like a kite. They almost lost her once. As they pulled her in, her legs dragged across the water. Together, they managed to haul her aboard.

Zoe looked over at Alya and Thea.

"We've lost her. Maria is gone," cried Alya.

Nadia sensed Ellie's silent words. *There is no way we can turn in this storm. If we return during the calm, the conobawns will have already taken her, and surely they will take us as well.*

Nadia was still breathing. The mask and its filters kept her alive. Zoe and Dina laid hands on Nadia and attempted to heal the burns as the rocking, creaking boat continued to fill up, and the crushing waves rocked the boat about and weighed it down.

Nadia felt life pump back into her drawing gloom. She succumbed back to some repressed memories to distract her from the agonizing wounds.

She remembered when Annie didn't come home. She was just sixteen. Nadia was thirty. The next day, she and Thea visited the Sym-Set she was allocated to, and none of them said they had seen her. Each one of them acted like she was never there. It was an obvious lie. An Ovidian who worked nearby verified that she was seen working with the Sym-Set in the morning. He had seen violent and abusive displays on a couple of their coats. It took them four days to find Annie. The trampled corpse was kicked into a ravine.

Two years later, her sister Lisa didn't come home. She was five years younger than Nadia. All of the Sym-Set told Thea that they didn't know anything about it in spite of the fact that she had been working with them for years. Only one of them refused to lie. He just refused to say anything. When they found her sister, she lay disembowelled and missing an arm. Lisa had been dragged into a nest of a venomous snake-like creature in the jungle.

Nadia was determined to kill each and every one in the two Sym Sets. The unnatural lying of all the members implied that someone else was influencing what had happened. Antonis notified her that three toddlers had been killed on their side of the sea by another group.

"It was Sym-Set Farnag that was responsible," she told him. "It's a high caste that was struggling to be noticed. Ranting against foreigners suits their purpose."

"It would be good to delay for now," was all Antonis said. She didn't understand the reference, but within three weeks, an explosion happened in the hive, and every member of Sym-Set Farnag was killed.

So as not to be noticed, Nadia waited another four years before providing a slow-action poisoning of the food for the Sym-Set that killed Annie.

Two years later, Thea used a flamethrower to burn all the Sym-Set that Lisa was associated with.

When the first action was done, she told Antonis, "Nothing out of the usual. It's just a bit sunnier."

For the second, she just said, "Things are looking up."

Ellie, Maria, and Adela were born shortly after that. Adela, unfortunately, died from a venomous bite while in the jungle.

Nadia was left guiltily asking herself, "Oh my God, Maria, where are you?" It was what forced her to open her eyes.

By the time the wind died down, Zoe, Dina, and Alya had gotten much better at emptying the boat. Everyone needed healing from the acid burns. The safety equipment they wore provided some protection, but not enough. While Nadia was lying on the deck, they weren't able to keep the acidic water away from her.

As soon as the sun appeared, the limbs of conobawns broke the surface. As soon as Ellie heard banging on the hull, she let a small sail out. She had everyone apply force to push the vessel to quickly get to a friendlier patch of water. They didn't have to go far before the wind picked up and took them to the next shore.

Nadia's sisters did not own anything outright, but after living in the same place for four and a half centuries, the family managed to exert considerable control in the region. They lived in an earthen-style house. It was only one floor, but the campus sprawled over three square miles. They had access to technology that few in Ovidia were aware existed.

In practice, they directly managed thirty low-caste Sym-Sets and maintained considerable influence and control. By handling the flow of natural resources, they manage to acquire access to top-caste information. The family, on both sides of the sea managed multiple operations remotely and through intermediaries. It had taken great effort, but Nadia was proud of what they had accomplished from very little.

For Antonis to tell her she had to leave was terribly grating, thought Nadia. *That her father and two of her brothers were going to be mutilated and tortured for no obvious reason was hard to deal with.*

The message that Nadia resented the most came from Antonis. He told her that 'everyone had to leave—Barrly is at it again.'

After the crew landed, Nadia staggered across the beach and found Ellie tinkering with a broken bilge pump.

"Didn't help much, did it?" Nadia asked as she gave her a bowl of water.

"I suppose not."

"Toss it in the boat and destroy everything. You won't need it," Nadia demanded.

"What?" Ellie asked.

"I received word from Natalie. I have her location. We have to hurry. We won't be coming back."

"But are you up for this?" Ellie asked.

Nadia waved for everyone to follow.

Alya and Thea cut a path through the undergrowth while the rest kept watch for predators. Dina and Zoe marched at the end of the line.

"How did Barrly become such a threat?" asked Dina.

"Barrly had a miserable start in life," said Zoe. "Ovidians send their young far away at an early age. The adults tend to stay with a hive for life, but maintain a connection to the world virtually. If there isn't a bid made from the other side or the local Sym-Set does not find the amount reasonable, the young one is normally placed with a lower caste. Rarely would the local Sym-Set take a young one back. Unfortunately, an exception was made in Barrly's case. He has spent a lifetime trying to rise above the social insult. Since he was never accepted as a caste member equal, he has striven to become more than any of them. Although desperate to please, he has become a self-serving, lying megalomaniac. Barrly has gained influence by ruining projects and rebranding their best parts."

Zoe forcefully pulled Dina towards her. Her hand went to her shoulder. She relayed a message that said, "Freeze." Zoe tossed a swath of powder in the air. A half-meter-wide head of a salamander-like creature poked through the leaves. It was orange with red dots. It coughed, shook its head, and retreated.

"Was that—"

"Yes, it was a Vrak," Zoe said.

"But how did you—"

"The others are too fond of cutlery. It wouldn't hurt for them to watch and learn, would it?"

"Dina, our parents and me have outlived all the Ovidians that lived when they first arrived. Although these creatures are organized and advanced in many areas, they adapt slowly. Over the years, their society has become progressively isolationist and regressive. Barrly is the antithesis of a normal Ovidian. He makes quick, forceful, and risky decisions.

"Our family does not have a legal foothold for any of our operations. We don't even have a legal right to exist. Until now, we have made ourselves useful. Barrly is the first to realize that he can acquire an advantage by having us killed. Fearmongering provides a distraction from his incompetence and ruthlessness."

Ellie walked in front of them. Nadia trudged stoically ahead of her.

"Is Nadia going to be alright?" Dina asked.

"Nadia's physical wounds won't stop her. She's pining for Maria, as do I. On the surface, Maria was quiet, but she was very much in control of her life. Maria was more intelligent and dependable than the lot of you. It wasn't obvious, but she was someone who everyone relied on. Nadia thinks that she failed her. Best not to distract her. Getting back on her own feet won't be easy, but she'll come around. Maria isn't the only soul she's carrying. If she needs help, she'll ask for it when she's ready. Just give her some space."

At a nondescript spot in the jungle, the sisters were greeted with hugs by their sister Natalie. It was getting dark. The sun was slipping away on the horizon.

"Antonis sent me confirmation an hour ago. They made it into the Space Centre and were strapping in to leave. That means that by now, Mom and the boys should have left."

"As in, we won't hear from them again?" asked Dina.

"No," said Natalie. "The system was mothballed for centuries, but they managed to figure out how to get it working."

"Barrly wants us all dead," cautioned Nadia. "We have to move as fast as we can. If they block us from the launch centre, none of us will be going anywhere, except maybe to an operating table or under their feet."

"Antonis told me that Barrly by proxy will soon have complete administrative control of the Science Centre," Natalie disclosed.

"Won't someone, somewhere, notice that the system has been tinkered with?" asked Thea.

"Hopefully not. The boys created a test scenario for a project that should explain why there was a need for a high energy drain if someone was not paying too much attention," said Natalie.

"Revving the system up on a different day would definitely attract way too much attention. So it's now or never," Nadia divulged.

"I have been inside the Space Centre," Natalie affirmed. "It is a small section of the large Science Centre complex. I don't have access to the door codes, but I left some entry points unlocked. We have to get back before someone discovers the security breach.

"I also learned that surgery has been done on Dad, Jamal, and Ahmed. The frame augments have been removed," Natalie disclosed.

"But won't that kill them?" asked Zoe.

"Before leaving, Antonis told me that they survived the operation," Natalie acknowledged. "That doesn't say much. The planet's gravity will crush them soon enough."

"How can Barrly be so brazen?" asked Zoe.

"He has been pretty open about wiping out every last one of us for a long time," Natalie said. "Antonis told me that he learned that Barrly had evidence that Dad murdered some Ovidians. Barrly says that the evidence comes from Nikos."

"Nikos? What the hell? That's nonsense," Dina said. "Well, I hope Mom hasn't heard that. She would be devastated."

"So why not take Dad with us?" Jena asked.

"Barrly is expecting a rescue attempt," Nadia counselled. "Actually, he's counting on it. It will be a lot easier for him to round us all up if we enter a trap of his making rather than him trying to hunt for us later. Antonis was convinced that a rescue now was destined to fail.

"It was also not clear if Dad and the others, in their weakened state, could survive being moved. The journey off-world might also be too much for them.

"And there are still so many other things that could go wrong in attempting two off-world trips on the same day. Collectively, everyone decided that it was better that some of us survive rather than none of us." Natalie put her hands on her hips.

"What do you mean, everyone?" asked Jena.

"Antonis asked me, and I agreed," said Nadia. "Jamal, who is staying with Dad, also agreed. Jena, I know this is hard."

"But what do we know about accessing a space portal?" asked Thea. "And why didn't they wait for us?"

"There weren't enough seats for all of us," said Nadia. "Over the years, I have been discussing the project with Antonis. He prepared detailed training information for processing another launch to Earth. The console procedures will get us to the other side. I and Natalie will share what we have with all of you."

Zoe wound a circle in the air and said, "Sym-Set Sari-Khalil."

Everyone huddled for a family share circle and yelled in unison, "Sym-Set Sari-Khalil."

"Forever," added Zoe, and everyone repeated.

"It wounds me to say, but we can't do a memory share of those that we've lost. I know that it is difficult, but that's for another day." She made another circle in the air, after which the plans and travel instructions were shared."

"Some might not think they need their goggles, but please wear them. You'll need the heat sensors. For the squeamish, remember that everything is out to destroy us. We are in a whatever-it-takes run. So let's go." Nadia waved for everyone to follow as she followed Natalie's trail back to the hive. It was pitch dark, and Zoe strong-armed her way next to Nadia.

"You'll need me, girlie. You don't want the little nippies to slow you down, do you?"

"Right," answered Nadia, and laughed. "Just keep your boots tied."

"Jena's really pissed about not attempting a rescue," whispered Zoe. "Better get her to work hard cutting. She likes to mimic someone else I know."

Nadia kept clearing a wider opening in the trail.

The Space Centre was two hours away. It had become pitch black, and not all predators were warm-blooded.

When the group reached a wide, well-cleared trail, Dina lowered Alya to the ground. A Vrrm, which was a meat-eating plant, had taken a chunk out of Alya's arm. Ellie reexamined the dressing.

"What about the poison?" Dina asked Zoe.

"I may not have gotten it all out, but we've given her a chance," Alya said. "What she needs is healing, care and rest. Everyone needs to pick up the pace. We'll catch up."

Jena took Ellie's place. Alya sat on a stone, which was levitated by Zoe. Jena held on to her so she wouldn't fall over.

The Sym-Set Sari-Khalil sisters staggered their approach to the entrance of the hive. They entered in pairs.

The group walked for miles through the complex. It was an active, unsecured public space. Besides the thundering Ovidians, the place was alive with smaller creatures. The main hallways were alive with thick vegetation. Leaves grew from the ceilings and floors as well as the walls.

Natalie led the group to a column. She showed Nadia and Jena that there was a break in a hollow column. It was hidden within a wall of thick vegetation. Each one followed Natalie's climb through the column. Jena was given a sling that Zoe made. Jena Alya sat in a sling, which wrapped around Jena's shoulder. Thea followed below and tried to lighten Jena's load. Without a firm surface matter nearby, attempts to levitate weren't particularly effective.

The hollow space within the column was tight as everyone forced themselves up through vegetation. The women climbed up through three floors. When they emerged from the column at ceiling level, none of them complained about being bitten. Natalie, however, saw that Dina's blade was dripping with something's goop.

Above the visible ceiling, the group kept crawling until they reached an exhaust that vented outside. Natalie pointed to the climbing ropes that she had previously laid out. Natalie went first. The rope was fastened to a column, and the other end led to the roof. A blast sucked her out feet first, but she was able to grab hold of the rope. Outside, she managed to get her feet to leverage her as she pulled herself up from the vent ridges to the roof foliage.

Dina got to the roof without a problem. Thea, however, also got sucked out by another blast. She lost hold of the rope.

Jena leaped into the vent headfirst. She repelled Thea from the far wall hard, to slow her slide out. Jena grabbed the rope and swung her legs around for Thea to grab.

Once Thea had regained a grip on the rope, she moaned, "Damned if I want to do that again. This isn't going well at all."

"Sorry to ruin your moment," Jena said. "But Alya is going to need a step up," Jena said.

"Just lovely. Sure, what else could go wrong?" said Thea.

Another rope was lowered from the roof.

"Natalie, why wasn't it here in the first place?" Thea muttered.

Jena, with a finger on her lips, told her to shush.

Thea gave her a hand kiss back.

Ellie lowered Alya in a sling. Jena grabbed her and fed an end of the sling to Thea. Thea attached the rope and the others pulled her up. Thea followed her up. Everyone else got up to the roof without another interruption.

On the walk across the roof-covered jungle, Natalie blasted a reptilian Colderzang as it lunged at Tanya's leg. The black reptile-like creature with red stripes had a meter-long body and a knobby tail. Its jaw would have taken her lower leg off in a single bite. Tanya moaned as she fell, and thorns ripped through her jacket. Blood dripped from her arm and shoulder.

"Yuck," she said as she sat up. Zoe and Dina attempted to provide some healing before the poison set in. The tall vegetation shrouded their presence from anyone below. Some scavengers, which smelled the dead Colderzang and Tanya's blood, sneaked around the underbrush. Jena killed two, and the other scurried off.

"We'd better keep going," Natalie said. "It's not safe to stay here." She led the others to another vent. Alaya and Tanya were lowered down another column with the use of the second rope.

Each of the sisters left the column and crawled out into a poorly lit hallway on the first floor. The group followed the hallway. It apparently led to a dead end. Natalie moved a set of rocks, and the wall opened.

"I thought you said that you left it open," Natalie said.

"It's set at a default setting. The long pass codes haven't been engaged. The door to the pods was left open. Each of you has that information."

Jena heard something approaching from down the hall.

"Shit," she whispered. She waved and told the others to scoot. "Close the door. We'll handle it," she said.

As she tiptoed towards the noise, Thea messaged her to let her know that she was behind her. Jena cringed when she heard the sound of the wall closing.

Jena rushed to reach the next hallway turnoff before the Ovidian came within eyesight. Thea followed. Jena sent her a written message that said, 'Don't kill. Let's rescue Dad.' Jena hurried down the hall to find a door that opened. Both stood there until the Ovidian stepped into view in the hallway.

Thea drew her finger across her neck.

"No, I have a plan," Jena whispered.

Thea pointed a thumb back to the others.

"Really. I have a plan. It will work. We're leaving tonight."

Before Thea could respond, Jena walked out into the hallway and yelled, "Hey." She waved at the creature. As it turned, she walked closer.

"We're lost. Perhaps you can help us."

The Ovidian would not have understood the words, but it could sense the vibrations. It would have sensed that the human had opened one of the doors.

Once the women got close, they exchanged messages and scents with the Ovidian. Jena repeated her request.

"Yes, you are not supposed to be here."

"We were in the Science Centre. We are not sure where we are. We were on the second floor. Perhaps you could escort us to where we should be."

"That's not near here. I will lead you out. Count yourself lucky to-day, that you have been shown mercy for your stupidity. It is true that recycled materials contribute to the hives' givers of life."

"We thank you, good sir, and praises should be sung. May you rise in status and always be hailed for all that you do. Thanks be upon you," said Thea.

Once on the other side of the secured entrance, Jena clapped. "I knew that would work. What an airhead. So full of himself. He's got stinkyboos for brains."

"So what was with 'don't kill it'?" asked Thea. "The goddamn fucker deserved it. I, for one, wouldn't have minded knowing that he was going to be added to a compost pile."

"It was about Dad and the others," Jena said. "We got in once, so why shouldn't we be able to get in again?"

"You do know that Dad and our brothers are ill and can't walk. The Ovidians are expecting us, and we have to get them through the hive. And how are we going to get them up to the roof? I almost died up there."

"Don't be a complainer. I know we can do it. We're not Tanya."

"What's with you and Tanya?" She looked back at the Space Centre door and looked around.

"I'll tell Nadia to leave. It's too big a risk to go back right now," said Jena.

"You do know it is an all-or-nothing plan for the rest of us here?" asked Thea.

"Sym-Set Sari-Khalil, all the way," Jena said.

"You know you're fucking nuts," Thea said. "Sym-Set Sari-Khalil, all the way," she repeated and raised a fist. "This is going to get messy."

As they walked, Jena sent a written message to Nadia saying, "Go. Don't wait. We're going to make our own way. We hope to bring back Dad and the boys. Give my love to Mom. Bye Jena/Thea."

Zoe and Ellie managed to follow Antonis's launch instructions successfully. Dina and Nadia managed to spend a brief healing time with Alya and Tanya. Zoe told the others that the system hadn't received a return signal from her brothers.

"That doesn't mean they weren't successful," said Ellie. "It just might mean that it might take a long time to cross over."

"I am willing to risk it," said Dina. "I am not staying here to be dissected."

"Jena and Thea have confirmed that they are not coming with us. They are going to try to bring Dad, Jamal, and Ahmed back. Maybe even Michalis. I believe their chances aren't good. If anyone wants out, the time is now; otherwise, into the pods."

Ellie hesitated, but after looking at the state of Tanya and Alya, decided to remain. Realizing that the trip using a very old and possibly unreliable system might kill them all, they gave each other a last solemn, meaningful hug before initiating the launch sequence. Zoe was the last one to climb into a pod.

Nadia was the first to roll out after the transit. The room was poorly lit. Although the air was breathable, it was stale and different. There was more oxygen. She felt remarkably light. Nadia was naked. She wandered around looking for clothes. She found some etchings on the wall. Nikos's name was there. Khaled was beside it. Someone with the last name of Winters was also there. She scratched in her own. When she finished, she found a stack of clothes at her feet.

Tanya was in a weakened state when she emerged. Zoe and Ellie tended her wound and laid hands for a healing session. When done, Zoe slapped Tanya's back and said, "She'll live."

Everyone in the group rolled out but Alya. Nadia pointed out to the others where the clothes were.

She knocked on Alya's pod and said, "Time to come out, sleepyhead, we're here."

The knock wasn't returned. She knocked a few more times. After checking the controls, she confirmed to the others that Alya didn't survive.

Dina opened the pod and found only a lot of dust. She checked the remaining pods and found that each was empty.

"We can't leave her there," Ellie reminded. "We will have to bury her somewhere else. The pods have to be cleared for the next transit."

"Let's find out where we are first," Tanya advised.

"What if it's not?" snapped Dina.

"Earth, you mean?" ventured Nadia. "It feels like it. Nikos was here, and so was a stranger."

"Yes, it's time to find out what we are up against, but first, Dina, make an urn and put your sister in it," said Momma Zoe.

Nadia led her sisters through a dark, winding tunnel. A hologram of a thin man in bright clothes stood in front of them.

"We've been expecting you," he said. "Nadia, welcome to Earth."

"Finally," said Tanya, who was following Zoe. "But so far it doesn't look like much."

"Good to hear that you still have a sense of humour," the image said.

Nadia stepped closer to the hologram and asked, "So, how do you know who I am?"

"A program cross-referenced your appearance with stored memory images that your brothers provided. A surveillance system was installed around the transit site."

"Who are you?"

"I'm an electronic avatar of Alex Winters. Alex and others are being notified of this exchange as we speak. Alex is an Earthling."

"But you look so different," Nadia said.

"It's what your parents used to look like. Please follow this way."

"But you're not real?" asked Tanya.

"Alex is listening in to this call. I pick up what he wants shared, and I adapt my responses."

"So you are him minus the swearing?" asked Dina.

"Perhaps," the avatar said with a dour face. "Since he speaks Spanish, I am translating his responses into Old English."

The avatar moved on. Zoe, who was behind Nadia, yelled, "They're coming, and they've got your DNA."

"Don't be concerned. We have theirs."

It took hours to get to the end of the tunnel. A stone door swung open. The image disappeared. They followed a stairwell upwards in complete darkness. It took a very long time to get to the next level. When they got to the top, a wall door opened. They proceeded into another tunnel.

A holograph was waiting for them.

"How do you know our brothers?" asked Nadia.

"My great-great-great-grandfather was Andrés Winters. Khaled adopted him. It's a long story."

At the end of the tunnel, Nadia stepped out into a six-meter space. The flooring was natural stone, as were two walls on both sides. In front of her was a glass wall. On the other side, there was a small lake that was within a towering arboretum. Some creatures with wings floated on the water's surface. On a wall overlooking the lake, there was another window. People who looked like Alex waved. She waved back.

Once everyone entered the small space, the doors behind closed up. The avatar did not follow.

"What is going on?" asked Zoe.

Nadia drew back from the glass and surveyed the others.

"Nadia, don't worry. I can't welcome you formally yet. You can see me in the window that overlooks the lake." She could see him waving.

"Like astronauts, we have to check if you are bringing infections back from the other world that we need to be concerned with. You will be in isolation for about six months before I will be able to show you around."

A door in the rock wall on Nadia's right opened outward into an adjoining space. A glass wall on the left let them see the lake and the arboretum. A figure wearing a hood with a thick mask and white medical garb approached them.

"Andrés, who is wearing a hazmat suit, will deal with you directly," Alex

Winters said.

Andrés waved and said, "You must be Nadia. Antonis told me to expect you. 'However long it takes, eventually, she will get here,' he said. So as you can tell, he believed in you."

"Is he still alive?"

"No, unfortunately, there's only one of your brothers still alive."

"What happened to them?" Dina asked.

"It will take a while to tell it. We'll have lots of time for exchanging family stories. Only Khaled is still alive. He developed the cure right here, in this lab."

"Cure for what?" asked Zoe.

"The genetic changes that the Ovidians made created an infection that stimulated a plague among Earthlings. It was passed on by direct contact and remained communicable even after death. It was a horrendous threat. Together, my dad, Antonis, and Sami developed a cure."

"Your dad?" asked Zoe. "You mean you're the original Andrés?"

He nodded.

"So you're not like them?" Nadia said as she pointed to the window of the onlookers.

"I have the same augments that you do."

"But you look like them."

"The augments help the body to adapt. It takes time, but eventually you will look like them, as does Khaled now."

"Where is he?"

"He inherited Antonis's aerospace properties in Australia. It's a country that is located half a world away from here.

"I have something to give to Jena."

"She didn't come."

He showed them an image of a pair of mittens.

"What are these?" asked Zoe.

"I suppose it wasn't cold where you were from."

"No," she said.

"They are mitts. They are worn in cold weather to keep the hands warm."

"The design on the mitt matches what was on Jena's sweater," said Zoe. "It was her first attempt. Mom was teaching her how to knit."

Before she asked, he looked away and said, "She sacrificed herself for everyone. All of us will have much to share."

"When did Antonis die?"

"It was about a century after he got here. It was a terrible accident. Sami, near the time your mother died, was hurt severely. His augments helped regrow much of his lost limbs, but his health never fully normalized. He died thirty-five years after his accident."

"Did you have children before or after your operation?"

"It was after. The augments actually saved my life. As I got older, I realized that Earth wasn't prepared for accepting this kind of change. I have made sure that my descendants don't inherit my abilities."

"Why?"

"Oh, on a personal level, there would be a big demand for it, but eventually the people with power would make sure that they continued to be the only ones who could have it. A minority of super-powerful immortals would control the world, and I doubt it would be for the better. I don't believe that our people will ever be able to deal with this technology altruistically."

"I don't think that all of your children would like that idea," said Dina.

"You're right. Not everyone agrees with me."

"When can we speak to Khaled?"

"You will be able to see him remotely all of the time, but you probably won't meet him until the quarantine is finished."

"We have much to share," said Zoe. "There's so much about those that had to stay behind."

"A family conference isn't the same as a family share, but I believe you will find it meaningful, nevertheless. Things are going to be different than what you are used to," Andrés said. "It might be a little cramped, but it won't be for long."

While the others were shown around the living space, Zoe and Nadia stood together staring at the park beyond the glass that their brother built.

"What are you thinking about?" Zoe asked.

"About whether I should have gone for the others."

"Nadia, there wasn't enough time to prepare, and there was no going back once they drugged Mom. In the end, getting us home was your job. Trying to make it possible to bring Dad and the boys back was Jena's."

"But—"

"You don't understand. Jena did it because you would. She believed she could get them here because she watched you get us here. If you didn't prove that it was possible, she wouldn't have volunteered to follow behind. Don't overthink it."

They watched the view outside quietly for another couple of minutes.

"What are you thinking about?" Nadia asked.

"Earth."

"Like how?"

"He made it with the Earthlings, but they look so alien and breakable to me," said Zoe.

Nadia laughed and looked back at her sisters.

"Use it or lose it," said Zoe. "Nadia, you realize that he's the only one of us who is eligible.

"He's unusual looking but—But when we get to be a little more like that—"

"You never know," Nadia interjected. "But the augments would have come from our brothers. Doesn't that mean they are genetically part of him?"

"Maybe not a problem. Have to do more research," said Zoe.

"Fuck," Nadia said, and then she screamed, "Life is..." and both of the oldest sisters yelled at the same time, "a BITCH."

A Last Stand

Crimson bleeding twists flared across the morning's lava-coloured sky. Electric flashes danced within wisps of terracotta and greyish-cream shadows that rolled as dusty orange clouds towered upward. The sun was rising. Jena felt Natalie's words burn in her chest.

She sat on top of a rock cliff that overlooked an expanse of rolling hills that was covered with lush vegetation. The hills were huge Ovidian interconnected hive mounds. They were covered with dense tropical vegetation. On a high-gravity planet, buildings tended to be low-standing, with only one or two stories. Inside and out, they were airy, spongy, and jungle-like.

The pathways between the buildings were kept clear, and the ground was overladen with thick, leathery, six-meter-wide leaves. The hives connected to the Science Centre. The pods were in the Space Centre, which was a department within the Science Centre complex. The Space Centre was attached to a mountain.

While Thea worked on plans and acquired equipment for the break-in, Jena reviewed the information that her sisters, Natalie and Nadia, had given her. She was surrounded by pinkish plants with green veins that stood five meters high.

They had thick, meter-long trunks. The undergrowth was dense and full of colour. She had collected some antiviral herbs and some poisons. Jena took a bite from a large piece of fruit.

She watched a memory image, from Natalie that was taken two days before the others had escaped off-planet. It was the comments about Michalis that alarmed her.

Within the image, she saw Natalie. Her white blouse was dyed with dabs of blue, pink, and light orange. She, like the rest of the women, wore thick pants and boots. She was watching Khaled approaching an entrance into a hive from four stories up. Natalie was in a roof vent of the Science Centre Administration hive. She held sections of the lattice tightly as her feet dangled in the wind. It was sucking her away.

"Whoa," she cried, and with both hands pulled herself back.

"Does Michalis really deserve to die? And why me?" Those were the words that still burned in her chest.

"It's obvious," Jena said. "There wasn't anyone else."

Jena moved the memory snippet ahead. It was after Natalie connected with Khaled in front of the entrance to the hive. He showed her a cane-like cutting.

"Kivi soup? Yeah, it's been a while. I see that your arm has healed."

"It has been eight months."

"Considering the damage, you still have use of it."

"Natalie, why are you really here?"

"I heard that the launch date moved up."

He folded his arms.

"We're going to follow you," she said. "Have you talked to Michalis?"

"I sent him a message, but Gravis replied."

"Isn't Gravis the one who tortured Ahmed?"

"That's Nori—the same one who tried to take off my arm. No difference between those two, though. Michalis has no idea."

"You must hate Gravis."

"Natalie, again, why are you really here?"

"Tarek told you not to talk to Michalis. He's compromised."

"Michalis doesn't know anything, and I didn't talk to him."

"You do know that Nori and Gravis work for Barrly?" Natalie asked.

"Everyone keeps reminding me. Barrly's cruel, devious, and powerful. Yeah, I get it. Tell Tarek and Zoe that I get it. Just leave me alone."

"I need to speak to Michalis," said Natalie. "We need intel. We need to know where Barrly and his agents are going to be when we make our escape."

"He lives and works with Gravis."

"He doesn't get away—ever?"

"It's a price for working at the Science Centre. He puts up with it. They would consider him tainted if he moved anywhere else."

"So they don't trust him?"

"Of course not. Any of them connected to Barrly are like that. Find Gravis, and Michalis won't be far away. Barrly and his group, Sym-Set Overdrive, are corrupt and powerful. Gravis is part of Sym-Set Overbear. His group and a legion of others are mindless followers of Barrly's group."

"So why do they trust you but not me?"

"You're supposed to be busy with the launch."

"No, it's because I don't believe he should be left behind. Sorry, Natalie, but I have to go."

"But—"

"I told you already."

"Loser," she mumbled.

"Flake," he said as the door of the hive started to close behind him.

Jena looked out beyond the cliff she was sitting on. "What a pair of whacked-out lovebirds," she said. She took another bite of fruit and kept a watchful eye out for a coming storm.

After throwing the uneaten core to the valley below, she opened another memory clip.

She saw Natalie meet with Antonis outside in the jungle.

"Did Khaled go to see him?" asked Antonis.

"He tried, but no, he didn't," she said. "What's Michalis's relation with Gravis?"

"His connection is indirect. He works with Gravis, who is a disciple of Barrly's Sym-Set Overbear. Michalis has been involved with the Science Centre for a long time. It took him twenty-six years to establish access to the Astro-Genome project. He was really proud of his accomplishment.

"Gravis got close to Michalis's group to feed information to Barrly in preparation for the takeover of the Science Centre. Gravis forced himself on Michalis. It wasn't the other way around."

"What can you tell me about Barrly?" Natalie asked.

"Why?" asked Antonis.

"Because I want to know. Nadia asked me to give her some background."

"Barrly, has always been overly ambitious. He has developed a knack for learning how to brush the right scents. Getting Sym-Set Overdrive to adopt him changed his fortunes significantly. I believe it happened through extortion. The behaviour is considered foreign in this society."

"Khaled was asked to look for Michalis so that others wouldn't. You somehow knew that he would fail. And you told me to stop him. Fuck. Michalis deserves to leave just as the rest of us do. You're one fucked-up asshole, aren't you?"

"Maybe, but Natalie, you don't have enough time to worry about what Barrly is or is not going to do. The schedule has moved ahead, and we need you to share our plans with your sisters. Nadia is expecting you. Get them the plans and get away as fast as possible. Do you understand? I am in a hurry. I'd like to share them with you now."

She nodded. They held each other's shoulders. Antonis provided her with a message that mapped out where Nadia had arranged to meet.

"When am I supposed to meet her?" she asked.

"She's waiting."

"But I'm not prepared."

"You're not bringing anything," he said. "There's no time. Can you do this now, or do I need to send someone else?"

"Antonis, I understand, but you are still a royal arsehole." Without looking at him, she left.

Jena broke away from the memory clip. A strong wind was beginning to push.

"What a lark," she said and laughed. "That's Natalie all right. All this, with a last-minute jibe."

Jena retreated to the jungle, where Thea was. She gave her some herbs and poisons that she had collected. Thea gave a thumbs up and then showed her the gear that she had assembled.

"For the next part of the plan, we have to make arrangements with Michalis," Jena told her.

The walls in the hive that led to the Science Centre were made of thick coral lattice. The holes were large, almost big enough for a human to tightly squeeze through. They were contained and bound with thick tropical plants. Large, treelike plants lined the hallways. The spaces were very wide, and some ceilings reached six meters.

Ovidians didn't really need to see, but they created large mezzanine spaces that rose to four levels with sunlight beaming down. They seemed to like the feeling of it on their bodies. Although there were a lot of tree-like plants, few grew beyond two levels.

An Ovidian's back reached the top of Jena's head. The creatures were intimidating. They thundered through the hive at a pace faster than an augmented human could outrun. They didn't normally give way to anything that wasn't as big as they were. Her father told her that they acted like a cross between giant beavers and elephants.

She huddled close to a post as three barrelled towards her. Two more approached from a hallway on her right. She sprayed a noxious smell, and the two thundering from the hallway on the right moved away. The other three that were coming towards her forced her to move next to a column. One of the creatures brushed the vegetation that coated the pillar.

Upwardly mobile caste members. Full of themselves as usual, Jena thought. "Buggers. Just like Nori and Gravis."

Six-meter-long tropical leaves covered the floors. They tended to be half a meter thick and felt like hard rubber. Each was coloured with stripes of white, red, yellow, and orange shades with greenish veins. Another meter of vegetation thrived below amongst streams of alien ooze.

Her father's ankle scent sprays were less than perfect in warning off puffers. There were many of them. At half a meter in length, they gave a noticeable blow when they banged into a human's leg. They weren't poisonous and didn't bite, but they were fast runners, dim, blind, and thick and got mushy if they crashed into something.

The floor cover was kept clean by *Turd Mupples.* That was Alex's name for them. They were cream with red dots, slippery, with many short feet and very tough. They didn't get squished when stepped on. There were also thin, chameleon-like creatures called *Stickles* that gorged themselves on bugs. They made a multitude of cute whistle sounds after they ate.

Humans wore face coverings and caps when they walked through the hallways. They would regularly get blasted by foul-smelling, stinging fog sprays. Ovidians liked the sulphuric jungle sensation. It made vision for humans awkward, and the stink was offsetting.

The hive was always a busy place. The higher castes worked mostly on the top floors. The lowest castes operated in the darkest areas of the first floor.

Ovidians didn't use stairs or elevators. They marched up long ramps.

In dorm areas, humans slept in hammocks to stay off the floor, where they could avoid predators and clumsy Ovidians. All possessions were stored in handbags, which hung from tree-like plants.

Jena sent Michalis an image of a letter. The characters would appear on plants growing from sand. An outsider would interpret what was written as being parts of plants left on a picture. The letter in Arabic said, *Can you get away from the Ovidian? I am waiting for you in the open commons area. Come alone. It is important. Jena.*

Half an hour later, Michalis showed up. "Jena, what are you doing here? Aren't you supposed to be on the other side of the sea? Did they send you back?"

"Not exactly. I thought I would check in and see how things are."

"You mean, Dad, Ahmed and Jamal?"

"Something like that. What are you doing?"

"Still reviewing the history of alien studies. It has been like working in a tomb. It was difficult to get away. They keep me on a tight leash."

"Why does Barrly think he has a case against Dad?"

"About harming an Ovidian?"

"Did you tell Gravis?"

"No, I didn't."

"Michalis, you are lying."

"Gravis asked me if I was familiar with Sym-Set Farnag. It was a ridiculous question to ask me. He was asking me about something that happened long before I was born. For God's sake, it was five centuries ago. I told him that he might have. He knew a lot of different groups."

"And you told him that?"

"Well, I might have. I heard from Nori later that Nikos told the authorities that Dad never met them. I repeated what I told them before. I didn't know much because this all happened long before I was born."

Jena laughed.

"What's so funny?"

"This all happened because Nikos didn't tell the truth."

"That doesn't sound funny to me."

"You are right. It is not. Did Gravis ask you about it since?"

"No. I keep to my work," Michalis replied. "We are trying to find out where the other alien races that were brought here came from."

"Did you know that Dad, Ahmed, and Jamal are being tortured? Have you ever gone to see him?"

Michalis didn't answer.

"Do you know what it's like for a human to be on this planet? You can't breathe. You can't move. You can't think. To live here unprotected means agony. They are dying. Do you know why that is happening?"

"Why?"

"Gravis's group, Sym-Set Overbear, along with Barrly, want all of us dead.

That will also include you.

"No, they wouldn't do that."

"You belong to Sym-Set Sari-Khalil. If you have no loyalty to your Sym-Set, they would consider you to be less than the lowest caste. They'd consider you to be just an animal. They'd just step on you. You never really thought that any of them would ever respect you?"

"Well, it is just that it has been going so well. I've accomplished so much."

"Barrly and Sym-Set Overdrive wants to find out where we are from. Since they clearly want all of us dead, what do you think they will do with the coordinates once you turn them over?"

"Jena, that is an exaggeration. I don't believe—"

"Michalis, you have been drinking alone for too long. You are clearly out of touch. You could be here for another thousand years, and they still wouldn't accept you as one of theirs. It's time to sober up. This is what you are going to do."

"What are you talking about?" said Michalis. "I don't have to do what you say."

"Don't be an ignorant jerk. Your life depends on it. I will only say this once. You are going to do exactly as I tell you. You are going to tell Gravis that he needs to let you in to see Dad tonight. It has to be tonight."

"He's not going to do that," Michalis said.

"Yes, he is. You are going to tell him that it has to be tonight, after lights out, because you are going to get information from Ahmed about the brother who really was responsible for the death of Sym-Set Farnag. You are asking him this because you believe you can trust him, and you believe this will exonerate your father."

"So, how are you going to get in?"

"That's not your concern."

He was looking around. She interpreted that as if he were looking for a way out.

"Michalis, I hope you understand that failure isn't an option. I don't care whether you want to be there or not. We will be expecting you."

He went to reach for her arm.

"Don't. Whatever you need to say, you can tell it to Dad and your brothers."

She looked for the quickest way out of the hive. Jena was putting a lot on Michalis's shoulders and she didn't think he was up to it.

Jena waited with her sister, Thea, in an open mezzanine in the lower-caste section of the hive until it got dark outside. Both had canvas pouches slung over their shoulders. They entered a hallway that led into the Science Centre. From within the protection of a vegetation wall near a column, they were able to cut a way into the water channel below the plant floor.

Where they couldn't squeeze between huge stems, they cut a way through. Progress was slow, difficult, and risky. They kept moving on because they only had to pass a third of a kilometre beyond the Science Centre entrance. The women wore scented gear that matched the requirements of the scent-controlled traps.

The swim was dangerous. Some of the creatures darting around them were venomous. If they cut too much of the stems for the flooring, they might get crushed by an Ovidian. There was also the possibility that the filters they were using might not be sufficient.

Jena followed a large pillar-supporting tree up through the plant floor on the other side of the security station. Before slipping off her mask, she grabbed a rag and wiped her head. The material was soaked with antitoxins. Thea slipped off her mask and whispered, "What a stench!" Jena grabbed a red stinkyboo, squeezed its belly, and squirted her sister.

"Yuck," she cried as she unsuccessfully tried to protect her face.

"My turn," Thea said when she reached for it. She also used it to squirt her sister's head. Spraying themselves with an assortment of stinkyboos from the vegetation helped disguise their scent.

They used leaves from vegetation from the walls to wipe the worst of the shit-like goop off their wetsuits. Thea transferred what was in her pack to Jena's. After removing their wetsuits, Jena rolled both of them and slipped them into her long, thin shoulder haversack.

Thea reached for a scarlet stinkyboo, but a python-like creature lunged to bite her hand. Its head got blown apart. Thea's augments sensed its presence and reacted violently in kind. A leaf fortunately protected her face from the splatter, which was fortunate because the creature's head covering was hard and its internal goo was acidic and poisonous.

On their clothes, they had a dozen scent packets for communication and a device with an electrical current for deepening messaging broadcasts to Odvidian levels if they were confronted. Their supplies were limited.

Jena cut a thin hole in the column that was hidden within the thick vegetation. She crawled up an air vent within a thick pillar to reach the third level. Thea filled the opening into the column with thick leaves before following her sister.

Their climb was difficult because the tube was half filled with thin marine-like algae. A line for the haversacks was clamped to their waists and hung between their legs. Jena dissolved the clumps that were difficult to squeeze through. They wore metal protection on top of their gloves and boots. Both wore thermal vision goggles.

They climbed into the ceiling and stealthily kept crawling for a kilometre. Thea stayed back to watch for any reinforcements. To reach Jena's position, she had to kill a priddle and a scannon. The former was a python-like creature. A scannon looked like an otter with twenty hands and millipede feet. It had very gnarly teeth.

The women crawled until they got to the wall opposite the door of the lab where their father and brothers were imprisoned. It was a long wait before someone showed up. The big critters in the walls showed up in thermal vision goggles, but it was the smaller ones that freaked out, Jena. Poisonous things a couple of centimetres long that could blend in with the vegetation were what she feared most. She placed gel-soaked stringed traps alongside. After disintegrating the last of her four sets, she wasn't confident that she had the stamina to remain where she was. Jena hoped her sister was managing her situation better than she was. She knew that there were just too many things that could make this mission go so wrong.

When Gravis entered the hallway, Jena noticed that Michalis was following alongside the creature's right side.

Doesn't Michalis recognize Gravis's markings? On the portion next to her brother, the colours had changed to show disrespect for someone of the lowest caste. The rest of him was emblazoned in Sym-Set Overbear designs.

A door opened for Gravis and closed behind him. Down the hall, she heard something else. She crawled back until she was able to see. It was a member of Sym-Set Overbear. He stepped into a side alcove from the big hallway. Jena crawled ahead within the wall until she was able to hear the Ovidians' shifting and breathing. She removed a gun from her haversack. She heard something scurrying. She froze. It didn't sound heavy, so she took her shot.

The metal broke through the thick hide. A charge immediately incapacitated and shocked the creature so that there wasn't time for any of its augments to communicate. Next, the metal bored deep into the creature. A payload disintegrated much of the creature's insides. She confirmed to her sister, who was moving towards the door, that the creature was dead.

When Jena got close to Thea, she heard Michalis yell, "I am telling you she will be coming here tonight."

She heard her brother Jamal weakly yell, "Leave him alone."

Jena pounded the door with both fists.

"What?" asked Thea.

Jena mimicked a gun with her hand.

Thea pulled out a bomb canister and gave a pretend dumb look.

The door quickly swung open, and they were confronted with a very large Ovidian in front of them. Jena spun out of the way. Thea threw a canister under it. The explosion flew the creature to the ceiling and destroyed the door opening. Thea shot it to make sure that it was dead. Jena tramped over it, while it shook in oblivious agony.

On the far side of the room, she saw another Ovidian smash the containment glass that surrounded their father and the two boys. The gel in the pool that they were floating on spilled out across the floor.

Michalis stood against a wall on her left. He was about twenty-five meters from the door. Gravis moved towards him. He had blood on his pincers.

Michalis's arm was cut off below the elbow. He tramped towards Gravis and swung a couple of smells through the air with the other hand.

For Thea's attention, Jena made a gun motion with her hand and pointed to the Ovidian that was attacking the men. Jena was determined to save her brother.

Jena recognized the smell. *You're not worth pugslosh, is what he's saying, she realized.* It was the smell of the burnt plague-infested.

Gravis tossed heavy pieces of lab equipment at Jena. The graze caused her to misdirect her first shot. Gravis was so mad at Michalis's insult that he took a running leap. He managed to trample his chest with his right hoof. The colour pattern of the right side of the beast changed to match the rest.

Since it had turned slightly, Jena was able to shoot its vulnerable underbody. Gravis was still able to smear her brother's body across the floor and tear at him with his pincers.

Jena got closer and shot his underbelly a second time. A nervous twitch from its foot tossed her to the wall. Her head got smashed.

From the floor Jena dizzily watched her father and brothers attempt to crawl on the floor. They were trying to move away from the other stamping Ovidian. She noticed that Ahmed had lost an arm and his skin didn't have any colour. She also saw some bleeding, but she couldn't determine where it was coming from. Thea, who had been thrown across the floor, stared back. Jena made a pantomime of an explosion.

Jena tried to get up, but she couldn't. She was too weak.

Thea threw a piece of crumpled metal at the creature. "Come on, you motherfucker," she yelled. When it turned towards her, she threw some noxious smells and backed away. She madly waved her arms and yelled at it.

"That scent got its attention. I don't recognize it, though," Jena muttered.

Just before it had time to rush at her, Thea rolled a canister under it. It blew up and opened its insides. Thea took out a gun and fired at the open wound.

"Fucking right, is what Nadia would say," muttered Jena. "Damn it. Time to get to work." She shakily stood up and stumbled towards the others.

Thea slipped on the goo and almost fell.

Fares and Jamal crawled to get next to Ahmed.

"That was the easy part. Now for the hard part," Jena said.

"You're kidding, right?" Thea asked.

"No, not really."

"Will there be a problem with Gravis?" Thea asked.

"As good as it's going to get," Jena answered. "Obviously, I fucked up."

"If you brought in an army, it could have still gone down the same way," Fares said. "Michalis wasn't a fighter, but he made a noble stand today."

"It's a miracle he was able to get Gravis here on such short notice," Jena said. Jena crouched close to Ahmed. "It's sad that none of the family has shared any of his recent memories."

"You got here. Jena, I honestly didn't think we'd ever meet again."

"I hope the rest of the plan works."

"I have confidence that it will," said Ahmed.

"Ahmed, you're bleeding," Thea said. "Let me help."

"You didn't tell her?" he asked.

"No."

"But there must be a way."

Fares shook his head. "It's not just the gravity. There were severe problems caused by a careless operation. His organs are failing, and there are severe infections. There are also severe bone breaks throughout his body.

"Please, a sharing before you go," Ahmed asked.

Although only the women could exchange memories, they hugged each other. Jena took special care of what Ahmed wanted to share with the others on earth. Jena shared her oldest memories before she had to move. She also included the good times on the other side of the sea and highlights of their trip for the transit.

After the share, Jena gave him a fast opioid, followed by something that put him into a coma.

The women gave their father and Jamal the wetsuits that they wore.

"They will smell," Jena said.

"Do you really think that's going to matter?" Fares asked.

"No, but we're desperately out of time."

Thea rushed to Gravis's corpse and slit its chest open.

Thea carried her father to the creature. She was shocked at how frail he felt and how alien he looked. She fitted him with a mask with an air attachment. She put on thermal vision goggles and checked them both to verify if there were any holes in the clothing. Her father had a small tear near the knee. The clothing had to protect them from the acid. After the repair, her father and Jamal were placed inside the creature on the thin floating beds that were used in the gel vat. She also gave them spare bottles of compressed air. Once they were inside, she gave Jena a nod. Jena nodded back in agreement.

Thea, with the help of her augments, sealed the creature's wound.

Jena returned to Ahmed, who she sensed was now in a coma. The small bag of possessions that he promised her was next to him. She cried as she stuffed it into her pocket. She stared at the remains of Michalis and Ahmed and froze.

Thea put a hand on Jena's shoulder, and said, "Steal up. We need you."

Jena took a deep breath, and then groaned, "Fuck." She vaporized Ahmed's body that was in front of her and walked over to Michalis and did the same.

Thea used a small medical crane to haul the dead Ovidian away from the doorway. Next, she used it to raise Gravis's carcass.

Jena helped position the dead Ovidian onto the low-sized cart. The two unstrapped the harness and checked the body for balance and control.

"Just enough room," Thea said. "The feet don't drag. Wheels don't show. It's wide enough."

"This was Ahmed's idea. It's a Trojan horse," Jena said. "Jamal built the cart."

"A horse?"

"Ask Dad."

"What if it rolls off?"

"We just have to get to the other side of the Science Centre on this floor. The place we're going is embedded in bedrock. It can roll off after we get there, not before. We can use our augments to manage the feet and force them forward from behind. Preventing it from rocking is going to be difficult, but we can do it; we just have to be in sync. Oh, another thing, if one of them approaches us, I'll move up alongside to initiate scents."

"But its back isn't going to change."

"They'll just think they're full of themselves."

They steered the body out the demolished door and spun left in the hallway.

They were fortunate that the hallway was empty because it took them another ten minutes of walking to get the feet and multiple legs moving almost naturally.

Jena, who was continually watching the legs move, wasn't convinced it would fool anyone who was paying attention. The escape was done late in the evening because there would hopefully be fewer bodies around at this level. Research into galactic travel had taken on a very low priority.

"Why did you say that getting them out was the easy part?"

"The others are going to know that there is something wrong with the Ovidians that we killed. The building is going to be surrounded, and soon they will come in for us. There is no way we can fight them off. The other thing that I am afraid of is that they might just turn off the power."

"Yeah. That's a biggy for sure. And what if they are waiting for us?"

"Actually, I'm counting on it. Barrly will want to have confirmation that the program works. That's the one reason the power stays on at least until we get there."

"One of the reasons I didn't want that Ovidian killed is because up until now, they haven't considered us a serious threat. So far we're just a foreign-looking inconvenience."

"The murder of a lowly caste would normally be severe," said Thea. "Gravis's Sym-Set must be really confident about the approaching takeover of the Science Centre."

"But we're legally not a caste. That's our problem, and Barrly doesn't give a priddle's fart," said Jena. "Gravis wouldn't move in on us unless it was sanctioned by the Barrly boys."

The women got the cart moving in the hallway. The wheels were making noise as they moved across the thick leaves. The two tried to levitate it slightly. The plopping sound faded, but the cart wobbled a bit side to side.

"What about the stomping sound?" Thea asked.

Thea stopped the cart, and each of them used their augments to gently make a swatting sound on the leaves. After a dozen trials, Thea was able to produce something that didn't sound ludicrous.

"Shit," said Thea.

Jena saw an approaching low-caste Ovidian. "Real slow," she said. She sprayed out an obnoxious scent.

Gravis's legs swished back and forth like a bad mop.

The Ovidian passed without releasing any scents or changing markings on its back.

"That one pretended it was invisible. It didn't do anything," said Thea.

"I gave a mild scent suggesting it had a contagious stomach ailment and a don't-bug-me attitude."

"Goodness, it would take six people to make this work," Thea said.

"Buck up, Thea. Remember, Michalis and Ahmed. Fuck this girl—let's move."

The cart waddled back and forth, and the wheels kept making sounds as they rolled up and down over different leaf thicknesses. They actually pushed the cart for another half an hour before meeting another Ovidian. They slowed and levitated the cart again and waited for the creature to pass. This time, he said something, but Jena didn't have any idea what it said. She just kept moving. It stopped and turned back.

"Just keep going. We need to get to the other side. It belongs to a low-caste, and it's not on the other side. So, fuck it."

When they reached the secure door of the Space Centre. The security doors opened. The sensors reacted to his DNA and scents. The guard ignored them as the corpse rolled past.

"Not a word," said Thea. "What a waste of space."

"Shush," Jena said. "Any more of this and I will be shitting myself. Let's hurry."

The women escorted the body to the next hallway. They made a turn and followed it towards the end and veered into an alcove.

"That is one of the dumbest things that I have ever done," Jena moaned.

"Damn fucking right," Thea said.

They removed the men from the corpse. Jena tethered her father to herself. Thea did the same for Jamal. Each woman pulled herself upwards through a column to the roof of the top floor. They secured their weak cargo tightly between their legs. Once above, they lowered their passengers from the ceiling. Something had given Jamal's thigh a small bite. Thea did a quick sanitize and patch and told him, "Hold it together. Not much farther." As expected, he didn't look well.

The women pulled the lying men behind. While the bodies hovered a couple of centimetres above the vegetative floor, a very small scannon rushed around to check them out. They heard something ahead, so they left the men leaning against the vegetative wall. They crawled up into the ceiling.

There were two Ovidians in front of the entrance to the Control Centre. A blue light shone from under the doorway. The women shot the guards a couple of times. One of them kept moving. The women dropped from the ceiling. The one still alive kept smashing into the wall. It went down after Jena shot at its vulnerable underbelly.

When the women heard the door open, they leaned back into the vegetative wall. An Ovidian came out. When it was fully out of the door, Jena squatted and shot it in the underbelly.

She looked inside. Stinkyboos, like a family of scared rabbits, bounced around chaotically. A scannon fell onto the floor from the wall of plants. Its arms and legs kept running while it lay stunned. Jena made its head explode. She proceeded inside. The small sixteen-square-meter room was empty of furniture. There were, however, two walls that had mounted pull-down control units. There were four doors on the left of a long attached hallway. An Ovidian came out from the third door. Jena shot it. The first time, she grazed its back. The second time, she hit it just above its pincers.

She opened the first door to the left. It was a large control room. There were three more Ovidians inside. The room was 125 meters long and empty of furniture. Controls were mounted on the wall at the far end. The banner showing on their hide identified them as belonging to Sym-Set Overbear. Jena rushed in and shot one. Thea, from behind, shot another.

The one that remained free was one that was farthest away from the door. He raced towards Jena. She moved in front of the wounded bodies and tried to take a shot, but she was out of bullets. With its appendages, it attempted to squash and dismember Jena. She scurried behind the closest Ovidian. Thea, who was also out of bullets, tried to distract by waving and shouting.

Jena dropped her gun and pulled out her knife.

When the creature turned to reach Thea, Jena ran past and made powerful stabs at the creature's back elephantine legs. The creature tried to twirl around and body slam her. Thea took out her knife and kept cutting. The creature kept stomping around. Jena pulled a flare gun and threatened the creature with fire. Fire did not directly intimidate an Ovidian, but they knew that it could do serious damage to plants in the hive. It caused the beast to back up. It was enough of a distraction to permit Thea to get a bomb canister from her bag. As it was backing up, Jena saw another Ovidian watching from the hallway. He tramped away.

As Thea threw it under the Ovidian, Jena rushed to the other side of the room to get away from it.

"Thea, check every other room. If there's nothing else, turn everything on," said Jena. I've got to get him. That was Barrly. I can't let him give the order to turn everything off."

Without grabbing her gun, Jena rushed after Barrly. She entered the hall and saw that he had already gotten a good head start on her. "Damn it, they're fast buggers when they want to be," she groaned.

She was going to try something that she had seen Dinos do many times. She had mimicked him a couple of times, but it was decades ago. She squatted low and put her palms on the ground. She levitated herself slightly, a couple of centimetres, and tried to accelerate.

"I really don't know about this," she moaned. The first attempt got her five hundred meters. She crashed and rolled and almost knocked herself out. It took another two tries, but she reached him.

She hesitated to land on him because the Ovidian had the ability to force sharp things out of its body. Nevertheless, she bumped into him because she hadn't figured out how to stop.

The fall had gotten Barrly's attention. He stopped.

She rushed behind him and kept cutting his back legs deeply. Before he kicked her, she backed away. The beast turned around to gore her. She used the flare gun to keep it from getting close while she searched through her pack.

He called her vermin. She called it a bottom-of-the-barrel lowlife. On Ovidia, the latter was worse.

Barrly, in spite of wounds to his back legs, lunged and meant to squish her. Jena threw a bomb canister under him. The explosion tossed her against a plant-covered wall.

The bomb had thrown Barrly over on his side. The stomach was cut, but he was still moving. Jena pushed another bomb into the cut and quickly rushed away.

Barrly didn't move. The mess from his belly gruesomely showed her that he would never do so again.

"Damn you. Serves you right for messing with Sym-Set Sari-Khalil." She raised her fist in the air.

She took a quick final look through her pack and learned that it was the last of her canisters.

"Damn it. Better not be any more of them, or that could be the last of me," Jena groaned.

When Jena returned to Thea, she found her father and brother on the floor. They were in the long room with the three bodies. They were still breathing from canisters, but both men seemed to be in great distress. Thea was trying to open a door into the next room. It was at the end of the room and was next to some control panels.

"The passcode I was given doesn't work," Thea complained.

Ahmed put up his hand.

Jena brought both of the men to the door. Thea brought Ahmed up to the console. He tried a couple of different codes, and the last one unlocked the door.

"Looks like Barrly had someone change it, but they didn't change my back door," said Ahmed. "They definitely weren't the brightest."

"Don't let it go to your head. The existing staff may have left it that way for their own reasons. There is a lot not to like about the new wrecking balls," said Fares.

"What?"

"Just an old expression. Fart heads, shitdisturbers—"

"Fine, fine boys. Into the pods, please," Thea said. "Any time now, we're going to have visitors."

While the system was booting up, Jena and Thea moved the dead bodies to brace the door in the front room. Thea had told her that she had taken out another Odvidian while she was gone.

"It's amazing what you can do with knives when you have to," Thea said.

"I'll bet. I'm sure you will tell me all about it once we're out here."

Thea gave a thumbs up.

"How many blades?"

"Four."

"I definitely needed more," Jena said. "Remember that when it comes to my birthday."

When they placed the men into the pods, they weren't given breathing aids.

"Looks like they are suffocating. Jena, it is now or never," Thea yelled. "They are fading."

The smashing of the door began.

"Shit," Jena muttered. She set the timer. After closing the door behind her, she jumped into her pod.

There were no guarantees that what they were doing would work, but at least they were given a chance. When in dire straits, pondering hope was far better than a certain death, any day.

As Thea closed her pod, she cried, "Damn them to hell."

When Jena closed hers, she stared into the blackness.

"If this is the way we go out, Sym-Set Sari-Khalil," she said. "Then fuck 'em all." Then she smashed the lid of her coffin. She thought she heard others smashing. Maybe she just imagined it.

When Jena rolled out of her pod, she saw that Thea was naked. She was leaning against a wall and throwing up. Jena rolled out to a crawl and did the same thing.

"Damned. That was brutal," she moaned.

"We're here," Thea said.

"Of course, we are."

"No, I mean, Khaled and Nadia's names are here."

"Well, that's a start, isn't it?" Jena said as she stood up.

A bug came out of the wall, and left a stack of clothes and boots. It retreated back into the wall.

"Why the hell did it rip off my clothes?" Jena asked.

"Because they would have reeked?"

"And what if the bug wasn't working? And which boots are yours?"

"Mine are the ones that fit."

"Of course. Why did I bother to ask?"

Jena got dressed and looked at the signatures. She put her forehead against the wall and moved her palm down the wall. She found an etching that said Nikos.

"They're alive," she breathed.

She cried and folded her arms tight. She sank into a crouch.

Thea knocked loudly and told the men to wake up and get out. Both of them rolled out to a crawl. Jamal was the first to throw up.

After putting on his coveralls, Fares tried to stumble to where Jena was crouched.

"It's too early," Thea said. "Start by putting on your boots."

"Jena, seeing that her father was stumbling, rushed over. Her father hugged him tight. She recoiled.

"I know, it has been a while," Fares said.

"Never is too long a time," she steamed.

"It's not like we didn't talk."

She saw the other two staring at her. She returned a hug to her father.

"Ow," Fares groaned. "Humans are scrawny, remember. You'll have to get used to them."

She let him go and made a long hoverboard for him to lie on.

"So, who came up with the clothes idea?" Thea asked.

"Dinos. Definitely Dinos," Jamal said.

"Why didn't we just strip and store our clothes somewhere?" Jena asked.

"The way I remember it, everyone was rather distracted," said Jamal. "Besides, you were the one who was supposed to have read the flight manual."

"How are you, Dad?" asked Thea.

He wobbled and threw up again. Jena helped him walk to where Jamal was.

"I can breathe. It doesn't feel like I'm being squashed, but I am still pretty weak."

"Why are all the coveralls the same?" asked Jamal.

"That's not a serious question, is it?" Jena said. "Everyone is so stressed out here, and you want to fight over colour coordination? Jamal, you're with Thea. Dad, you're with me."

Jena pulled her father's lying body behind her. Thea followed with Jamal. Fares groaned and tried to roll off his board.

"No," Jena said. "You'll slow us down. You know better. I'd like to make something that you could just sit on, but the board has to be really close to the ground. Just put up with it until we are out of here.

The tunnel was pitch dark, and they couldn't see a thing. They made their way forward by feeling the walls. After about ten minutes of blind navigation, the space brightened with the appearance of a hologram. It was of an old man with long white hair and a beard.

"Halo Fares," he said. Mi nombre es Raúl Winters.

"Hello," Jena said, but the speaker kept talking. "It's just a recording," she said. None of them could make sense of what he was saying.

The image fluttered. He turned and kept walking.

Jamal, who was staring at the back of the ghost's head, asked, "How are we going to stop them from following us?"

"There must be a relay station in orbit. If we take it out, it would take them a long time to send another. The Transit Centre that is here is just a beacon. Once this site was created, I don't believe the Ovidian had any use for what was left in the destroyed part of New York."

The group kept walking for another hour and a half. The hologram was the only thing that provided any light.

"Michalis was researching other alien species. Was anyone else?" asked Thea.

"I did some in my early days," her father said. "Michalis's work was built on what Alex and Dinos discovered. Unless you know something that I don't, Ovidia is the only planet that we have to worry about right now."

Fifteen minutes later, the group came to a rock wall. The hologram turned to look at them and then faded.

"What the hell?" cried Thea.

Both women stepped back when they heard the sound of moving rock. The sound stopped.

"It's a small staircase. We'll have to carry them," shouted Thea.

"I've got Dad. Thea, hurry before it shuts," said Jena.

The staircase seemed to go on forever. "You told me that it was small," Jena said.

"I meant that it's cramped. And where did that Raúl guy go? We could have used the light."

Once they reached the top of the stairwell, a portion of the rock wall opened into another tunnel. The space was pitch dark like the stairwell.

Jena heard two cries; one was from Thea and the other from Jamal.

"What is it?" asked Jena.

"We bumped into another damned wall," Thea moaned.

A stone door crept open.

The daylight was blinding. Jena saw a cobblestone street outside. She hurried past her sister with her father in her arms. To the far right, there was a small water fountain. The buildings on both sides were high-rise towers. There were dozens of aliens passing by. The sky was a strange colour. It was blue.

"Looks like Earth," Fares said. "But it's not like what I remembered. Looks like we've created a scene."

A half a dozen people had stopped and were staring at them.

The women set the men down on a street bench.

"Is this Brooklyn?" Fares asked.

"Brooklyn, No. Sí."

"Spanish, I think," Fares said. "New York?"

An old man waved a hand in front of him. "Sí," he said.

"I think that means sort of," Fares said. He pointed to Jena and Thea and asked, "Have you seen any of them?"

The old man pointed to the sky and said, "Jovianos."

Fares looked towards the sky, raised a grabbing hands, and cried, "Alhamdulilah."

Seeing Jena's perplexed look, he said, "Jupiter. They've gone to Jupiter. Fuck. They don't make it easy, do they?" He stood up, hugged his daughters and his son, and said, "Welcome to Earth."

For News, and Behind the Scenes

c
Lawren e. visit my Canadian website (my name). *Story Giveaways and Discounts can also be accessed from the newsletter tab.* Other features are available from my Facebook site.

Honest reviews posted on vendor sites, are much ppreciated. And for your curiosity and perseverance, go raibh míle maith agat; many thanks—in case you were wondering :)

www.ingramcontent.com/pod-product-compliance
Lightning Source LLC
LaVergne TN
LVHW091123080826
845145LV00008B/2027

* 9 7 8 1 7 7 7 8 1 5 5 9 2 *